**Jack found himself nearly in tears**

at the thought of Kate, the special, sweet girl he knew years ago, living in such hell. He knew the shelter demanded confidentiality and the chances of Mary Anne even telling him whether Kate was there or not were very slim. But he had to try. If she was there, he needed Kate to know he would do everything possible to keep her safe.

Mary Anne stood. "Now Jack, you know I can't tell you the names of the women in this shelter. I would be risking their safety, their very lives, if that information got out."

Jack's shoulders slumped, he'd known she wouldn't tell him. "I'm not going to put them at risk, Mary Anne. I'm trying to protect these women. I'm trying to help."

"I appreciate your concern and know when you've thought about this, you will understand it's the only thing we can do to keep these women safe. I think you'd better go."

The door clicked open behind him. He turned, expecting a security goon to escort him to the door.

Instead, framed in the sunlight spilling through the open door, stood Kate.

# Killing Her Softly

## by

## Barb Warner Deane

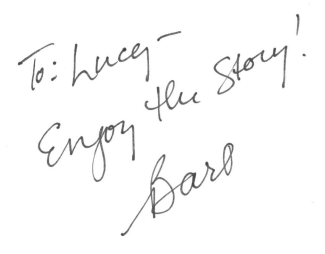

To: Lucy—
Enjoy the story!
Barb

**Killing Her Softly**

Cover Art by *Kim Mendoza*

The Wild Rose Press, Inc.
PO Box 708
Adams Basin, NY 14410-0708
Visit us at www.thewildrosepress.com

Publishing History
First Crimson Rose Edition, 2017
Print ISBN 978-1-5092-1666-6
Digital ISBN 978-1-5092-1667-3

Published in the United States of America

## Dedications

In memory of author Nancy Richards-Akers
and other victims of abuse.

~*~

This book is dedicated to my daughters, sisters, nieces,
aunts, mother, mother-in-law, sisters-in-law,
critique partners, and friends.
To all the women in my life, may you be safe, healthy,
and happy.

~*~

Many thanks go to my editor, Rachel Kelly,
everyone at The Wild Rose Press,
Mike Wood and Mike Maloney,
formerly of the Schuyler County sheriff's office.

~*~

And as always, to Chris.

http://www.barbwarnerdeane.com

Chapter One

Kate lifted her head off the pillow, trying to be certain the knocking was real and not just the pounding in her battered head. Her stiff neck creaked and a stab of pain shot from her shoulder straight to her temple. But the pounding in her ears was gone. No, there was definitely someone at the front door.

Although her body moved slowly, thoughts raced through her mind. Would Tony have come home from his trip early as a way to trick her into angering him again? It could be him, testing her. If she answered the door looking as she did right now, with no make-up and messy hair, he would explode.

She peeked out the bedroom window and breathed a sigh of relief at the sight of an unfamiliar car in the driveway. Tony wouldn't go to the trouble of renting a car simply to punish her.

She eased her arms into the sleeves of the cotton robe and slid her feet into tattered slippers. Tony had been rougher than usual. He must have wanted her to have something to remember him by all week long. Whoever was at the door was going to have to accept her like this. She was too sore and too tired to get dressed.

She finally made it to the door and inched it open. The stranger outside peered in through the small gap she provided, fortunately blocking the most direct of the sun's rays.

"Katherine Finelli?"

How did he know her name? Could Tony have put him up to this? She scanned the driveway beyond the stranger to see if anything outside was peculiar, but there was nothing more than her quiet neighborhood on a typical Monday morning.

"Are you Katherine Richards Finelli?" He stepped closer to the door and Kate pulled back. Whatever he was selling, she wanted none of it.

"Who are you?"

"I'm Patrick Morris. I'm the attorney of record for the estate of Linda Richards. I believe you are Ms. Richard's niece?"

"Yes."

Kate hadn't seen Aunt Linda in several years. Tony wouldn't like it if she saw her now.

"May I come in?"

"No, I have nothing to do with my aunt any longer. You'll have to talk to her directly." He shifted uncomfortably, but Kate wasn't willing to let her guard down.

"You misunderstand, Mrs. Finelli. I'm sorry to say your aunt has passed away."

A wave of nausea swept through Kate. She turned and fled to the bathroom. How had it come to this? Her only relative had died, and she had to learn it from some lawyer.

She thought of the day of her parents' deaths. Aunt Linda held her as she cried before they both fell asleep entwined on the couch. She'd held tight to Linda all night long and by morning, the ache of her loss stung a little less.

As the pain tore through her body, Kate doubled over to keep a scream from flying out. She couldn't fall apart in front of a stranger.

After splashing cold water on her face, Kate walked out of the bathroom. Mr. Morris was standing inside at the doorway, watching her.

He looked her over. "Are you all right?"

She couldn't take the sympathy. It only made things worse.

"Yes, I'm fine. Was there something else you needed to tell me?" Maybe he'd take the hint and leave.

"Are you sure…is there something I can do…" When she shook her head and started to turn away, he spoke again. "I'm deeply sorry for your loss."

"Hmm…" Her loss? How could you lose someone who had been torn away from you long ago? The loss was only in what might have been, what she had dreamed would be, but now, never could.

"The funeral is scheduled for tomorrow. Your aunt had been ill for a long time and knew the end was imminent. She made all the arrangements herself, not wanting to burden you in your time of grief."

He sounded so reasonable and understanding, but he understood nothing.

"If she made all the arrangements herself, why are you here?" She'd have to make sure she and Tony read about her aunt's death in the *Harper's Glen Express*. She'd have to act surprised. Of course, with the funeral tomorrow, the news would be in the paper coming out on this Wednesday.

"Ms. Richards made you the sole beneficiary of her estate, Mrs. Finelli. My law firm has handled her legal matters for many years; I can give you all the help you need in understanding the complexity of this situation. Essentially, you have inherited all of her real and personal property as well as any liquid assets remaining after her final expenses have been paid."

Kate almost laughed. He would think she was crazy, so she held back. He would think she was stupid if she told him she had no idea what he was talking about, as she knew nothing of assets, liquid or otherwise, but better he think her stupid than crazy.

"What…what does it all mean?"

Kate sank onto the sofa in the living room. Apparently taking this as an invitation, the lawyer walked farther into the room and took a seat in the armchair opposite her.

"It means you now own your aunt's house on the lake, all the furniture and furnishings inside of it, and the money left in her bank accounts after her funeral costs have been paid. Here's the breakdown of the property."

He handed her a sheet full of numbers and letters, but Kate couldn't ask him to explain and she couldn't admit it meant nothing to her. She felt the heat rising in her cheeks and looked intently at the sheet. Hoping she'd given it enough time, she glanced back up at the lawyer.

"She gave me her house?" It sounded too unreal to believe. The house she loved and hated and missed terribly was now hers. Linda's house on the lake, where she'd been alone much of the time as a young girl. But where she'd learned to love the lake and its moods.

"Yes, Mrs. Finelli. Here are the keys."

She shivered at the cold metal in her hand, all new and exciting and hopeful. But the concern etched into Mr. Morris's face reminded Kate she was a mess; like she'd lost a battle with a backhoe. How could a house make everything better?

"I know this is a lot for you to take in, especially after the disturbing news about your aunt. I will leave these papers for you to review at your leisure."

He handed her more papers full of nonsense words.

"The house is yours now. You can move there, sell it, whatever you wish. There is no mortgage and the utilities are being billed directly to my office until the estate is probated."

She looked up at him, wishing he could take her away from her life and bring her aunt back. Wishing he could make her cuts, pains, and bumps go away. Wishing so many things.

He suddenly placed his hand on her arm and gazed into her black eyes.

"Your aunt loved you very much and wanted you to be happy. As her legal representative, I am bound to do everything I can to ensure her last wishes are carried out…to help you as she wished, now that she no longer can."

Kate cringed, expecting him to say she wasn't worthy of getting Aunt Linda's house. Or worse, that Tony had already learned of this and sold it all off before she could walk through her aunt's door again.

"Mrs. Finelli, if there is *anything* I can do in my capacity as a lawyer to help you, please tell me."

Kate pulled back, unwilling to let her weakness show more than it already had.

"I'm fine, Mr. Morris. Thank you for your offer, but I won't be needing any legal help."

He looked her over as if his Superman eyes could tunnel through to her bruised and splintered bones, making her a liar without saying a word.

"Mrs. Finelli. I cannot help but notice you have terrible bruises and—"

Kate stood and walked toward the door.

"I fell off a ladder yesterday, Mr. Morris. That's why I'm home from work this morning. I appreciate your concern and your offer of help. I'll review these papers and let you know what my husband and I would like to do with the house."

She opened the door and held it for him, willing him to take the hint and leave quickly. She couldn't stand the thought of this stranger pitying her. Another day or two and the worst of the bruises would fade enough for her to cover them with make-up. She wouldn't leave the house until then.

He must have figured their meeting was over. He picked up his briefcase and walked out the door. When she thought to close it, though, his hand reached out and stopped her.

"Mrs. Finelli, you are the only person who knows about this bequest. I work alone and have no partners. The paperwork has not yet been filed with the probate court. There is no reason this will become public knowledge any time soon."

His eyes seemed to say much more, but when

she didn't answer, he turned and left. She watched him drive off and eased the door closed.

This was their secret then. Maybe, just maybe, she could keep it that way.

Kate grabbed the railing and pulled herself up the stairs as quickly as her broken body could go. A hot bath would go a long way to easing her aches and pains. It would also give her time to think, time to plan. Maybe this was her chance.

****

"Did you go visit your folks yet, boy?"

"Yes, get off my back already, okay." Jack knew the old man meant well, but he could be a pain sometimes, especially when he was trying to make a point.

"Are they okay with it, your mom and dad?"

Deke leaned back in the old wooden chair and winced. His wrinkled skin had a gray cast to it and his eyes were more sunken in. The cancer had spread too fast and too far. Jack made it back to town just in time.

"They are fine with it. I honestly don't think my father cares one way or the other, but my mother is pleased, I guess."

"Of course she's pleased," said Deke. "Her stray chick is back in the roost. Even with your brothers here in town, she still worried about you. I'm sure your dad's pleased too, he just doesn't show it as much."

"Yeah right." Jack tossed his hat on the coat rack and plopped down in the chair opposite Deke's desk. He started to put his feet up on the desk top but stopped when Deke's eyebrows went up in that way he had. Jack's feet dropped back to the floor.

"Did you talk to your brothers too?"

"Nope."

"What are you waiting for? You want them to learn you're back by running into you around town? You need to tell them you've moved home."

Home. Hmmm…he wasn't sure he really thought of Harper's Glen as home anymore. And certainly the Finelli brothers had never been close; well at least, Tony and Tom had never been close to him. After Deke…well, without Deke here, Jack would never have returned.

"My mother told me they are both out of town this week. Big hunting trip, you know how it is. No worry of running into them at the Quik-Mart."

"And did they leave their cell phones at home?"

"What is it with you, old man?" Jack got to his feet and paced the small room. He wasn't sure how Deke had worked in here all these years. The tiny space was cluttered with newspapers, pictures, trophies, and letters—a lifetime of memories in an eight by eight office. And many of those memories involved Jack.

"Don't get your back up, boy. I just thought you'd want your family to know you've moved back to town. Still can't believe you didn't tell them about it before you got here. We talked about this over a month ago. What have you been doing since then?"

Jack actually chuckled. In the six weeks since Deke had called him and practically begged him to come back to Harper's Glen and be his undersheriff, Jack quit his job with the FBI, packed up and sold his condo in Silver Springs, Maryland, and moved himself to the backwoods of upstate New York. Only when he left Harper's Glen after graduating from college had he ever moved faster.

"I was busy winding up some cases. Getting ready to come back here took all of my time. Besides, why would I bother to tell Tony or Tom I was coming? It's not like we talk all very often."

Jack stopped in front of his favorite picture. It showed him and Deke, arm and arm, in front of his dorm at Dartmouth. The four years of college had filled Jack out in a way he'd never been when Tony called him a skinny geek in high school, but he'd never gotten taller. He and Deke were about the same height back then, before Deke had started slumping over with age and illness.

"That was a good day, wasn't it?" Deke's voice sounded suspiciously deep.

Jack would never forget how happy he was when he saw the crusty old sheriff on graduation day.

"Yeah, it sure was. You made it great."

"Not me, boy. You're the one who graduated from that fancy, Ivy-league college. You're the one who got the honors. All I did was watch."

Jack turned to Deke, unable to ignore the moisture he saw in the old man's eyes.

"You drove eight hours each way to sit there and watch me graduate. Which is more than I can say for anyone in my family."

"They had their reasons. No matter what, they're still your kin."

"You can say that because you don't have any." Jack regretted the words the minute they left his tongue. What kind of a heel reminds a dying man he's alone at the end of his life?

"Sorry, Deke—"

"No, it's true, boy. I got no kin. I wish I did. But, as far as you and me are concerned, I always kinda' thought of you as the son I never had."

Jack walked to Deke's desk and gently squeezed the old man's bony shoulder. "I would never have come back for anyone but you."

Deke took a moment to collect himself and then, slowly, gingerly, stood and walked around the desk.

"Let's go through some of the files and paperwork. You're going to need to take over for me as soon as possible. I can't keep up with it anymore, even in this little ole town of ours."

Jack followed Deke out of the sheriff's office and into the reception area. A bank of file cabinets covered nearly all of one pea-green painted wall.

"Now, you know Thelma would be all too happy to help you with whatever you need. She has been here longer than I have, which is saying a lot. Of course, she looks a heck of a lot better than I do. She'll probably outlast you, too."

As it was late in the day, the ever-efficient Thelma had already left. The evening dispatcher handled any incoming calls from an inter-departmental office down the hall.

"Is there anything in particular you think I'll need help with?" Deke knew better than anyone, other than Jack himself, what he'd been through in his years with the FBI. Deke was the only one in town who did.

"We pretty much get your standard garden-variety petty crime. Some DUIs, some drunk and disorderlies, more drug use than we used to get, some minor theft here and there, and too much domestic violence. Nothing unusual for a town of two thousand people."

"Well, it'll be a nice change for me. I can handle a lot of nothing too exciting right now."

Deke looked back at him but must have been satisfied with what he saw, since he moved on with the rest of his tour.

"Well, that's pretty much it. Small potatoes to you, I'm sure, but it's been a nice life for me."

"You're not done yet."

Jack couldn't stand the thought of Deke dying. There was no way he could envision a world without Deke in it. Even when he didn't get to visit with the old man more than a couple of times a year, he was forever calling him for advice and well, just to hear his voice. Deke was all the family Jack needed. But, if the doctors knew what they were talking about, Deke would be gone within the year, or even sooner. He couldn't deal with it.

"Nope, not yet." Deke moved back to his desk and picked up his hat.

"Larry's on duty tonight, so I think we should go to Minnie's and get some dinner. Monday is meatloaf night and I remember how much of a sucker you used to be for Minnie's meatloaf."

"Oh man. I've dreamed of Minnie's meatloaf with a side of fries covered in gravy. You can't get a dinner like Minnie's in DC, you know."

Jack grabbed his hat and turned toward the door. He was just in time to run into his sister-in-law, Brenda, walking toward the front counter. When he

11

entered the room, she turned her gaze on him.

"Jack? What are you doing here? When did you get into town?" She graced him with one of her genuine smiles and pulled him into a firm hug.

"Hey, Brenda. I got into town this weekend. I stopped by Mom and Dad's, but they said Tom and Tony are on a hunting trip."

"Yeah, until Saturday. They will be surprised to see you. Will you still be here then? I hope they don't miss you."

"I'll still be here."

Deke cleared his throat and Brenda jumped.

"Oh, yeah," she turned to Deke. "I'm here because I'm worried about Kathy. She hasn't answered the phone all day, I tried calling at least three or four times. I swung by there on my way home from the Quik-Mart tonight to see what was up. Even though the car is in the drive way, she didn't answer the door and no lights were on." Brenda's gaze switched between Deke and Jack and she wrung her hands. "It's her day off, so I'm sure she's not at Ruby's. I'm worried about her."

He hadn't seen Kathy, or as Jack always thought of her, Kate, in over ten years. Not since he'd left for college after she married his brother.

Jack tried to be reassuring. "Do you have a spare key to their house? Maybe she's not feeling well. You could let yourself in to check on her."

Brenda shook her head. "No, they never gave us one. And I already asked your parents, they don't have one either. This isn't like Kathy. I don't know where she could be."

Jack turned to Deke, wondering if his years of

experience might add anything to this situation.

Deke nodded. "There's no sign of trouble, right?"

"No."

Deke patted Brenda on the back. "I wouldn't worry about her, Ms. Brenda. I'm sure she's fine. Probably has a case of the flu or something. I bet she'll be back at Ruby's in a day or two. Try calling her again in the morning."

Jack watched for the anxiety to return on Brenda's face, but she was nodding instead.

"Deke's right," Jack said. "I'm sure there's nothing wrong. Maybe she had somewhere to go today and forgot her phone. She might have been late getting home."

"No, not Kathy. She's never late, ever."

Jack had trouble believing anything sinister could happen to Kate in a town like Harper's Glen. "Did you call any of her friends?"

"Well, she doesn't really have many friends I know of. She pretty much keeps to herself; Tony and her."

That didn't sound like the vibrant, young girl Jack knew in high school, but it was many years ago. Lord knew, he wasn't the same man he was back then, either.

"Well, give her another try tonight and then tomorrow and if she doesn't show up, we'll start a serious search. I'm sure there's a perfectly reasonable explanation for everything."

Brenda seemed more relieved. "Okay, I'll give you a call in the morning, Deke, if I still can't find her…"

After a few hugs and a kiss on the cheek, Brenda left.

"What do you think? Is there some kind of family feud going on I should know about?"

Deke shook his head. "Not that I know of. Kathy is a quiet little thing, keeps to herself mostly. I sometimes think Brenda doesn't understand her."

Jack and Deke closed up the office and headed off for the diner.

"Why don't you ride with me?"

"What? You think I'm too feeble to walk two lousy blocks to Minnie's?"

"No, it's started to cool off. I thought maybe you'd rather drive."

"Nope. It's a nice night for a short walk." Deke started walking, and Jack quickly caught up.

"What did you mean when you said Brenda doesn't understand Kate?"

"I don't know nothin'." Deke's gate slowed and he glanced up at the stop lights as they crossed the street. "I've wondered sometimes."

"Wondered what?"

"Well, seems to me that little girl was a shy, sweet thing when your brother married her. Always took time to speak to a person and pass the time of day. All I'm saying is, over the years, she sure has changed."

Jack was more worried by what Deke wasn't saying than by what he was.

"What do you mean?"

"It's just... I remember when you used to help her with homework, back before she started dating Tony. She was beautiful on the outside but more, it went clear through," Deke said. "I haven't seen that side of her in a long time."

"Do you think there's something wrong with her? Is she sick? Maybe not being able to have children threw her into some kind of depression."

"Well, I surely don't know. I think the light went out of her eyes somewhere along the way. She's not a happy person."

"Okay. Then she's probably off somewhere Brenda doesn't know about. Or else, she's sick and turned off her phone to get some sleep. I don't know why Brenda got worried so fast, anyway."

"Don't ask me to explain women to you. They're a mystery, for sure."

Chuckling, Jack held the door as he and Deke entered the diner. The scent of grease from the grill did battle with the harsh taint of empty coffee pots left on the heaters. Cigarette smoke hung like a cloud over the counter and clung to the walls of the tiny diner. He could almost taste the meatloaf already.

****

Kate circled the lake house slowly, careful to stay in the shadows of the trees as much as possible. She didn't want to believe this all was an elaborate ruse of Tony's to give him cause to punish her, but ten years of his "tests" gave her ample reason to be cautious.

She had waited until long after dusk, late in the evening, to make her move. She couldn't chance being seen, even this far from town. Fortunately, once she turned off the lake road, onto the road leading to her aunt's cottage, there was no other traffic. At least, no other humans. And animals didn't

15

worry her.

She dropped her plastic grocery bags in the trees on the edge of the driveway. Even though she wanted to run into the house, to relive the pleasure of the normal life she'd had there, she didn't.

No light shone through the windows, the only sounds came from the lake, and Kate started to breathe again. Nothing about thc house made her think Tony was waiting inside, nothing to make her believe this was one of his sick jokes. She retrieved her bags and quickly ran to the front door.

The sweet click of the lock made her heart flutter, and she pushed the door slightly ajar. Her pulse hammered in her throat, her skin instantly clammy, as she feared Tony's smooth, dark voice scolding her again. She listened, willing her ears to pick up the tiniest noise in the house, beyond the slight wheeze of her own breathing.

She would never know if she was safe unless she went inside, but she couldn't make herself take the step. Gripping fear rooted her feet to the floor of the porch, just as desperate longing urged her to move.

She'd dreamed of her escape so many times, in so many different ways, it didn't seem possible it was now within her reach. If this house was truly hers, if the lawyer was right, she might be free at last.

But if Tony found her, if he learned about the house and the money, there was no way she'd be able to stay here. He'd drag her back, literally. Just knowing she had taken this step to get away from him would spike his anger enough he might kill her.

Her hands shook, causing the beam from the

flashlight she held to dart across the far wall of the living room. Before she could decide whether to go in or run home, the light fell on the piano. Sitting on the top right corner, where it had been for the past twenty years, sat the last picture taken of Kate's parents.

Everyone always said Kate inherited the best of both of her parents. She had her mother's silky blonde hair and petite, feminine build. From her father, she'd inherited the cornflower blue eyes and fair complexion. When they died she was too young to remember much about them. She had spent hours, probably months all told, staring at their picture, trying hard to make them real again.

Her father had surprised her mother with an elaborate vacation cruise for their tenth wedding anniversary. Luckily, before they left port, a photographer took a photograph of them dressed to the nines, young, beautiful, and in love. They must have paid the photographer in advance, because he mailed it directly to the house.

The picture made it home, but they never did.

When Kate was about fifteen and having a rebellious, angry day, she demanded her aunt pack it away, claiming it made her too sad to be faced with their smiles every day. Aunt Linda calmly replied that even if Kate didn't want to see her parents, they wanted to look down on her. So, the picture stayed where it was.

Glancing one last time at their smiles, Kate hustled her bags into the house and quickly locked the door behind her. Her legs were shaking too much to continue standing, and she slid down the door until she was sitting.

With her arms wrapped tightly around her knees, she soon found herself rocking back and forth in the dark. Silent tears warmed her face, reducing her panic with each drop.

How long she sat there, she wasn't sure. When the last tears finally dried and she recovered her strength, she stood and scurried through the dark house.

In the kitchen, she set down the two grocery bags containing all the food she'd been able to carry. Dry soups, cans of pasta, baked beans, tuna, and vegetables. Breakfast bars and cereal. She didn't eat much; it should last her a while.

Kate moved back to the front of the house and down the hall to the back. Her aunt's bedroom was filled with wonderful memories. Even through the smells of dust, mildew and disuse, she could detect a trace of lilac water. The old bedstead and dressers still filled the room and she could make out the outline of the antique dressing table by the window.

She put her two bags of clothes on the bench at the foot of the bed, but wouldn't go upstairs to her old room. This would be her room now as it was on the back of the house, facing the lake.

This haven was going to be her sanctuary, but, she quickly pulled the curtains closed.

Kate made the rounds of the house, making sure all the windows and doors were locked tightly with no lights on anywhere. She'd lived there long enough to find her way in the dark and use the flashlight sparingly.

Even though no one could see a light from the

nearest road, she couldn't risk anyone knowing she was here. Any boat going by on the lake would notice the lights, especially on such a dark night as this.

Her plan, her escape, her very survival depended on no one knowing where she was. Tony could not find her here. She couldn't risk anyone telling him of a strange light out at her aunt's old place. No one could suspect or he would know. He would know and he would come. He would kill her here or back at their house, but either way she would die at his hand.

Making her way back to the living room, Kate walked to the piano and picked up her parents' picture.

"Are you there, Mom? Dad? Is Aunt Linda with you now? I'm here and I'm all right. Help me, please, help me stay safe. Help me hide here and I'll be all right. Please don't let anyone find me."

She put the picture back in its place of honor, checked the locks once more, and climbed into bed. After tossing and turning for hours, listening for any telltale footsteps or the tires of a car crunching on the gravel drive, she finally gave up her fear and fell into an exhausted sleep.

## Chapter Two

She must be dreaming—the hum of a boat motoring down the lake, chatter from a few crickets in the trees, and the tart scent of the lake on a cool fall morning. Kate didn't want to open her eyes and leave the dream, because reality never measured up.

Suddenly, she remembered that today's reality was different. Today she was waking up at Aunt Linda's house, in her bed, safe and hidden from Tony and his pounding fists.

While the thought of Tony caused her heart to race, the memory of Aunt Linda made her ache. Today Linda would be buried. If Kate didn't go to the funeral, no family would be there. Linda had plenty of friends, but she was old enough that most of them had passed away already. She couldn't let Linda's passing go unnoticed, unmourned. Somehow, she had to get there.

Kate made her way back to Tony's house; it was no longer hers anymore, to find clothes for the funeral. Fortunately, it was early and no one was out yet. She drove the car to the grocery store, where it wouldn't draw notice. From there, she walked down the back alley to the cemetery behind the little, Episcopal church.

In a town full of Catholics, Aunt Linda had been one of this church's strongest supporters. Hopefully, the good ladies of the church had been a comfort to her in the past few years, since Tony forced her out of their lives.

Tears threatened to slide from behind her dark glasses, but she didn't want to attract any attention. She stayed to the tree line and walked back toward the small group assembled in the far north corner. She could hear enough to follow the service without actually participating.

An enormous maple had shed a few orange and red leaves; the musty, bitter scent lacing the air. The sun shone brightly from above and the bell tower of their pretty little church was clearly visible. Aunt Linda must have picked this spot. Yes, she would love it here.

The tears filled her eyes, even though she was sure she'd lost the ability to cry years ago. She couldn't believe she would never have a chance to explain to Aunt Linda why she practically abandoned her not long after her marriage to Tony. This woman scrimped and saved, and did her best by Kate for ten years. It had been nearly as long since she'd even seen Kate.

After the first couple of years, Linda stopped trying to visit and rarely ever called. Though they lived only a couple of miles apart, Tony ensured Kate never got to even talk to her aunt, her only living relative. He warned Linda never to approach Kate at work and somehow scared her strong, stubborn aunt into complying. Now Kate would never be able to apologize or explain. She could never hug her aunt or thank her or even listen to her talk about Kate's parents again. She was gone and

Kate suddenly was more alone than ever.

When the funeral was over, Kate waited for the other mourners to leave before walking back to her car. She made it to the car without drawing any notice and took the back roads to Tony's house.

She parked the car in the driveway where it always sat and walked to the front door to let herself in one last time.

"Kathy, thank God! I've been worried about you."

Kate nearly jumped out of her skin at the sound of Brenda's voice. She pasted on as serene an expression as she could manage, hoping most of her bruises had faded overnight, and turned to face the woman who was supposedly her best friend.

"Oh hi, Brenda. Why in the world have you been worried about me?"

"I've been calling you for two days. Where have you been?"

Brenda followed her into the house and grabbed a chair at the kitchen table. Long ago, they were close enough Kate would have thought it the most natural thing in the world.

"Me? I haven't been anywhere. I went to the grocery store, but mostly I've been here. I must have misplaced my phone."

Kate pulled out a pitcher of water and offered Brenda a glass. As she placed it on the table, Brenda placed her hand on Kate's arm and gasped. Kate winced and tried to turn.

"What happened to your face? Were you in a car accident? Does Tony know?"

Kate almost laughed. *Oh yeah, Tony knows.*

Instead, she sat at the opposite end of the table, out of the direct light.

"No, I wasn't in a car accident. I fell down the back stairs. I'm fine, only a little banged up. It's no big deal, really."

Brenda moved closer and Kate pulled back.

"Not a big deal? When did it happen?"

"Uh…yesterday, in the morning. I went to bed with an ice pack. That must be why I missed your call yesterday."

She'd gone to bed with an ice pack many, many times. Tony had splurged on the automatic ice maker when they bought a new refrigerator a few years ago probably for that very reason.

"Oh. You know, Deke and Jack said it was probably something like that when I spoke with them."

Kate's head whipped around quicker than was comfortable. "Jack?"

"I went to see Deke yesterday, because I was worried about you, and Jack was there. I guess you didn't know he was in town either."

"Jack Finelli?"

Brenda laughed. "Yes, Jack Finelli. As in the younger brother of our husbands."

It'd been a long time, ten years, since he'd left town. She figured Harper's Glen had seen the last of Jack Finelli forever.

"What's he doing in town?"

"You know, he didn't really say." Brenda didn't seem as interested in Jack's return as Kate. "Well, as long as you're okay, I'm going to head home. I have a ton of stuff to do before the school bus pulls in, and then homework, sports practices, and all the rest."

Brenda grabbed her purse and walked to the back door. She paused and turned back to Kate and her bruises one last time.

"Are you sure you're okay?"

A tiny voice in the back of Kate's mind screamed *tell her, tell her* but the rest of her rational brain knew better. If Brenda never suspected anything in all these years, she'd never believe Kate at this late date. Brenda and Tom worshipped Tony, as many people did. A few bruises, cuts, and scars couldn't outweigh his perpetual charm. No contest.

"I'm sure. Thanks for stopping by." She walked to the door and closed it. Then, she sank back down into the chair, her legs no longer able to support her.

How could she think she could sneak off and no one would notice? Heck, if Brenda went to the sheriff when she didn't answer her phone for two days, what would Ruby do down at the beauty shop when Kate didn't show up for her afternoon shift? And how long would it be before Deke, Ruby, Brenda, or someone else called Tony and told him his wife was missing?

Her hands began to shake. If someone interrupted his hunting trip with the boys, and told them Kate had disappeared, he would hunt her down like the deer he had his sites on right now. He would be embarrassed in addition to being livid, and she'd seen that combination enough to know, it could kill her.

Automatically, she began picking up the kitchen, putting her glass in the dishwasher, and sweeping up the leaves that blew in when she opened the door.

While she ached to return to Aunt Linda's to hide out, to escape her life, she also knew she was fooling herself.

Maybe if she was smarter, she could pull it off. Of course, if she'd been smarter, she might not be in this situation to begin with. Tony told her all the time it was a good thing she was pretty, since she was a dumb as a rock. How could a rock ever escape Tony?

Kate climbed the stairs to the bedroom and got ready for work. She layered on her makeup, making sure to cover the bruises completely. Ruby was not stupid and would want more of an explanation than falling down the stairs. Kate had already taken a number of "falls."

**\*\*\*\***

"Why don't you go home early, Deke?" Jack could tell the old man was hurting more today. He'd hardly moved from his desk chair all afternoon, yet he didn't seem very comfortable there.

"Why in the world—"

"You know as well as I do why. My question is, why not?" Jack looked pointedly at Deke. "I think I'm perfectly able to handle all the excitement around here this afternoon. And if anything comes up I can't handle, I'll call you at home. Okay?"

Deke started to argue some more, but it just wasn't in him to keep up the fight. "Okay. I guess I could use a break today."

"Want me to drop you home?"

"No, thank you very much. I'm not feeble. I can drive myself home."

Never one to be coddled, Deke didn't take Jack's offers of help too easily. Jack figured Deke's resistance was a good sign; the old man hadn't given in to his illness completely.

Jack listened to Deke talking to Thelma and then it was quiet once again in the office. The sheriff's office in Harper's Glen didn't have a lot of business during the middle of a weekday afternoon. Definitely a plus to moving back here. Of course, it was also a minus.

Working and living in DC had its ups and downs, as well. He always thrived on the excitement, the fulfillment he got from doing his job and doing it well. The satisfaction he got from figuring out and tracking down the bad guys kept him going through many long nights.

Until his job followed him home one too many times. Until the reality of his career choices came crashing in on his home life. Yeah, he definitely could use a break from the scum he'd been dealing with at the FBI. Small town drunks and traffic violators sounded like heaven about now.

Jack jumped when the intercom buzzed, pulling him from his review of the files.

"Yeah, Thelma?"

Thelma's voice was always the epitome of professionalism on the phone. "Undersheriff Finelli, there is a call on line one I think you should take."

"Who is it?"

"She wouldn't say, but it seems rather urgent."

Shaking his head, Jack said, "Okay. Put her through."

"Hello. This is Jack Finelli. How can I help you?"

"Uh…well…uh, is Deke there?" the timid voice

on the line stammered.

"No, he's not. May I ask who's calling?"

"Uh…well, I thought maybe Deke could…"

Jack wasn't always the most patient of men, but something about this woman's voice worried him.

"Deke has left for the day. What's your name, miss?"

"I can't tell you…I…I can't tell you," she whispered.

Red flares lit up in his brain, but he tried to keep his voice calm and casual. Meanwhile, he pressed Thelma's extension on the phone and when she entered the room, motioned for her to get a trace on the call.

"Okay, okay. No name. But I promise, I can help you with whatever you need. If I can't, I'll call Deke for you. Now, tell me, what's the problem?" Jack swiveled in his chair, taking out a note pad and pen.

"Well, I'm wondering…" she began. "If a woman leaves her husband and, well, she has her reasons and all, is there anything the sheriff can do to keep her safe?"

"I'm not sure what you're asking, miss. Maybe you need to talk to a lawyer, if you want to get a divorce." The thin, reedy breathing let Jack know she was still on the line, even though she didn't respond.

"Do you want to divorce your husband? Is that what you're asking?"

"I don't care about a divorce. I want to get out." The woman hesitated. "This was a stupid idea. I'm sorry I bothered you—"

"No. Don't hang up. I want to help you, ma'am, but I don't understand what's going on." Jack

27

absently clicked the pen he had been holding in his other hand. "Where are you right now? Maybe I can take a drive over there and talk to you in person. I'm sure we can figure out whatever you need to know."

Jack was certain if she hung up, she'd never call back. If this was a domestic violence case, as he was beginning to suspect, she might never make it out alive. He couldn't lose her now.

"No, you can't come here. He'd go crazy if he found out you were here."

The panic in her voice glued him to the phone. Whatever doubts he had about her home-life flew out the window.

"Okay, okay. No problem. What do you want to do?"

She hiccupped. It sounded like she was trying to hold back her tears.

"I want to get away. I don't know how, though. He'll find me and then it'll be worse than ever. I just can't ever get out."

"Don't give up, honey." Right now, Jack would have traded a dozen drug dealers in DC for a broken, battered woman in his quiet hometown. He didn't know if he could help this woman. He didn't know what to tell her. "You can get out. We'll find a way."

"No, there is no way. I was a fool to think there was."

Jack knew he was losing her, in more ways than one. Whoever this woman was, she sounded young. She had a lot of life left to live, if the bastard who married her didn't kill her first. He had to find a way to help.

"Wait, don't hang up." He flipped through the

old rolodex sitting in the corner of Deke's desk. He'd never been much of a believer in divine providence until his finger landed on the business card for the Southern Tier Domestic Violence Shelter.

"Listen, honey. I've got a phone number for you to call."

"No, I can't tell anyone else about this." She sighed. "I should never have called you in the first place."

"Please. It's the women's shelter. They have professionals there who can help you."

"I can't go to a shelter. Aren't you listening? He'd kill me if I tried."

"You don't have to go there. Just call them. Let me give you the phone number, and you can call and talk to them. They can help you."

"I don't know. If he ever found out…"

"Take the number and call later or tomorrow or whenever. Take the number, please. These women can save your life. They can help you get out."

Jack was afraid she had given up on him. His pulse pounded in his ears and he was sweating like he'd run a marathon, even though he'd never gotten out of his chair. The silence on the phone dragged.

"Okay. Give me the number."

He did and said a silent thanks to the heavens above while he did.

"Can I…can I call you again, too?" she asked.

Jack almost laughed with relief. He couldn't have messed up too much if she wanted to talk to him again.

"Of course." He rattled off his cell phone number for her. "When you call here tell them

Honey's on the phone. Anytime, day or night, and I'll be there."

"Thank you. I gotta go."

With the sound of the dial tone, he found himself able to breathe again. His shirt was soaked with sweat and he had a whopper of a headache starting in his neck. But he knew, even still, it couldn't compare to what that young woman had been through.

Deke told him there was some domestic abuse in the county. In fact, he knew there was a problem with incest and child abuse, as well. These things tended to be self-perpetuating and among the hardest crimes to prosecute. He didn't expect to get up close and personal with abuse the first week back in town.

He walked to the outer office and leaned one hip on the corner of Thelma's desk. If the pained expression on her face was any indication, he'd guess Thelma didn't appreciate a casual office atmosphere. How could she have worked for Deke all these years?

She handed him a pink memo slip. "Here's the phone number and location of where that call came from."

"Thanks." He checked the slip and read "*Ruby's House of Beauty*," which was only a few blocks away on Main Street. "Can you do me a favor, Thelma?"

"Of course. What do you need?"

"Can you take a walk down to Ruby's for me right now, let me know who all is in there?" He didn't dare go himself, especially not in uniform, in case he scared the woman off. Maybe Thelma could find her.

"Okay. I can schedule my next appointment while I'm there."

"Perfect," Jack said. "But quick, before you go, can you show me where I can find the current or pending domestic violence files?"

It was as if her whole body snapped to attention. If there was one thing Thelma could be counted on for, it was having perfectly organized files. She could probably find the file on last time the mayor's son got caught pinching a candy bar from the Quick-Mart in ten seconds flat. A true believer in the cleanliness is next to Godliness motto.

She pulled open three files drawers along the far wall. "These files are divided into spousal abuse, child abuse, and sexual abuse."

"I'm interested in the spousal abuse ones."

She clicked two drawers shut and pointed to the one left open. "Everything you need should be in here or cross-referenced to one of the files in the back room, where the closed cases are."

"Great. My guess is I won't need those, as this case is probably still open. Well, if it's ever even been reported."

After Thelma took her purse and walked out the door, Jack pulled out the first file from the drawer and started reviewing it.

By the time she returned from the beauty parlor, his blood pressure had risen twenty points, his collar button was unbuttoned, and his attitude had seriously deteriorated. Damn, there were some worthless human beings in this county.

"Here's the list of everyone who was in Ruby's. I can't guarantee the caller was still there, of course.

It wasn't very busy."

"Good." He grabbed the list and then stopped, took a deep breath, and raised his gaze to Thelma's. "Thanks for your help. Please be sure to keep this confidential."

"Yes, of course. That goes without saying for all office business."

She almost seemed insulted he even mentioned it. He'd have to remember to do something nice for her this week, flowers or something. She was an asset around here and he didn't want to piss her off.

Jack walked back into Deke's office and stared at the list. She wasn't kidding about the number of people in the shop. Ruby and her customer, Mildred Shafer, a seventy-two widow, an unlikely candidate to be the caller.

Thelma had listed two more customers, neither of whom he knew, as well as two more stylists. Rita Perry was unfamiliar to him but not the last name on the list, his sister-in-law.

He forgot Kate worked there. If he could narrow down the list a bit more, Kate might be able to help him find out the identity of the caller. He couldn't ask her about it yet, but when he had a little more to go on, he would.

He took the rest of the day to cross-check open spousal abuse cases with the list of names from Ruby's but had no luck. He knew it was entirely possible the caller never reported the abuse.

The next logical choice was the hospital; since it was likely the caller had required medical care at some point, especially if the abuse had been going on for years. However, they would never show him anyone's medical records without a warrant, which he couldn't get yet, based on what he knew thus far.

He would have to wait, talk to Deke, and follow up with the women's shelter staff. And most of all, he would pray Honey stayed alive long enough to call the shelter.

**\*\*\*\***

By the end of the week, Aunt Linda's house, and the freedom it promised, was becoming a distant memory for Kate. She spent her days working, cleaning, cooking, shopping, and keeping up appearances, as she had for the past ten years. She didn't know how to do anything else.

When she awoke on Sunday morning, she was longing to go back to church, maybe to connect with Aunt Linda on some level. She hadn't been religious growing up, but had enjoyed the security and peace which came from sitting in the sanctuary and participating in the familiar rituals.

Why had she stopped going? Truth be told, she never gave it much thought. When she married Tony, it was in the big Catholic church in the center of town. But even though Tony's parents went regularly, she and Tony never did. At some point, though, when she talked about going, Tony refused. She could have used it today, with him coming home soon. But if he found out, it wouldn't be worth it.

She started laundry and put a roast in the slow cooker while she cleaned for Tony's return. When she finished, she showered and did her hair and makeup the way he liked. Fortunately, she was ready when he came home, several hours earlier than she expected.

"Kathy? Kathy, where are you? I'm home."

She tried to stomp down the panic rising up her spine at the sound of his voice. If she didn't rush to greet him, she'd pay.

He stood in the kitchen, all six-foot-four-of him, scrutiny in his deep brown eyes, a sickly-sweet smile on his chiseled face, and not a dark hair out of place on his head.

"Welcome home." She walked into the kitchen and kissed his cheek, took his duffle bag, and hung up his coat.

She was trying, desperately, to judge his mood, which then would decide her fate. If things went well with his brother and friends and the hunting had been good, it should be a peaceful evening. If not, then any little thing could set him off.

"Did you miss me?"

Did this mean he was happy? Could it be a set up?

Kate looked up into his dark eyes, pasting on her best sincere-style smile. "Of course. You know how quiet it is around here when you're away."

After she set his things on the basement stairs, she started pulling together their dinner. Her fingers wouldn't work right, probably because they had turned to shards of ice.

"What did you do all week?" Tony asked, settling at the kitchen table with the glass of beer Kate knew to have ready for him.

She prayed he couldn't read her mind. She couldn't say she ran away but then chickened out and came back.

"The same as ever. I had Monday off, but

worked every other day."

"Where are your tips for the week?" He controlled all the money in their house, said it was "the husband's job." And since her earning depended heavily on tips, he collected those weekly and then gave her back an allowance to live on.

She grabbed an envelope from the counter and took it to him. She tried to calm her erratic breathing and the shaking of her hands.

"It was a pretty slow week at Ruby's, but I made some decent tips anyway." She didn't add it was always when she had the most bruises that she got the most tips. She never knew who left them, since they were tallied at the register, but it scared her to think someone knew what was going on.

He leafed through the money, and, apparently satisfied, stuffed the envelope in his pocket. He placed his hand on her arm. Not quite a grab, but enough pressure she couldn't pull away without making him angry.

"I stopped at Tom's with him on the way home." Tony's voice was tense. "Brenda said she was here on Tuesday because she was worried about you. What the hell was that all about?"

Kate took a shallow breath, trying to summon up enough volume to eke out an answer.

"I had trouble getting around Monday, so I napped most of the day. Brenda tried calling and got worried when she couldn't get a hold of me."

Each of the five fingers tightened slightly on her arm. No more short-sleeve shirts this week.

"She said she finally came here on Tuesday and found you?"

"Yeah. She must have tried calling when I was at the Quik-Mart. I walked in the door from shopping and she was right behind me."

No let up on the pressure, but no twisting of the skin either. "She asked me if I knew about your fall down the back steps."

"She noticed some bruising, so that's what I told her. It was no big deal."

The twisting started and she sank down in the chair next to him, trying not to cry out. Experience taught her it would only make things worse.

"Don't tell me what's a big deal or not. I walk into my brother's house after a week away and his wife starts hounding me about did I know you fell, shouldn't I have come home to check on you, when had I talked to you last. It was embarrassing," Tony spat out. "Tom stared at *me* as if I'd done something wrong."

She couldn't keep the sarcasm out of the voice in her head, even if she never spoke it out loud. *God forbid Tony should ever be embarrassed. As if he'd done something wrong.*

"I'm sorry, Tony. I told her it was nothing, and I was fine."

He stood, making the angle of the pressure more intense and more painful. "Did you have any makeup on?"

"Of course I did, just like every day. It was a little harder to cover than sometimes." When she thought the bone in her forearm was finally going to snap in two, he let go.

"Don't be so careless again. I don't want my brother or his nosey wife accosting me like that ever again."

"Yes, Tony. I'm sorry, Tony." She kept her eyes down and held her left arm gently with her right hand. When he started eating, she picked up her fork and ate. There would be time for more ice later.

\*\*\*\*

"This is Mary Anne. How can I help you?"

It was a slow Tuesday afternoon and Ruby had run out for supplies. Kate grabbed her chance to call the women's shelter, hoping for something, although she wasn't sure what.

"Hello? Is anyone there?" The woman on the phone sounded friendly enough, but Kate wasn't sure she could tell another soul what her life was like. It was killing her to know Jack knew, even if he didn't know he knew.

"Uh…yeah. Hello," Kate started.

"Hello. Who's calling, please?"

"Uh…is this the Southern Tier Domestic Violence Shelter?"

"Yes, it is. What can I do for you? Do you need some help?"

Man, did she ever. But she wasn't sure anyone could really help her get away from Tony. "I…uh…I wanted to ask some questions, you know, about what can be done to protect a woman if she, you know, leaves her husband."

"Are you being abused?" Mary Ann asked.

"Well, uh…it's my husband, well, he gets mad sometimes. I don't know if I can take it much more." Kate found the words hard to say out loud.

"Where are you? Let me come and get you and bring you to the shelter. He'll never know where you are and we will protect you. What's your name?"

Kate nearly hung up the phone. Panic ripped through her. She took a deep breath. "No, you can't. He'll know, believe me, he'll know."

"I understand you're afraid of your husband, and if he abuses you, you have every right to be afraid. But believe me, he plays on that fear. He makes you think he'll find you, no matter what. But he won't. Let us help you."

"I can't...I'm afraid, for sure. I'm too afraid to leave. If I did and he found me, he'd kill me."

"We can protect you. Really we can."

The woman on the other end, Mary Anne she'd said, had a strong and caring voice. But so did Tony, when he wanted to.

"I want to know how a wife could be protected. I mean, how does it work? What are the chances of stopping him...I mean, how can you keep a man from hurting his wife?"

"We can hide you in this shelter or another initially, until we are able to get legal proceedings under way. We'll help you find a lawyer, even pay for one, and get a protective order on file. Do you know what a protective order is?"

"It means he can't hurt me anymore or they'll arrest him, right?"

"Right. Usually, it means if he comes within one hundred feet of you the police will arrest him. Once you have one, you can file divorce papers, and begin to rebuild your life. We'll help you find a new job, a new apartment, or daycare if you have kids. Whatever you need, we can help you to achieve it."

It sounded too good to be true, so Kate knew it

was.

"You don't understand. I have nothing, I know nothing, I am nothing. He's used me up and left me with nothing."

Mary Anne was silent for a moment. Kate thought she might have given up hope and hung up. But when she spoke again, her voice was a little deeper, a little huskier.

"Not true, not true. You have the sense to want to get out and to call us to help you. He hasn't left you with nothing. You have your heart, your soul, and your brains. That's all you need to survive."

The bell rang on the front door, as a customer entered the shop.

"I have to go."

"Wait. Can you give me your name?"

"No…uh… Honey will have to do."

"Okay, Honey. Will you call me again tomorrow?"

Kate gave up making promises long ago. She couldn't keep them if she had no control over her life and she couldn't bear to let people down.

"I'll try." It was the best she could do.

"Okay. You try. I'll be here."

Kate slipped the phone onto its charger and pasted a smile on her face.

"How can I help you today, Mrs. Johnson?"

Chapter Three

"Did you talk to your brothers yet?" Deke pushed open the door to Minnie's, waving to the hostess as they took a booth in the back.

The lunch rush was in full swing. Jack's eyes stung as he waded through the cloud of grease hovering just below the ceiling, mixed with the stench of stale cigarette wafting off many of the customers. Minnie's catered to truckers passing through town, in addition to the regular working guys from the salt company or down off the farm.

"They just got home this weekend. It's only Tuesday so, no, I haven't had a chance to visit them yet. Why are you so concerned about me seeing my brothers anyway?"

Deke looked him in the eye. "I thought you'd want to talk to them, now you've moved back to town. You could call them, at least."

"I will, eventually. There's no rush."

Jack turned his head as the waitress approached with a coffee pot. Her brassy blonde curls were piled high on her head. The name tag on her tight pink uniform read *"Debbie."*

"Hi. How are you gentlemen doing today?"

Deke smiled at the woman as if she was a cute little twenty-year-old rather than a road-worn fifty-something. He pushed forward his coffee cup and she filled it.

"We're fine, sweetie."

"Great. Today's soups are chicken noodle and split pea, and the blue plate special is roast turkey with mashed potatoes and gravy." She turned to look at Jack as she started to fill his cup as well. "Are you ready to order?"

"Yeah, I'll have—"

"Wait. Aren't you the youngest Finelli boy?"

Jack nodded and examined Debbie's face. She still wasn't familiar.

"I haven't seen you around town in years. Are you passing through?"

"Uh, no. I'm working for Deke now," he said.

She set the coffeepot on the table and braced her hand on her hip.

"No kiddin'? Great. I see your brothers in here a lot and they never mentioned you were moving back to town. I bet the family is thrilled."

Jack tried to keep the sarcasm out of his voice. "Yeah, thrilled."

He gave up on her ever pouring the coffee, and picked up the pot to do it himself. She didn't seem the least embarrassed by it, in fact, she hardly noticed.

"I'm sorry, sugar, but I don't remember your first name."

"It's Jack."

"Jack, that's right. Well, it sure is great to see you again, Jack."

He mumbled his thanks, not wanting to admit he had no idea who she was.

"Guess I'd better get back to work." She took

out her pad and pen again. "What's it going to be, boys?"

After the both ordered the blue plate special, she finally retrieved the coffeepot and headed back to the kitchen. When Jack turned back to Deke, he was smiling.

"You have no idea who she was, do you?"

Jack had to chuckle himself. "None."

"Billy Michaels's mother."

"That's Mrs. Michaels? I couldn't even recognize her."

Deke's smile faded a bit. "It's Mrs. Standish now. She and Billy's dad divorced about eight years ago."

"She looks much older. I know it's been ten years, but she's aged more like thirty."

Deke took a sip of coffee and nodded. "She's had a hard time of it. Ed, Billy's dad, beat her some, but nobody ever knew until Billy finally graduated from high school and left home. I guess his father got even rougher with her than usual and she landed in the hospital. She wouldn't press charges even then, but she did agree to leave the bastard. Years of getting beat will age a woman."

Jack sipped his coffee and thought about Honey. Would she call again? If so, could he convince her to leave her husband before she ended up in the hospital, or worse? He decided to put it out of his mind for now, since there was nothing he could do about it.

"You haven't seen your brothers much in ten years. Don't you think it's time?"

Jack sighed. He'd hoped they were finished with

this part of the conversation.

"I can't imagine they've changed very much. I'm sure Tom is still a decent-enough guy. He loves life and thinks everyone loves him, and mostly they do. But Tony, well, let's just say, I haven't been honored with his presence yet."

"Now see, that's why you need to call 'em."

Jack tried to swallow his hot coffee before he sputtered. "What do you mean?"

"It means, you let those boys run ya' out of town ten years ago. Don't you think it's past time to let it go?"

No one else in his life had ever spoken to him the way Deke had, never pulling any punches. Maybe that was part of the reason he loved the old man so much. But it sure made him uncomfortable at times.

"They didn't run me out of town. I left Harper's Glen to go to college, got busy with my life, and never came back, until now."

Debbie delivered their lunch, refilled their coffee, and left them to themselves. Jack's gaze met hers and he smiled, aching for the pain she'd endured. He'd have to leave a big tip.

After taking a bite of his mashed potatoes, Deke started waving his fork in the air. Jack knew it meant the conversation was not finished.

"Don't try to fool me, boy. Your father, and dang near everyone else in this town, idolized those two boys because they were the stars of the football and basketball teams back in high school. There was no way you, at five-foot-eight, could compete with those two boys on the basketball court, with both of them topping six-four. You and I both know it was the main reason you left. And it's still between you now, you and your brothers. It's time ya' laid it to rest."

Jack chewed his turkey in silence. He thought he laid it to rest long ago.

Sure, he was disappointed his father never had time for him the way he did for Tom and Tony. His father was a man's man. He liked hunting, fishing, drinking, and sports. Just because none of these appealed to Jack in any great way didn't mean he wasn't the man's son. But his father certainly implied as much.

Maybe if his brothers hadn't been so popular, athletic, and, well, so damn tall, he wouldn't have seemed so nerdy, serious, and short to his dad. Maybe then, his father would have celebrated Jack's valedictorian speech in high school, his cum laude graduation from Dartmouth, or even his appointment to the FBI.

But those weren't things his father noticed.

"I never think about high school anymore, Deke. It's ancient history."

"Good, because here come your brothers." Deke leaned in with a conspiratorial smile on his face.

Jack turned around in time to catch sight of Tom and Tony approaching. Watching them together, strolling through the diner, shaking hands and patting backs, Jack couldn't ignore the picture of vitality and popularity they created; even now they were in their thirties.

Still the big men on campus, big fish in a little pond, and loving it. Especially Tony.

He could tell the moment they noticed him; their gazes switched from jovial greeting to utter shock. Tom's turned quickly to delight, but Tony was harder to read.

Jack stood when they approached the booth and held out his hand. Tony took it first, shaking it briefly and then letting it go. Tom grabbed his hand and pulled him into a hug. He always was the most affectionate one in the family.

"Jack! Hey man, what are you doing in town? Brenda told me she ran into you, but didn't know how long you're staying." Tom slid into the booth next to Jack. Tony glared down at Deke, who slid over to make room, and sat as well.

"Hey yourselves. How are you? I arrived last week while you two were off saving the world from helpless animals. I stopped at Mom and Dad's, and they told me you would be gone all week."

"Yeah, we got back Sunday."

While Tom was as exuberant as ever, Tony was more reserved. When he finally spoke, something in his voice grated on Jack's nerves.

"What's with the sheriff's uniform, Jack? Were you fired or are you slumming it in some kind of small-town undercover assignment? Maybe there's word of price fixing in the local grape market? Or maybe the salt plant is really a cover for the mob?"

Jack glanced at Deke and then turned to Tony. "Actually, I quit the FBI and have moved back here. I'm working for the sheriff's office now."

"Oh how rich. Coming down in the world a bit, aren't you, little brother?"

Jack had always hated it when Tony called him

'little brother' in such a condescending tone.

"Only making a geography change, Tony. DC was starting to get to me, and I decided the quality of life must be pretty good here if you two liked it too much to ever leave."

Tom chuckled.

Tony didn't.

"Why should we leave when we have everything we could ever want here, as well as being near Mom and Dad and the rest of the family?"

"Well, I decided to find it out for myself, Tony-old-man. If Harper's Glen is indeed paradise, I think it's my turn." A ripple of annoyance, or maybe anger, shot through Tony at the old-man remark. Verbal sparring was always fun.

"Where are you living?" Tom asked.

Jack turned to Tom again, leaving Tony to steam.

"I found an empty apartment up in the Morris house on the south end of town."

Tom shook his head. "Sure, I know where you mean. Wait 'til I tell Brenda you're staying. She's going to want to have a big family dinner to celebrate. I'll let you know when."

He turned to Tony. "Do you think Kathy will be up to coming?"

Tony stood. "We'll be there. Be sure to tell Brenda to make leg of lamb."

Jack couldn't miss the interaction between his brothers. Tom seemed amused but confused, but Jack had already guessed where Tony was headed.

"I didn't know you were big on lamb, Tony."

"It's only appropriate, Tom, to welcome home

the prodigal son."

As his brothers walked away after promises of getting together, well, at least from Tom, Jack turned to Deke, who was shaking his head.

"Are you happy now I told my brothers I moved back?"

Deke shot him a look that Jack knew equaled exasperation. "You and your brothers have a long way to go before I'll be happy."

****

"Turn it up, would ya Ruby?"

Kate was surprised Ruby had the television on while customers were in the shop. The customers seemed to like it, though, as all four women were riveted to the talk show.

Ruby flicked the remote and then turned to Kate. "Did you cut Ed Michaels's hair yesterday?"

"Yeah, why? Was something wrong?" Kate often felt nervous around Mr. Michaels. He was big and gruff and always seemed a little off. Sometimes he called Kate by the wrong name.

"No, nothing was wrong. He came in this morning and said he'd forgotten to tip his hairdresser yesterday. I figured it had to be you, since he said it was a pretty blonde, but he called you Debbie. Anyway, here's the tip."

Kate took the folded bills from Ruby. There was a note clipped to the money saying *"Debbie,"* with a rough heart drawn around it. Probably harmless enough, but she tossed it out to keep it away from Tony.

"He forgets my name every time, but he's a good tipper." Kate sighed. "I think I remind him of his ex-wife."

Kate pocketed the bills and Ruby went back to her customer.

Ruby's customer, Mrs. Miller, pointed to the T.V. "Look Ruby, doesn't that woman write those romance books you like?"

Kate glanced over at the beautiful, dark-haired woman on the screen. Ruby was a big reader of historical romances, especially when between customers. She even kept a rack of books she'd read for customers to borrow at their leisure.

"Yeah."

Kate turned her attention back to taking out her customer's rollers, but almost ended up with a handful of hair when the woman shot up in her seat.

"Would you look at that?" Mrs. Miller slapped the arm of her chair. "Your writer's husband killed her, right in front of their kids!"

Everyone in the shop, Kate included, stopped in their tracks, absorbed in the story.

The reporter stood in front of a beautiful, old Victorian home in a lovely neighborhood. "Friends of the couple claim they had no idea this was an abusive relationship, at least not until it was too late for this famous author. The police are alleging she ran from the house in an attempt to escape his abuse, but he apparently followed her. When he caught her in the driveway, he beat her to death."

The camera closed in on a picture of the author at a recent conference, surrounded by her books. "The world of romance and happy endings was how she made her livelihood. But it was the complete opposite of her daily life. It's hard to imagine where she came up with her story ideas. Her own story has no happily-ever-after ending, especially for the children she left behind."

"Oh that poor woman," mumbled Mrs. Miller.

Kate pulled herself back from the story on the screen and tried to ignore the way Ruby was gazing at her. Her eyes seemed a little red around the rims.

Mrs. Miller crossed her arms over her chest. "I just don't understand why she didn't leave him the first time he hit her. I would never put up with abuse from any man."

Mrs. Miller was in her early fifties and had worked in the county offices for as long as Kate could remember. She'd never seen the woman take grief from anyone, but couldn't help thinking how different it was when it was someone you loved, someone who supposedly loved you.

Ruby seemed to understand. "I don't think it's easy, Helen. In the beginning, I'm sure she was hoping he'd change. She probably stayed because she thought it'd get better. Or maybe she was afraid to leave, or had no money."

Kate's pulse quickened. She wanted to run screaming from the shop. Or at least run into Ruby's arms. But instead she concentrated her entire focus on keeping her face a benign picture of mild interest.

"Well, he never did change, did he? They never do. The only difference this time is he finally killed her. I think it's a little late to be worrying about fear of leaving or public opinion or finances or whatever. She's dead. Would have been better off broke, divorced, and frightened, but alive."

Everyone immediately agreed with Mrs. Miller

on this one. Everyone but Kate. She was frozen in place by the thought of living frightened versus being dead.

She couldn't seem to make her fingers work. She pulled a roller from her customer's hair and dropped it to the floor. The woman made some remark, chuckling, but Kate couldn't focus. The room was suddenly spinning and devoid of air. She couldn't breathe.

"I'm sorry...uh, I'll be right back." She ran to the bathroom and slammed the door behind her. Chills overtook her body. Her legs could no longer support her, and she slid to the floor. She wrapped her arms around her knees and began rocking, trying to calm the powerful shaking in her body.

Change. She'd been waiting ten years for a change. But she had to face the facts. Tony wasn't going to change. He didn't have to. She voluntarily let him go right on hitting her, apologizing, and moving on. She couldn't make him change. And if he didn't, he would kill her.

"Kathy? Are you all right, sugar?"

Ruby's voice rang through the door, but Kate couldn't seem to speak. When she tried to stand, she doubled over the toilet and tossed up her breakfast, her morning coffee, and maybe, finally, her belief that Tony would ever change. Her belief in happily-ever-after for the two of them.

When her violent spasms finally started to subside, she sank back to the floor, wasted and spent. Her head was too heavy to even lift off the floor, although the shaking had stopped.

She'd been a fool for too long. She'd fooled

herself, and tried to fool everyone else in her life. It was time to face reality. If she didn't get out now, she would end up dead, either on the inside or outside. It didn't matter. Dead is dead. And she wanted to live.

"Kathy? Do you need some help?" Ruby's warm, loving voice cut through the nausea and shame.

Help. Yes, she definitely needed help, and more importantly, she wanted help. She'd kept this secret too long. The secret was killing her softly, slowly, just as Tony was.

She pulled herself to her knees and then slowly to her feet. The room spun for only a moment before she got her bearings. Turning the knob, she pushed the door open.

Ruby stood outside the door, frantic worry etched on her face. Kate took a step and found she was still a little weak, grabbing onto Ruby's ample arm for support.

As she gazed into her dear friend's face, the tears she'd hidden for many years started clouding her eyes.

"Yes, Ruby. I need help. Please, help me."

\*\*\*\*

Jack had made the mistake of stopping off at his parents' house on his way home that evening. He promised his mother he would, but then she wasn't even home.

"Hey, Dad." As Jack walked into the family room, his father briefly glanced up from the newspaper which sat in his lap. The ball game was already on the TV and probably the first or second of tonight's beers stood on the end table.

"Jack."

"Mom asked me to stop by." The fact he had to explain his presence in his childhood home made him sad and a little mad.

"Don't know why she did, as Tuesday is her bunco night. Always has been. 'Course, you wouldn't know, living in Washington and all."

Jack swallowed his retort to the dig about DC. "Especially since she *told* me to come tonight."

"Well, you can sit if you want to. I had supper already. Leftover lasagna from Sunday. Always better leftover, ya know."

Jack didn't sit, but walked around the perimeter of the family room, stopping to peruse family photos along the way.

"That's the party Tony and Tom threw us for our thirty-fifth anniversary. You were out west somewhere, on some case instead, right?"

"Yeah. I was in Los Angeles, Dad, remember? It was a joint investigation with the DEA; hundreds of teenagers killed by overdoses because the stuff was bad. I couldn't get back in time for the party."

"Right."

Jack could never understand his father's lack of interest in his work with the FBI. It wasn't like he was a dance instructor. Chasing bad guys and drug smugglers and mafia bosses ought to be as manly as shooting Bambi's mother. He couldn't figure the old man out and really ought to stop trying.

"Tony said you're back to work with Deke now, huh?"

"Yeah."

"Not going back to Washington any time soon?" Even though his father wouldn't meet his gaze, Jack knew he was getting at something, although not what, exactly.

"No. I've moved back and plan to stay. Deke needs the help, like I told you."

"Hmm…"

Jack moved to the mantel over the fireplace, amazed it still held the memorabilia from Tom's and Tony's high school days. Laminated newspaper clippings, ribbons, trophies, and more pictures.

He found some new pictures at one end. The three of them standing in their hunting gear with a deer carcass hanging behind them. It was a shrine to his favored sons. A testament to the success of their manly endeavors. Jack's image was nowhere to be seen.

"I figured you woulda left after Melanie was killed."

Jack didn't say anything, waiting for the other shoe to drop.

"I mean, after your job followed you home and killed your wife, how could you keep going back day after day? Was it so damn important you be a fed even then, after you buried your wife?"

Jack spun around and faced his father. Rage seeped through every pore. He did his best to rein it in, although he was starting to wonder why he even bothered.

"You don't know what you're talking about. I suggest we consider this conversation over."

"Of course. I mean, if Deke's health is important enough to finally get you to come back to town, we should be grateful, right? You wouldn't come back for us, but at least you came back for Deke."

"Right. He asked me to come back. And I guess I'm lucky Deke saw his way to attend Melanie's funeral, since you were probably too busy hunting or fishing or polishing trophies for your other sons to worry about a murdered daughter-in-law."

His father's lips were moving, but Jack didn't wait for the pitiful excuses. He couldn't leave fast enough.

"Be sure to tell Mom I stopped by."

Jack muttered curses to himself all the way to the car. He flew out of the driveway, turning to the lake rather than back downtown. He was in no mood to sit in his empty apartment alone.

What was he thinking? Why did he think anything would be different because ten years had passed?

He pulled into the parking lot of the community park at the end of the lake. The season was long over and the tourists gone. A few die-hards had probably been sailing today, but it was getting dark now. The lake was empty.

Jack got out and walked across the park to the water's edge. The rocks and gravel glistened in the day's last rays. The clouds hanging over the west hill were dancing with pinks and purples in incredible hues. The quiet evening air was broken only by the sound of the waves on the shore.

He missed these sunsets when he lived in DC. The sight of the sun slipping behind another high-rise or into a mist of ozone didn't have the same connection to his soul this nightly display did. Even as a young kid, the lake had called to him at twilight.

Seneca Lake is the deepest and widest of the Finger Lakes, a living, sleeping giant of water with a personality all its own. Somehow the eternal battle between night and day, as reflected in the calm and quiet surface of the lake, spoke to Jack.

It was time to face facts. He and his father were very different people and always would be. Jack took after his maternal grandfather, and, lord knows, his father never had much respect for him, either.

With his thirtieth birthday recently behind him, it was time for Jack to stop fighting for something he'd never have. If he'd learned nothing else from Melanie's murder, it was life is short. As long as he had his own respect, he didn't need his father's.

But unfortunately, he didn't think he could live his life in Harper's Glen without it. The thought of other nights like this one, family gatherings where he didn't fit in and the pain it would cause his mother made it clear to him he couldn't stay.

He was fooling himself and Deke, to think anything would have changed.

He promised Deke he would move back and he had. He'd stay as long as Deke did. But after his friend was gone, Jack would have to move on. He would have nothing else to hold him to Harper's Glen. Even if he had nowhere else he wanted to be, it would be better than staying where he wasn't wanted.

The fresh air washed away the heat of his anger, leaving only resignation behind. He would never have the relationship he wanted with his father, but he was lucky to have found Deke. He would help

Deke through this tough time and then, when it was over, he would move on.

Jack returned to his car, surprised to find he was actually getting hungry. He started the engine, turned around, and his cell phone rang.

"Jack Finelli here."

"Undersheriff Finelli. I'm sorry to bother you, but there's a phone call that appears to be important."

"What's the call?"

"It's a woman. She'll only identify herself as Honey, but she insists on speaking to you—"

"Put her through. Thanks."

Her voice, quiet and timid, came through on the line. "Hello?"

"Honey, is that you?"

"It's me."

Jack released a breath he must have been holding for days. She was alive, hopefully well, and still willing to talk to him.

"Are you okay?"

"I'm okay. I wanted to call and thank you for giving me the phone number for the shelter." She kept her voice to a whisper.

"Did you call them?"

"Yeah, I did. I called them a few days ago and then again today. They are going to help me get out."

Jack leaned forward, resting his forehead on the steering wheel. "I'm glad."

"Yeah. Me too."

"Do you need help with anything?"

She laughed. He decided it had to be a very good sign if this woman could still laugh.

"I need help with nearly everything. I realized that today and I guess I'm finally willing to ask for it."

"What a great start."

"I talked to Mary Anne at the shelter this afternoon. She helped me pack a few things and then took me to the shelter. We're going to talk tomorrow about what I need to do from here."

"Are you scared?"

"Absolutely. I know he'll go through the roof when he gets home and I'm not there. But he won't be able to find me. Mary Anne says they'll keep me hidden as long as necessary."

"Good. Please, be careful. You can get a restraining order against him. Do you know what that is?"

"Yes. Mary Anne and I talked about it and I'm going to meet with a lawyer tomorrow. She's going to file the papers with the judge for me to keep…my husband…well, to let him know he can't come near me or hurt me anymore."

"Good. And you know Sheriff McAllen and I will do everything we can to help you. If you have trouble, you call us and we'll come running. Okay?"

"Okay."

"I'm glad you took this first step. I know it's going to be very hard. Promise me you'll be careful and do everything Mary Anne and your lawyer say you should do to be safe."

She was quiet for a moment and Jack wondered if she'd answer.

"I will."

Her voice quaked with tears and exhaustion.

"You should get some sleep now. You're going to need your strength."

"Okay. Can I call you again...you know, to talk?"

"Anytime. I am proud of you."

"Thanks. I couldn't have done this much without you. And it helps me a lot to know I can call you for help. I know I'm going to need it."

Jack swallowed, trying to force down the lump that appeared in his throat.

"I'll do anything I can to help. But remember, you're the one who made the decision to leave, a brave and wonderful and strong thing to do. Be careful, but don't be hard on yourself. You're doing great."

Through her quiet crying, she mumbled something like thank you and hung up.

Jack dropped his cell phone and closed his eyes. He forced a few deep breaths in and out of his lungs. He sat in the stunned silence of his car and wondered if he had put this woman in more danger than she'd already been in.

What did he really know about dealing with abused women? Sure, he had basic training, but not much real experience. His work for the FBI had involved a lot of bad stuff over the years. Drugs, gangs, the mob, gun-running, the whole gambit of industrial-strength crime, and corruption. But nothing could hold a candle to a fragile voice on the phone, a woman fearing for her life and turning to him for her personal salvation.

Thank God she didn't know about Melanie. She'd never have called him if she knew he endangered his own wife, and his job had gotten Melanie killed.

Jack put the car into drive and wove slowly back through the empty streets of town. He pulled into the lot behind his apartment and crawled from the car.

He was suddenly beyond exhaustion. He'd done a kind of battle today, slain a few dragons and killed an ogre or two. He only hoped it was enough to keep the fair maiden safe, at least for tonight.

Chapter Four

"Once we get some of the details taken care of, you can go up to your room and relax. You might want to take a nap." Mary Anne's voice was calm and soothing. "This is extremely stressful, and you need to take extra care of yourself to keep your strength up."

"Yeah, never know when I will need it."

Mary Anne tilted her head, her gaze meeting Kate's after Kate's sarcastic retort.

"How are you holding up?"

Kate took a deep breath, trying to hold in a scream which threatened to escape whenever she opened her mouth. It made sense for her to be frightened and a little overwhelmed. After all, she'd left Tony and was sitting in a battered women's shelter.

What she didn't understand was this compulsion to run screaming from the building. Even though there was nothing here to fear. The only thing that could hurt her, Tony, was somewhere out there, on the prowl for her.

"Kate?"

"Sorry. I'm okay, I guess. Everything is a little numb."

Mary Anne smiled and her kind face reassured Kate somewhat.

"It's completely normal. You have made a huge change in your life today. But it's a good one, the right one. I won't try to tell you it will be easy or you'll never be frightened again, but I promise you the only way you have a chance to make a new life, a healthy life, is away from your abuser."

Her husband was now known as her "abuser." Boy, Tony would be pissed.

"I know. And I can't tell you how grateful I am for your help."

As she watched a pained expression flit across Mary Anne's face, Kate suddenly wondered what brought the woman here.

"Let's not worry about gratitude right now, Kate. Let's get your life together, okay?"

"Okay."

"Now, the first order of business, since we have you out of the house, is to apply for an order of protection. Our staff attorney has written this draft for you to read and approve." Mary Anne pushed paperwork across the desk toward Kate. "You also need to write up a list of anyone or any place our attorney can contact for evidence, such as friends, family members, your doctor, or hospital. She'll use these in court to convince the judge to give you an order of protection."

Kate picked up the small stack of papers and then set them back down. "I'm sure everything is in order. Your lawyer does this all the time. Where do I sign?"

When Kate reached for the pen, Mary Anne's hand stopped her.

"You can't sign it without reading first it, Kate.

You need to make sure everything is correct. She left blanks for you to fill in, since she didn't have a chance to meet with you herself and I gave her only the basic facts."

Kate swallowed. Tony's mocking words came back to her, *You can never leave me; you're too stupid to make it without me*. Maybe he was right.

"Do you want me to help you with the legalese? I'm pretty familiar with the terms she uses in these applications and I can explain some of the more complicated stuff to you."

"Yes, thank you." Kate slid the papers back to Mary Anne, pasting a smile on her face to hide her shame.

"Okay." Mary Anne began explaining the concepts and procedures for obtaining a restraining order.

"Once the judge signs the order, Tony will be forbidden from coming within one hundred feet of you at any time, except when we are back in court at some future date. If he violates the order, he will be arrested."

"Assuming someone is around to see it, right?"

"Right. This is part of the reason we strongly advise you to stay here until you have a secure place to live with people around you. You are in the most danger when you are alone."

Kate's thought drifted to her little house on the lake and the quiet solitude of the place still called to her. It was hard to imagine she could be in danger there.

"Kate?"

Mary Anne handed Kate a pen and pointed to an

open space on one page.

"I'm sorry." Kate shook her head. "I drifted there for a moment."

"No problem. I was saying you need to fill in this section. Meanwhile, I'm going to get us some coffee. It's been a tough day for you and it's not quite over; I'm sure you could use a little jolt."

When Mary Anne left the room, Kate picked up the paper trying to focus on the area she was supposed to fill in. She wasn't certain what she was expected to write.

After making sure she was still alone, Kate picked up the sheet and tried to read each word aloud, hoping to make sense of it all. She followed the words with her fingers, but still couldn't figure out what was expected of her. As she threw the papers down in frustration, Mary Anne entered the room.

Mary Anne handed her the coffee and then bent to retrieve the order. "What's the matter? Is something wrong with this?"

Kate took a sip and tried to regain control of her nerves and to drown out the taunting refrain of Tony's insults going through her brain. *Good thing you're pretty, honey, because you sure are dumb. In fact, the phrase dumb blonde was coined for you.*

"Can't you ask me what you want to know? I…I'm tired, and my head is killing me. I can't read all of this right now." *Or ever.*

Mary Anne smiled and picked up the pen. "Sure thing. I'm sure you're wiped out; let's get this thing finished and back on the attorney's desk."

When they filled in all the information needed

for the order and prepared Kate's list of witnesses and evidence, sparse as it was, Mary Anne handed Kate some more paperwork.

"I know your brain is fried right now, Kate. Why don't you tuck these flyers away for tomorrow? They pertain to the various counseling options we have available for you, both here and when you move out on your own. You should read them over, but you don't need to make any decisions about anything today."

Kate breathed a sigh of relief and shoved the information into her purse.

"Why don't we go to the kitchen and have a couple of sandwiches? Then, you go have a nap or a bath or relax for a couple of hours and you can meet with our staff counselor before dinner. Okay?"

The thought of food made Kate cringe. "I couldn't eat anything right now."

"Just try, okay?"

Kate surprised herself by scarfing down almost an entire ham and cheese sandwich and a glass of milk. She walked to the dishwasher and stowed her plate.

"I guess I was hungrier than I thought."

"A good sign, for sure."

Kate turned after the voice answered her. A tiny mouse of a woman dressed in warm colors of brown and gold stood in the doorway. She couldn't be more than twenty-eight. Kate had to wonder if she was another resident.

"Hi. I'm Stacy, the staff counselor."

Mary Anne stood and took care of her own dishes. Mary Anne was a tall, statuesque black woman in her mid- to late-fifties and the two were more like Mutt and Jeff than colleagues.

"I wanted you to meet Stacy now so you can find her after your rest. Her office is next to mine, just down the hall."

Stacy smiled and took a seat opposite Kate. "You're free to come and talk to me at any time. If I'm not in my office, our secretary can find me. Day or night, Kate. We're here to help."

Kate nodded, unable to find her voice through the thick swell of emotion in her throat.

She had been alone for too long. It was hard to believe anyone was willing to help her.

\*\*\*\*

He couldn't understand what she thought she was doing. If he hadn't followed her to this plain, white house, he would never have found her again.

What was she thinking, straying this far from home?

A man was entitled to expect his wife to be waiting for him at the end of the day. What possessed her to pack a suitcase and get in that woman's car?

Was there a man in there with her?

She shouldn't be in there. It wasn't right.

She belonged at home.

\*\*\*\*

Jack rang the bell attached to a small intercom system. Almost immediately, a voice came out of the speaker.

"Who's there?"

Realizing a camera was attached to the intercom, he leaned toward it and spoke into the speaker.

"I'm Undersheriff Jack Finelli. I called earlier and spoke with Mary Anne Porter. Would you please tell her I'm here?"

He was actually shuffling his feet, although he tried to shake the tension from his body. It was almost as if the nondescript building itself was radiating a message of "No Men Allowed." He didn't belong there and everybody knew it.

He held up his badge to the camera, to prove he was really an office of the law. After a few moments, the door swung open.

"I'm Mary Anne. Please come in, Undersheriff Finelli."

The shelter administrator had a warm smile and a kind face. With her firm handshake and direct gaze, Jack immediately began to relax.

He followed her down a small hall off the living room into her office. The shelter was able to be business-like and professional, but still project a homey, comforting image. Jack admired the effort the staff had gone to in creating this haven.

"Thanks for seeing me today."

Mary Anne smiled. "I'm pleased the sheriff's office is interested in updating and improving their domestic violence policies and procedures. Often the village and county police are our best security in these types of cases."

Jack coughed. "I am here because I've been getting phone calls from a victim who only identifies herself to me as Honey. I gave her your number and when I spoke to her last, she said she'd called you. I guess I wanted to make sure everything is okay."

The woman visibly bristled at his response. "I'm

sure you're aware I can't give out any information on women sheltered here without a warrant."

Jack raised his hands, shrugging. "I know, I'm not asking for specifics."

"Then what are you asking?"

"Well, I guess... I wanted to reassure myself I gave Honey the right advice. I was with the organized crime division of the FBI before I moved back to Harper's Glen. I haven't had much experience with domestic violence matters."

Jack always favored honesty and it seemed to be working now. Mary Anne lowered her defenses a bit.

"Undersheriff Finelli, if you advised a battered woman to come here and she did, you did the right thing. Her battle isn't over, but she's taken the first step. The safest step. As long as she's here, she's safe."

"What can we at the sheriff's office do to help these women?"

She jumped out of her chair. If not for the broad smile on her face, Jack might have been worried. After she pulled a pile of literature from her credenza, she returned to her seat.

"Knowing you want to help is great progress. Here's some information for you from the Commission on Domestic Violence. Please read it and if you have questions or want more information, I would be happy to meet with you or your staff anytime."

Jack leafed through some of the papers. A couple of things jumped out at him.

"You told me coming here was the safest thing a woman in her situation could do, but it says here women who leave their batterers are at a seventy-five percent greater risk of being killed by him than those who stay. Will my advice get her killed?"

"It's true that a battered woman is at a higher risk of death immediately after she leaves her abusive spouse." Mary Ann put down the papers and folded her arms on the desk. "That's why we have such elaborate security here and do not publish our address anywhere. If her spouse was able to get his hands on her, after she's left him, he would likely kill her. It's up to us to use the courts, the available police protection, and our own resources and intelligence to keep these women as safe as possible."

"What's the incentive for them to leave, then?"

"The incentive is to escape the emotional and physical abuse, to try to make a better life. To survive."

"Well, it's going to be damned hard for her to make a better life if she's dead now, isn't it?"

Mary Ann wasn't smiling anymore. "I appreciate your concern, I really do. But, you have to understand what life is like for these women. In many cases, they would rather be dead than live with the abuse and the fear of more abuse every day." She shook her head. "We give them financial and legal assistance. Hopefully, the courts and police can provide protection while we get their abusers arrested, tried, and convicted. Then the woman has a chance to start again."

Jack tried to imagine Honey's face. She sounded frail, scared, and lost on the phone. He didn't want to think of her being in more danger now than she was yesterday. He stood and prepared to leave.

"I don't envy your job, Ms. Potter. But I admire your dedication and sincerity." He offered her his hand, which she shook but held for a moment longer than usual.

"And I admire your willingness to admit you don't know everything there is to know about law enforcement in Harper's Glen. Having someone in the sheriff's office willing to learn more about domestic violence is a good thing for all of us."

As they walked back to the front door, Mary Anne pointed out the reinforced doors and windows, emergency hotline with instant access to local hospitals and police offices, and other security measures barely evident in the homey interior. There weren't any other people milling about, but Jack assumed they had been warned he was visiting.

"Please give me a call if you have any more questions, or if you'd like one of us to come and talk to you and your staff about ways we can improve the services available to victims of domestic abuse in Harper's Glen. I would be happy to help in any way I can."

"Thank you. I'll let you know. I plan to discuss this with the sheriff to update our policies and procedures in this area."

Jack walked down the front steps of the porch and got into his car. He was again glad he'd driven his own Explorer instead of one of the department vehicles.

As he started the engine, he glanced at the inconspicuous clapboard house. Out of the corner of his eye, he noticed one of the living room curtains fall back into place. Either Mary Anne was still watching him or someone else, maybe Honey, knew he was there.

He kept his eye on the window a few seconds longer and then pulled away.

\*\*\*\*

"Don't worry." Mary Ann laid a hand on Kate's arm. "He doesn't know you're here and I don't think he knows who you are, either. It seems like he's really concerned about you, without even knowing you're his sister-in-law."

Kate turned from the window.

"Even though I disguised my voice on the phone, I was sure he'd figure out who I am. I mean, he is more than my husband's brother. He and I were good friends a long time ago."

"He's still being a good friend."

Mary Anne put her arm around Kate's shoulders and walked with her down the hall.

"You can continue to call Jack as a mystery woman named Honey. I probably would recommend you do, since you don't know for sure how he'll react to the news that his brother has been abusing you for years. But, you might want to talk to Stacy about this all in more depth."

As they stopped in front of the counselor's door, Kate decided it was time. She needed the push and was glad Mary Anne literally put her in the right place to admit it. She knocked on the door.

When Stacy called "Come in," Kate took a deep breath and opened the door.

Stacy sat at her desk, smiling. "Kate. I was hoping you'd stop by. Have a seat."

Kate sat in the overstuffed arm chair facing Stacy's neat desk. Two needlepoint samplers and a stunning seascape print hung on the walls of the tiny office. Soft jazz played in the background and a desk-top fountain gurgled smoothly. Leafy green plants hung in the window behind her desk, nearly disguising the reinforced glass and bars.

A shudder ran down Kate's spine, she knew those bars were designed to keep people out, not in. Though Tony had never actually put bars on their windows to keep Kate locked in, he might as well have. She'd been a prisoner in his house for so long. Too long.

"Kate?"

Kate shook her head, obviously having missed whatever she said. "I'm sorry. I drifted there for a moment."

"That's okay. Why don't you tell me where you went?"

Kate's fingers twisted in her lap. "I was thinking about our house, my husband's house. I don't want to go back there again."

Stacy nodded. "Okay. That's a start. Tell me about it? How did you meet your husband? When were you married?"

Kate took the bottle of water Stacy offered from the mini fridge under her desk. Her thoughts fluttered back to high school and even before.

"I moved to Harper's Glen when I was eight, after my parents died. I came to live with my great-aunt in her little house on the lake."

Kate had been shy and sad and lonely, but Aunt Linda had been upbeat, soothing, and a little bit quirky. It didn't take long for her to find her normal again. Well, at least what had passed for normal.

"I wasn't a good student and didn't make many close friends in school. It was hard, you know, since we lived outside of town. Not a lot of kids live on the lake road, at least once the summer's over."

Crossing her hands in her lap, Stacy gave Kate an encouraging nod. "Did you meet your husband when you started school in Harper's Glen?"

Kate laughed. "He didn't give me a moment's notice back then. And, I have to admit, I didn't really notice him, either. I was scared to death, starting a new school and all. I remember Jack…uh, my husband's brother, he was really nice to me, right from the start."

Jack had become her unofficial protector. When other kids called her stupid or laughed when she tried to read out loud, Jack would come to her rescue. He read her the books after school as she couldn't read herself. He helped her figure out word problems in math. He became her best friend.

"The summer I turned fifteen, I suddenly developed a figure, and the following fall, when I started high school, Tony finally noticed me. I couldn't believe he was Jack's brother. I mean, Tony and Tom are tall and popular, such jocks. Jack is smaller, leaner, and smarter. They were always incredibly different."

"Did you start dating Tony in high school?"

"Yeah. I made a friend, Brenda, who convinced me to try out for cheerleading. Amazingly, I made it. Then she started dating Tom and I started dating Tony and we sort of became a unit, the four of us."

"When did your relationship with Tony get serious?"

Kate paused, rubbing the lump on her left wrist where a break had never quite healed right.

"Well, I guess it was serious right from the start. Tony wanted to own me, sort of, to show the guys he had the pretty girl. He used to boast about how great it was he was dating the prettiest girl in school."

"Was he ever abusive back then?"

"I don't think so. At least, not that I realized at the time. I mean, he always had a temper, but he was sweet to me when he wasn't mad, I figured it was a part of him I had to accept. Like he had to accept I was stupid."

Stacy leaned forward in her chair. "What do you mean stupid?"

Kate stood and walked to the framed sampler on the wall. Although she could admire the precise stitches and blends of colors which created the piece of art, she couldn't quite decipher the words of the message.

"Kate, I know it's hard to go down these old roads, to dig up the past." Stacy's voice was strong but soothing. "But, please remember, everything you say in here stays in here. I have a duty to keep everything you tell me completely confidential."

Kate nodded, wiped away a tear which escaped from her eye and returned to her seat.

"It's true. I'm twenty-eight years old and I still can't read. I couldn't even tell you for sure what your sampler says."

Stacy sat silent, obviously shocked. She was probably amazed Kate had the guts to admit she was an idiot. Kate didn't want Stacy's sympathy, but, at least she'd been able to admit it.

"Oh Kate. Not being able to read doesn't mean you're stupid. Didn't your teachers try to help you read in school? How did you graduate if you can't read at all?"

"I had help, of course. Tony figured it out right away, but since he didn't want anyone else to think his girlfriend was an idiot, he helped me with my homework." Kate shook her head, moving back to her seat. "When the tests came along, I muddled through as best I could and was able to squeak by. The teachers always wondered why I did well on the homework and could answer their questions in class, but then froze up on the tests."

Stacy smiled. "See, you admitted it yourself. You could answer their questions because you are an intelligent woman. Obviously very intelligent, if you were able to make it through high school, taking tests you could barely read, and still graduate."

Kate shook her head, amused but unimpressed.

"No one has ever called me intelligent—a first, for sure. In fact, Tony's been telling me for ten years how stupid I really am." She took a deep breath before continuing. "You're very kind, Stacy, but I accepted my limitations a long time ago. You don't have to lie on my account."

This time, Stacy stood and walked around her desk, leaning on the front edge. Kate had to tilt her head up to meet Stacy's gaze.

"You are not stupid, Kate. You could not have survived what you've been through, not to mention getting away from your abuser, if you weren't a capable, resourceful, and intelligent woman. Don't sell yourself short. Stop listening to Tony's put downs. If he told you how stupid you were, it was because he wanted you to believe it. It made you vulnerable, Kate. It made you dependent on him. Don't give him an edge anymore."

Kate shrugged. "Okay, I can believe he told me how stupid I was in order to put me down, keep me from fighting back. But it doesn't change the facts. I can't read. How can I be intelligent?"

Stacy grabbed a sheet of note paper and a pen from her desk and handed it to Kate.

"Write down the name of the last movie or TV show you watched."

"But…"

"Just do it, Kate."

Kate struggled to remember as the familiar panic set in. She tried to sort the letters into the right order. When she finished she handed the paper back to Stacy. Stacy handed her another piece.

"Now, draw me a picture from the story. A scene, one of the characters, anything at all."

Kate instantly relaxed. This she could do. Doodling had always been fun, a way to escape her frustration in school. She handed the paper to Stacy, who's face broke into a huge grin.

"Incredible." Stacy took the two papers and walked back to her chair. Picking up an eraser, she tossed it to Kate, who caught it, but started to worry if her counselor was also a little quirky.

"Quick, Kate. Which hand did you catch the eraser in?"

Holding up her hands, Kate tried to envision the

thumb and index finger forming an L. "My right."

"You have trouble telling left from right, don't you Kate?"

Kate scowled. "I already told you I'm stupid. Do you have to keep trying to prove it?"

"Oh Kate." Stacy was shaking her head, smiling. "You are not stupid and you proved it, at least to me."

"What are you talking about? I wrote some gibberish, drew a picture, and caught an eraser. What could you possibly get from that?"

"Well, you're right, I don't have a definite answer for you." Stacy made a few notes in her file. "But I've done a lot of work with United Literacy Volunteers and know the signs of dyslexia. I think you may be dyslexic, which would explain your trouble with reading. Do you know what dyslexia is?"

Kate was stunned. No one had ever tried to tell her why she couldn't read. They always assumed her brain didn't work right or she was lazy or stupid. "I don't really know what it means, although I've heard of it."

Fumbling through her desk drawer, Stacy continued. "Dyslexia is a learning difficulty. Dyslexics have trouble putting things in order, following instruction, problems with reading, writing, and spelling. However, studies have also shown dyslexics are generally extremely intelligent and gifted people, particularly creative, physically coordinated, and often very empathetic. We can do some testing and I can do some more research. But, if it turns out dyslexia is the problem, there are lots of ways to work around it."

Kate tried to take in everything Stacy was saying, but it was almost too good to be true.

"It does not mean you're stupid, though, Kate." Stacy continued "If you made it to the age of twenty-eight, graduated from high school, maintain a job and a home, function well in society without ever knowing you're dyslexic, you have to be extremely intelligent and gifted in order to have been able to overcome your problems with no help or training."

Kate sat back in her chair. She was weary and exhilarated, ready to jump up and shout or break down and cry. Could it be true? Could there be a reason she was never ever to make words make sense? Could there be help for her?

"Do you mean I could learn to read? I used to love to listen to Jack when he read me stories. I really missed it when he stopped."

Stacy tilted her head. "Why did he stop?"

"Once I started dating Tony, he didn't want Jack helping me. Tony said I didn't need stories as long as he helped me do my homework. I missed those stories a lot, I even made up some of my own in my head. I always wanted a way into the world of books. Now you're saying it might be possible?"

"Yes, it's possible for dyslexics to learn to decode reading. But in the meantime, there is no reason you can't listen to all the books you want on CD. Have you ever taken an audio book out of the library, Kate?"

Kate's spine stiffened. "The library? Why would I go in there? I might as well announce to the town I was too stupid to read."

Stacy stood. "Oh Kate. I'm sorry. Of course. But listen, they have audio-books there. Some popular novels, some classics, all kinds of books you can borrow and listen to. No reading involved."

"Really?" Again, her pulse raced.

"Really. In fact, we have a few in our library here at the shelter. Let me dig up a CD player for you and you can try some out, okay?"

After Stacy left the room, Kate walked to the window without focusing on the lush grass of the fenced-in backyard. Was it possible Tony was wrong all these years? Could it be she wasn't stupid at all but really gifted and intelligent? Kate couldn't quite make such a stretch, but it would be great if there were books she could listen to, story worlds waiting for her to find them.

Her mind drifted back to Jack, the younger, more earnest Jack who had been her best friend, before Brenda, before Tony, before all hell broke loose. Having him back in town was a comfort, even if she couldn't face him right now. Maybe someday, after the worst was over, and if she survived to talk about it, she'd tell Jack how much he had meant to her back then. Maybe, if he was really here to stay, they could be friends again.

Then it hit her. Jack would never want to be friends again. She was about to tell everyone in town, everyone in his family, that his brother had been beating her senseless for more than ten years. Even if a judge believed her enough to give her an order of protection, the Finelli family would never forgive her.

Brenda and Tom wouldn't want to be her friends

anymore. Tony's parents would cut her from their lives. And Jack. Jack would have no reason at all to rebuild their special friendship. No, Kate would lose him forever when she left Tony. As much as it hurt, she had no choice. She couldn't go back to her living hell. She'd rather be dead.

Chapter Five

"Thelma, could you come here for a moment?"

"Certainly, Deke. I'll switch the dispatch calls down the hall and be right in."

Jack sat in one of the armchairs opposite Deke's desk and Thelma took the other. She gave them both a curious glance, waiting quietly for one of them to speak.

Deke started. "Jack here thinks we could stand to update some of our policies in spousal abuse cases. He met with those folks over at the shelter and came back with some good ideas."

Thelma whipped out her steno pad, pen poised to begin her note-taking.

"I think we all know a lot more spousal abuse is going on in this county than is reported," said Jack. "According to this brochure, it's the leading cause of injury to women between fifteen and forty-four; more than car accidents, rapes, or other attacks. I think we need to do more to educate ourselves and the community. We have to give these women real options and support to make leaving their abusive spouse possible. And we need to help keep them safe once they do leave."

Thelma took the brochure and made more notes. Then she glanced from Jack to Deke. "Once they have left, unless he violates an order of protection, what can we do? We're not the social services office."

Deke leaned back in his chair, scratching his chin. "Yeah, true enough. But I guess we can do more to let women know about the services available in this area, including the women's shelter, food stamps, social service, and the welfare office."

Thelma held her pen, poised for more note-taking. "Even when they know what's out there, they don't always want to leave. Remember Debbie Michaels or, rather, Debbie Standish? How many times did you try to talk her into leaving, Deke? She couldn't bring herself to even press charges against Ed."

A flicker of sadness appeared in Deke's gaze.

"True enough. But she did divorce in the end, even though he never would accept it. At least Bob Standish hasn't been shy about calling us to press charges when Ed gets after Debbie."

Jack shook his head. "What do you mean?"

Deke shook his head. "Every now and then, Ed gets it into his head that Debbie is still his wife and thinks he can beat the crap out of her. We've arrested him at least four times in the past six years. He's even done time in the county jail, but he can't let the poor woman go."

Jack wondered if Honey would be able to get free of her abusive husband, or if he'd continue to hound her for the rest of her life.

"We need to catch these people early in the relationship, before abuse becomes a habit."

"Maybe we can work up a program to present over at the high school or to some of the local women's groups," said Thelma.

"Good idea, Thelma," said Deke. "Why don't you call Mary Anne Potter at the shelter and discuss it with her? I'm sure she'd have some suggestions for us."

"Okay. And I'll put all the information in an inter-office memo, for Larry and the other guys, to bring them up to speed."

Deke smiled. "Thanks Thelma, that would be a big help."

After they discussed a few more ideas for public education and official response, Thelma went back to her desk. Jack closed the door after her, turning to face Deke again.

"Education is great, but if we can't protect these women once they leave, they'll wind up dead."

Deke raised his eyes, catching Jack's gaze in his. "There's only so much we can do, Jack."

"I know, but if we had some better way to stay on top of the situation, keep track of the husbands, we could prevent them from getting to their wives."

Deke leaned back in his chair. "Listen, I think this is a noble cause which seems to have gotten under your skin. But you better remember these women go back almost as often as they leave."

"Maybe if they knew support was available, they wouldn't go back," Jack countered.

"Maybe. But not necessarily. I've seen it happen many a time, Jack. Even though he never changes, she still goes back."

Jack shook his head. It didn't make sense to him. "But surely if these women knew something better was available…?"

"You can't force someone to change her life. If she's put up with abuse for a while, you can be sure she still loves her husband and doesn't want a divorce. Just because things get bad enough she walks out, doesn't mean she won't go back."

Jack stood. "If we could help keep them safe, they won't have to go back."

"They go back for many reasons. Usually there are kids involved. And if she's got no job or money, more than likely she has no way to support them without her husband. Women will do most anything to protect their kids."

Jack walked to the window, the sleepy little town spread out before him. How could such violence exist in Harper's Glen?

Deke leaned forward, resting his arms on his desk. "Was the gal you talked to over at the shelter?"

Jack turned back to Deke.

"I don't know." Jack walked back to the chair and dropped into it. "Mary Anne wouldn't discuss it. I have to go on the woman's word that she went there."

"If she went there, they'll protect her," said Deke. "If she didn't, it's not your fault. You're not her keeper."

Easy for Deke to say, but Jack wasn't sure he could leave her on her own.

"I know. It's just she sounded scared, and young. I hate to think of her staying with him when she could get out. She deserves to be safe."

Deke put his hand on Jack's arm. Jack looked into the old man's eyes.

"Don't let yourself get personally involved, boy.

Even though Harper's Glen is your hometown, you can't hurt for every person who gets hurt or you'll never last in this job."

Jack shook off Deke's hand, leaning back in his chair.

"I'm not a fool, Deke. I have worked in law enforcement for more than ten years. I know what I'm doing."

"No, I don't think you do. This is not the FBI. There's nothing impersonal about being a small-town sheriff. You may have left this town behind long ago, but it's still a part of you. You are going to have to figure out how to serve and protect without making yourself crazy here. You cannot take on everybody's troubles, Jack. You have to do your job and then let it go, best you can."

Slamming the chair legs back on the floor, Jack jumped up and began pacing the small space.

"Are you saying you don't take these cases home with you at night? Are you trying to tell me you aren't really on duty twenty-four/seven? 'Cause I don't believe you. I've seen you worry a case to death. I've seen it consume all your thoughts, even when you were four hundred miles away, visiting me in DC."

"I'm not trying to say you should, or even could, forget your job when you go home at night. What I'm saying is you have to distance yourself a little." Deke pulled himself to his feet and walked around the desk. After lowering himself into the other arm chair, he put his hand on Jack's arm again.

"It's great you are concerned about this gal, but you aren't objective about her. We don't know her name. We don't even know if we have a file on her claims of abuse. She hasn't filed a protective order with us. You referred her to the shelter, which is all we can do. Let it go for now."

Jack tried to shake it off. Indifference was not an option in this case.

"I don't know if I can let it go. I have this feeling that she's special and in danger. I don't know what else I can do, but I have to do something."

Deke sat silent for a moment. Finally, he released Jack's arm and folded his hands on his chest.

"More education for the community is always a good thing. If it helps this gal, then great. If it helps some other woman, sometime down the road, great. I don't want you to burn yourself out. You will be sheriff soon and for many years to come. You can't keep up this level of worry about every case."

Jack couldn't deny the concern in his friend's gaze. Nor could he tell Deke he really didn't plan on staying around in Harper's Glen any longer than necessary.

His main concern was implementing some changes which would last long after Deke's passing and his own resignation. Maybe his own guilt over Melanie's death was behind his sudden concern with battered women and how best to protect them. Maybe Honey's voice had gotten to him. Whatever, he could live with it, as long as it helped.

Maybe he could save somebody else's wife when he couldn't save his own. It didn't matter what his reasons were, as long as he was able to help.

\*\*\*\*

Jack pushed open the glass door. Ruby turned her head when the bell chimed. Her face held a smile, but it seemed to dim somewhat when her gaze met Jack's.

"Hey, Ruby. How's it going?"

Ruby turned with a smile. "Well, well. The rumors of you being back in town are true then. Seems like Harper's Glen must be pretty dull after living in the big city and working for the FBI."

Jack laughed as best he could, trying to maintain the facade it was a sacrifice for him to give up his life in DC. He walked farther into the store and took a seat in one of the empty chairs. The sharp sting of peroxide and hair spray made his eyes water.

"It's not the same, for sure." The shop was nearly empty. "It's pretty quiet in here."

"Yep, this is my down time. School's about to let out for the afternoon. Then I'll have kids and moms in trying to get a quick cut before dance or after basketball and then the after-work crowd comes in. I kinda' like having a lull about now."

"Calm before the storm, huh?"

Jack watched the buxom woman straightening supplies at the desk. Her bleached blonde hair was piled high on her head, much as it had been when Jack was a boy. Ruby was always quick with a smile and a laugh, and you could tell she truly enjoyed people. No wonder her place had been a central gathering place in town for years.

Ruby crossed her arms, tilting her head. "Yep. Now, what can I do for you? You want a haircut?"

"Not really, Ruby. I'm hoping you and Kate have some information to help me with a matter for the sheriff's office."

Ruby turned and edged farther toward the back room.

"Uh…Kate's not here today."

"Okay. Then, I can talk to her later. Maybe you can help me."

Still Ruby didn't turn to face him.

"Since you have a lull right now, can I ask you a couple of questions?"

"I can't imagine how I could help you with anything, Jack."

"Well, unless things have changed a lot in the past ten years," Jack said, chuckling, "this place is probably still gossip central in Harper's Glen. Maybe you know more than you think you do."

"Maybe." Ruby suddenly got very busy shuffling papers, straightening curlers, and sweeping the floor.

Jack stood and walked toward the sinks, leaning against the mirrored wall.

"I got a call from here last week, down at the station."

This made her stop and turn to him. "You mean someone called in a complaint or something?"

"No Ruby. I mean a woman called the sheriff for information about leaving her abusive husband; a scared, battered woman wanting to get out. I referred her to the women's shelter, but I am trying to find out who she is. I want to be sure she's getting the help she needs. Any ideas?"

She didn't speak or even move for the longest time. Jack started to wonder if she was even listening. Just when he decided she wasn't going to answer, she did.

"I have no idea, Jack. Sorry." Her expression was oddly indifferent and her tone flat, as if he'd asked her opinion on the latest laundry detergent or toilet paper.

"Too bad." He kept his gaze on her. "I was hoping you might be able to give me some idea who this woman is. I want to do whatever needs to be done to help her stay safe."

"Yeah, too bad. Wish I could help."

Again, this didn't sound like Ruby. It sounded more like she was disappointed to have missed the toothpaste sale at the Quik-Mart.

Jack moved a bit closer to Ruby. "Well, if you think of anyone, please let me know. Maybe Kate will know who it was. Will she be in tomorrow?"

Her eyes shifted to the door and back before she answered.

"Uh…um, I don't know exactly when she'll be in. Uh…I…I can ask her to call you. Okay?"

Whatever was going on, Jack needed to take it easy here. He was pretty sure Ruby knew who Honey was, but was afraid to say. He'd wait and ask Kate about it when he talked to her.

"Okay. Great."

She faced him, her expression neutral. "Well, thanks for stopping in, Jack. Good to see you."

"Before I rush off, do you mind if I use your rest room?"

The professional mask slipped back on. "Of course. Right through the back."

The minute he opened the bathroom door, Jack caught the raised voices sweeping the front of the shop. When he stepped into the back room, he recognized a much too familiar voice yelling at Ruby.

"What do you mean, she isn't here? Where the hell is she, then?" Tony bellowed.

Ruby's replay was muffled, which apparently didn't sit well with his brother.

"Don't tell me you don't know where she is. I don't believe you."

"Really, I don't know..." Ruby stuttered.

Tony raised his voice even louder. "Tell me where she is. I need to bring her home."

Jack inched his way around the corner of the doorway into the back room. Tony was practically climbing over the front desk as Ruby cowered behind it. Not exactly the picture of popularity and all-around good charm his big brother usually presented to the public.

Ruby backed away from Tony. "I told you, I don't know where she is."

"Right, like I believe you." Tony tore around the desk and pushed Ruby out of the way as he made his way to the back of the store. His fierce expression caused Jack to catch his breath. He'd never seen his brother so upset.

Tony stopped dead in his tracks when his gaze met Jack's. "What are you doing here?"

Jack stepped more fully into the salon. "Ruby kindly allowed me to use her facilities, if it's all the same to you."

"Yeah, right." Tony pushed past him and stormed into the back room. Jack followed him, righting the many supplies which went flying in

Tony's wake.

"What's your problem, Tony?"

Tony turned on him, his eyes almost glowing with something dark Jack refused to name.

"I'll tell you what the problem is, little brother. My wife is missing. Can the god damn sheriff's office do anything about it?"

"And you think Ruby has her hidden back here?"

Tony didn't answer, pushing past Jack once again. This time, Jack stopped him on his way by.

"How long has Kate been missing?"

Tony bit out his reply. "She didn't come home from work yesterday."

"Yesterday? Why didn't you call it in?"

"I have been a little too busy to bother calling the cops, Jack."

Tony sure sounded pretty sarcastic for a man supposedly crazed with worry.

Jack pulled out his notepad to jot down the details. "What about her car? Is it missing as well?"

"Listen, I have been searching all night. I'm a little too tired and worried to play twenty questions with you. Get out of my way and let me go find my wife."

Jack followed Tony back to the front of the store.

"Listen Ruby," he ground her name nearly to dust. "I'm sure Kathy will call you. Call me as soon as she does. She will need me to bring her home, wherever she is. Call me."

Jack reached out to Tony, placing a hand on his brother's sleeve. "Maybe I should check the hospitals, Tony, in case she's been in a car accident or something." There had to be more to this story, but Tony seemed reluctant to elaborate.

"Sure, whatever."

Tony shrugged off Jack's hand and ran from the store before Jack could get any more information or even ask where else Tony looked for Kate.

Jack turned back to Ruby. The otherwise feisty and robust hair dresser was suddenly old and frail. She slid into her chair and held her head in her hands.

"Ruby, are you okay?"

She jumped, apparently thinking he had left with his brother. "Oh, of course, I'm fine. Only a little tired, you know."

Jack moved a little closer. "If something's wrong with Kate, please tell me. If there's any way I can help her, you have to know I would do it."

Ruby's gaze met his straight in the eye. "I don't know where Kate is. I already told Tony. Apparently you Finelli boys have trouble listening."

Her anger was now directed his way. He took a step back and held his hand up in front of his chest.

"Wow. I'm trying to help here. I'm one of the good guys, remember?"

Ruby turned away and mumbled, but Jack thought he caught her dismissive, "Sure you are."

"Okay." Jack held his hands up in mock surrender. "Well, if she does show up and needs help of any kind, please call me. Or Tony. Or Tom and Brenda. I'm sure anyone in the family would be happy to help her."

"I'm sure," she said, not turning to look at him.

Jack wasn't certain what it was about Ruby's

tone of voice or body language giving him the shivers, but he knew without a doubt Ruby had no lost love when it came to his brother, maybe his whole family. What had happened here? And when?

When he got back to the sheriff's office, he wanted to discuss the situation with Deke. Even if Tony hadn't filed a missing person's report, Harper's Glen was a small enough community he could poke around for answers.

Besides, the possibility that something was very wrong with Tony and Kate and their marriage filled him, and he wanted Deke to tell him he was crazy. Unfortunately, Deke was having a bad day and left early. Jack would have to do the snooping on his own.

****

"Hello, this is Ruby's."

The warmth in her friend's voice was enough to make Kate smile.

"Hi, Ruby. It's me."

"I was hoping you'd call. Hold on."

Ruby was talking to someone in the background; Kate started to wonder if it was a good idea to call.

"Sorry," Ruby continued. "I wanted to take the call in the back, so I put Erma under the dryer first."

Kate hesitated. "If this isn't a good time—"

"Now stop that. You know any time is a good time. As I said, I was hoping you'd call. Your s.o.b. of a husband was in here demanding I tell him where you are."

Kate tried to swallow the mountain of cotton in her throat, but was only able to croak out one syllable. "When?"

Ruby kept her voice low. "He came in early this afternoon. He was in a fine state, too. I've never really seen him acting like a madman. I think he would have tried to force me to talk if his brother hadn't a' been here."

Kate couldn't picture it. "Tom was there?"

"No, not Tom. Jack."

"Jack? What was he doing there?"

"He says he was here to ask you and me about a call he got from a battered wife." Ruby didn't try to hide her wariness. "Says they traced it to the shop phone. He wants us to help him figure out who she was, because he wants to help her."

Kate bit her lower lip. If Jack knew the call had come from Ruby's, it wouldn't be hard for him to figure out it came from her.

"I'm sorry, Ruby. I should never have called from work. I was just…well…I didn't know what to do. I wanted to talk to Deke, but he wasn't there."

"Don't you dare apologize. I'm grateful you were smart enough to call and get the number for the shelter."

Ruby was starting to cry and Kate had to wipe a drop off her own cheek, as well.

She cleared her throat before continuing. "I don't want you involved any more than you already are, that's all."

"Don't give it a thought, girl. You concentrate on getting your life together and don't worry about me."

Swallowing her emotions, Kate continued. "What did Tony do when he ran into Jack?"

"He told him you were missing and he'd been

scouring the town. Of course, Jack wanted to know why he hadn't called the sheriff if you were missing. Tony growled at the both of us and tore out of here."

"That I can believe. He's probably crazy mad right about now. Ruby, if he comes back to the shop, call the police. Please. I don't want you to take a chance of him hurting you. Okay?"

"Okay, but I don't think either of them will be back. I wasn't too friendly and I think I made it pretty clear I wasn't going to help those brothers."

Kate almost chuckled at the mental picture she had of Ruby standing up to Tony, who was at least a foot taller.

"Don't lump Jack in with Tony, though. I think Jack is a good person. He doesn't know what his brother is like."

"Well, I got no reason to think one way or the other about Jack, as he hasn't been around in years. But until he shows me something different, I won't go betting he'd turn on his own brother, you know?"

Kate thought of all the times, back in high school, when Tony turned on Jack. She was still ashamed for not speaking up. It embarrassed her to even remember the abuse Jack took back then.

"I've gotta go, Ruby. I have a meeting with the lawyer."

"Good. While you get everything straightened out, I better go rescue Erma from the dryer. She'll be tight as a corkscrew by now."

For the first time, Kate let out a loud laugh.

"Thanks again, Ruby. Promise me you'll be careful. Stay away from Tony, and if he comes back, call the cops. Okay?"

"Okay, okay. Don't worry about ole Ruby. I'll be fine."

"Bye."

Kate held the phone a few moments after the line was disconnected. The thin connection to the real world kept her grounded; reminding her this was not a dream.

She had gotten out. As long as she was careful and accepted the help she was offered, she could start again. No, this was no dream. And she could only hope her nightmare was over, too.

****

She hadn't gone into work and she wasn't at home. He had waited in the dark alley outside her work for hours. No one noticed him, and she never showed up.

Was she with another man? What was it?

He'd have to go back to the little, white house.

If she was being unfaithful, he'd have to teach her a lesson. Then she wouldn't forget she belonged with him, again.

To him.

It was only right.

Chapter Six

"Over here, Deke."

Jack and Deke walked through the damp, dark woods. The light of their own flashlights led them to the clearing lit by Larry's lantern. The natural forest sounds were eerily absent.

Jack tried to hold Deke's elbow, offer him some support over the ragged path. Deke pulled his arm away.

"What have you got here?" Deke asked, turning to Larry.

"I got a call from a couple of teenagers," Larry stuttered. "The Parsons boy brought his girlfriend up here to neck, I guess. Anyway, by the time they called it in, the romance of the whole thing was shot all to hell."

"Where are they now?" Jack swung his flashlight around in the trees, scanning for the young witnesses. Larry's partner was standing about ten feet down the bank with his back to a small river running through the woods.

"They are sitting in my unit, back by the road," Larry said. "I called Victim Services to come talk to them as well as their folks. They are coming to be with the kids."

"Okay. What did they find?" Deke was hobbling through the underbrush, following Larry down to the river bed. Jack knew it wasn't an easy walk for the old man to make, but it was part of the job. And the job was who Deke was.

Larry stopped short at the water's edge. He turned back to face Deke and Jack. "This is bad, real bad." He shined his lantern over the river bed.

Even before the shaft of light hit the rambling river, Jack could sense the devastation and malice that had ravaged these quiet woods. Still he wasn't prepared.

"Shit." Jack crouched down, careful not to touch anything more than absolutely necessary, as this was obviously a crime scene now.

The body had been stripped of clothes, dignity, and even life. The raw stench of blood and body fluids mingled with the musty smell of damp leaves and pine trees. Something like this did not belong on this tranquil site, but unfortunately, it was only too real.

Jack knew instantly Larry had only called the EMTs to deal with the shock and grief of the poor couple who found the body.

"God almighty. How could anyone do such a thing?" Deke nearly crumpled to the ground, but pulled himself together. Or rather, duty and anger pulled him together.

The woman was laying spread eagle on the river's edge. Jack was no doctor, but he was certain she'd been raped as well as beaten. Whether it happened before or after her throat was slit was a question for the coroner.

Her neck was severed, leaving her head at an obscene angle lower than the rest of her body. Her face was partially submerged in the water. Given that it was still connected, Deke or one of the deputies could probably identify her.

"Have you made an I.D.?" While there was something familiar about her, Jack couldn't put a name to what was left of her face.

Larry's voice sounded far away, as if he was standing in a cave. "Yeah. I checked. It's Debbie Standish. Her face being bloated and beaten it took me a minute to be sure. The coroner will have to confirm, but I'm certain it's her."

Deke patted Larry on the back as he walked to the other side of the water. Deke's gaze was filled with the confirmation of identity, along with sadness and disgust.

Jack pulled himself to his feet. He'd seen the woman for the first time in ten years and now she was dead.

Deke couldn't hide his sadness, but became all business again.

"Larry, I want you two to stay here with the body until the coroner arrives. Be sure the crime scene is secured. I'll call in some relief for you as soon as I can."

"Okay." Larry shifted, shining his flashlight into the dark woods.

"Also, I'll call the state troopers and get their investigators in on this. They'll send out the forensic unit. Make sure nothing is disturbed until they get here."

Nodding, Larry said, "No problem."

As Jack and Deke walked back to their car, the final memory of Debbie Standish forever etched in his mind. By the time they reached the side of the road, the ambulance crew was treating the teenagers, whose parents had also arrived.

Deke spoke quietly with the distressed parents and moved on.

"Jack, you and I need to take a ride out to Debbie's house. We need to talk to Bob Standish. Then we'll have to go out to Billy Michaels's place. They're both going to take this hard."

Jack stopped in his tracks. "Where does Ed Michaels live these days?"

"He's up on Maple Hill, out in the back of beyond."

"We should go there first, Deke. Maybe he decided it was time to hurt his ex-wife again."

Deke turned back to stare at him. "Yeah, but, he did much more than beat her this time."

"Yeah. But, even if it was him, he may not have planned to kill her. He could be running scared and we don't want to let him disappear on us."

A fierceness filled Jack that had been gone a long time, at least since before Melanie's death.

He knew without question this woman had been murdered by her ex-husband. She may have escaped their marriage, but she couldn't escape his wrath.

As Jack was starting to learn, they rarely did.

He offered up a silent prayer for Honey's safety from the bastard she was trying to leave. Whoever her husband was, Jack's hatred for the man was so intense; he'd better not run into Jack in a dark alley. The devil wouldn't stand a chance.

****

The house was dark when they pulled up, but

more, it was deserted. Jack's gut instincts screamed that Ed Michaels was their man, but he was long gone. Wherever he was, it was going to take everything the sheriff's department had, even with the help of the state police, to track him down.

"Nobody's home at two o'clock in the morning. Seems mighty peculiar, don't you think? Unless you're running from something." Deke's observations echoed Jack's thoughts. No cars in the gravel drive, no dogs barking, or porch lights left on. No one answered the door when they knocked. The silence in the still air was almost spooky.

"He doesn't work second shift, right?" Jack scanned the side yard with his flashlight.

"No. I checked with Bob Mason at the salt plant. He said Ed has been on days for years."

Jack and Deke walked to the back of the double-wide trailer. The darkness was all-consuming out here, where there were no street lights for miles around. Jack could barely make out the thin line of light from his flashlight.

"Okay, where would you be, other than in bed asleep, when you have to be at work in five hours?"

Deke followed behind him, slowly. "Especially since it was last call at the Water's Edge an hour ago."

Jack shook his head. "Still a big drinker, huh?" A lot of the problems in this little county were connected to how much time people spent at one of the village watering holes.

"A regular. But I have to say, with all the hunting he's done over the years, Ed probably knows the back roads and trails of this county as well as anybody."

Jack stopped in his tracks. Something wasn't right. Deke was saying something, but Jack tuned him out. There was something in the air, an acrid smell that had nothing to do with country living and everything to do with trouble.

"Where are you going, boy?"

Jack turned his flashlight to the stand of pine trees at the back of the yard, carefully picking his way over the spare engine parts and household appliances which had been retired out here.

"There's something back here."

Jack shifted the flashlight to his left hand and carefully unlatched his holster, resting his right hand on the butt of his gun. He didn't sense anything alive out here, but he wasn't willing to risk his life or Deke's on instinct. Not when they'd proven him wrong before.

"Find anything?" Deke followed him to the stand of trees. His boots crunched across the fallen needles.

Jack worried at the old man's labored breathing. Although the days were still fairly warm, the fall nights were crisp and the cold air was hard on the lungs, especially sick lungs.

When Jack's beam of light finally landed on the source of the pungent smell, he was glad for the cold night air. The briskness of the weather helped dissipate some of the foul stench.

"He hated animals almost as much as women."

What used to be a dog, a mixed breed of some kind, lay hidden under a low-lying stand of pine trees. Jack moved in closer, but was almost bowled over by the strong scent of death.

Deke walked up next to him. "Yep, it's Bob's dog, all right. Bob and Debbie have had him for as long as I can recall. Hate to think of that poor old thing ending up like this."

Jack tried to swallow the bile rising up his throat. He'd always loved dogs and had already thought about getting one, now he'd left city life behind. He had to take a couple steps back from the carcass in order to catch his breath.

"You're sure this dog belonged to Debbie Standish?"

"Well, as sure as I can be, especially since it's tore up and we're in the pitch dark. But yeah, I'm sure."

"Okay, then I'll call in some more back up to come out and stake out this area. We have to search here, organize a search for Ed, get somebody to figure out what happened to the dog, and we still have to go to Bob's house and tell him the news."

Jack didn't relish the thought of telling the man both his wife and dog were dead, but telling him the man responsible had been caught would help him heal. They had to catch the bastard.

They radioed for back up, then called in the village police to handle what they could. "We need more help, Jack."

"What do you mean?"

Deke stuck his hands in his pockets and glanced at Jack. "I mean, there aren't enough people in the sheriff's department to handle a manhunt, a murder investigation, a search for your missing sister-in-law, and all the other day-to-day business. The village police don't have the manpower to take on much extra, their help won't go too far."

Even in the dim light of the car's interior, Deke's skin was more than pale. He looked downright translucent. This case would be too much for him, unless they solved it fast. Jack didn't want the old man overextending himself.

"Well, we need to contact the state police and get some of their investigators on the case. We should also call in help from some of the surrounding counties. Then we can figure out where to go from there."

"Good."

A couple of village squad cars pulled up behind them.

Jack nodded his head toward their car. "Why don't you make some calls while I go fill these guys in on where everything stands right now? Maybe the state police can lead us to Ed Michaels before something else happens."

"Okay."

Deke paused as he opened the car door. "Have the troopers check up on Kate, too. They may be able to help you track her down."

Jack watched Deke lead the local cops into the woods while waiting for an answer on his cell phone.

"Scott Randall here."

"Hi. This is Jack Finelli, Undersheriff in Stevens County. I'm calling for help on a murder case."

Jack explained the situation with the body, the ex-husband, and the status of the crime scene.

"Okay. I can get down there in about twenty minutes. Why don't I swing over and check out the scene before meeting you at the office? Can you give me directions?"

Jack described the location and then hesitated.

"Is there something else?"

Jack cupped his chin in his right hand. "Yeah. I haven't received an official missing person's report, but I need help tracking down a local woman who has been missing for two days."

"Man, things are really hopping in Harper's Glen tonight, huh?"

Shaking his head, Jack said, "Too much, for sure."

"Okay, who's the woman?"

Jack swallowed hard. "My sister-in-law, Katherine Finelli. She's twenty-eight, blonde, blue eyes, about five-foot-six inches tall, and around one hundred ten pounds."

"I'm sorry, Finelli. I'm sorry to hear it."

"Thanks. This has to take second to the murder investigation right now, especially since I can't get my idiot brother to file a report. But if you have some time, I'd appreciate anything you can dig up."

"I'll get it in the works here and let you know when I learn something more."

"I appreciate it," Jack said, nodding.

"Okay. As soon as I get someone on the missing person, I'm on my way."

"After you've been to the scene, call my cell phone and I'll meet you."

"Sounds good. See you then."

Jack decided there wasn't anything more he could do for Kate until Scott Randall came up with something, so he might as well try to help find Ed

Michaels. It was too late to be of any use to Debbie Standish, but Jack knew he had to try.

**** 

Jack opened the door to Deke's office with caution, afraid he might catch the old man sleeping. It had been a long night for everyone, and Deke needed his sleep more than the other officers.

Deke sat in his desk chair, facing toward the tiny, dirty window behind his desk. Jack couldn't see his eyes, but he didn't think Deke was asleep. His friend turned as Jack entered the room, pale and obviously tired. Worried and stressed, but awake. "Hear anything yet?"

"Yeah." Jack closed the office door and took a seat.

"I got a call from Scott Randall. He said they are working on the search for Ed Michaels. I faxed him our A.P.B. and all the information we had on file, including a copy of Ed's driver's license photo. He'll get back to us as soon as he can."

"What was he calling for, then?"

Crossing his legs at the knee, Jack took out his notebook. "He called about Kate. I wanted to talk to you before I go to Tony's. I'm not sure what to do next."

Deke turned fully back to the desk and leaned forward, concern etched deeply on his face. "What do you mean?"

"I don't know what to tell Tony. I can't think of anywhere else to find Kate. Her car isn't missing, she wasn't in an accident. I called all the area hospitals, but nobody's seen her."

"Well, that's good news," said Deke.

"Yeah, but where is she? I mean, I talked to Ruby, who says she doesn't know where Kate is."

"She says she doesn't, or she doesn't? Which is it?"

Jack shook his head. "I don't know. She was acting very weird, even before Tony stormed into the place. She was fairly hostile with me, even though I can't think of a single reason for her to act that way. I couldn't tell if she was being honest or not."

Deke nodded. "Tony came in while you were talking to her?"

"Yeah, he told me Kate was missing. I had gone there to talk to Kate and Ruby put me off, saying she wasn't working. But when Tony came in and demanded to know where his wife was, I learned she was missing."

"Did Ruby seem surprised or concerned?"

Jack stopped to think about the scene at the beauty parlor. "No. In fact, she seemed afraid of Tony and hostile to both of us, but she didn't seem very worried about Kate. It's been bothering me all day."

Deke ran his hand through the gray, scruffy hair on this chin he liked to call a beard. "Did the trooper have any information for you?"

"No. He checked their records, and I called the surrounding county sheriffs. But there's no one even remotely sounding like Kate. He's going to do some more checking but in the meantime, I'm stumped."

Jack stood and walked to the window. Somewhere out there must be the answers. But where?

"Maybe she's not missing."

Jack turned. "What do you mean?"

"I mean, maybe she's hiding."

Jack walked back around the desk and sat on the corner. "I was afraid you were going there. I've had a twinge of doubt about all of this, but I was hoping you'd tell me I was nuts."

Deke leaned back in his chair, looking up at Jack. "If you're wondering the same thing I am, then you're not nuts. Maybe it's no coincidence Kate disappeared at the same time Honey took off to hide out at the shelter. Maybe Kate is doing the same kind of thing."

Jack jumped to his feet, trying to pace in the small office.

"I can't believe this. Is Kate the woman I spoke to on the phone?" Jack rubbed his hands over his face. "Do you honestly think Tony has been beating her?"

"I'm saying maybe it bears thinking about." Deke's tone was calm and quiet. "I told you, Kate is not the same gal she used to be, and I don't think it's only because she can't have kids."

Jack stood again. "You have reason to believe she's been battered?"

"No. I don't have any proof. I got to thinking about why Ruby would act odd, being afraid of Tony and mad at you, but not crazy-worried about Kate. Maybe she knows Kate is at the shelter."

"Then why would she be mad at me?" He threw up his hands. "I'm the one who told Honey to go to the shelter. If Honey and Kate are the same woman, then Ruby would know I'm one of the good guys."

Deke raised a hand. "And you are brother to the

man who has abused that gal for years, if it is Kate. I expect Ruby isn't quite sure of your loyalties here."

Jack sank back into the chair, the weight of his thoughts pulling him down.

"I hate the thought of Tony beating her. He's always been a jerk, and, well, he inherited my father's temper, for sure. But you've been here, you've seen them together. What do you think?"

Deke shook his head, his hands folded on the desk. When his gaze met Jack's again, there was a definite sheen of moisture there.

"I think it's possible. That little gal has had fear in her eyes, like a dog somebody'd been kicking. I guess I never thought about it much until you brought back the information from the shelter. I think it bears consideration now."

Jack sat still in his chair, his thoughts racing and his pulse pounding. If Honey really was Kate, what hell had she lived through during the past ten years? Could he have seen or done something to save her if he'd come back to town to visit?

Could he have seen something in his brother all those years ago, something in the possessive way he kept everyone away from Kate, some indication his brother was more than a bully? Was it possible? How could Tom and Brenda not have seen it? What about his parents? How could they have been blind to it all this time?

"I think you'd better head on over to the shelter again, Jack. You need to find out for yourself if that little gal is Kate. If not, you have to keep searching for her. But if it is, you're going to have to figure out what to do next."

Jack looked into his old friend's eyes, seeing the unconditional love there that should have come from his own father.

"You're right. I'll call Mary Anne and let her know I'm coming. Hopefully, she'll be able to tell me, if not who Honey really is, at least who she's not."

Jack stood and walked to the door, pausing a moment when he opened it.

"Thanks, Deke. I know it couldn't have been easy for you to even suggest my brother is such a monster. But if it is Kate at the shelter, you can be sure I'm going to do everything I can to help her through this and keep her safe."

"I know you will, son."

With one last glance at Deke, Jack turned and headed for the car.

****

Mary Anne held the door open for Jack as he entered the shelter.

"Thanks for seeing me on such short notice."

"You sounded pretty serious on the phone, Jack. Come on back to my office and we can talk privately."

As Jack followed her down the hall, he didn't try to hide the fact that he was scanning the adjacent rooms for any sign of Kate. He had to know if she was there.

Not a soul was about. No one hiding in the corners or watching TV in the living room. They knew he was coming or he wouldn't have been let in the place. Now they hid. Was Kate hiding from him, too?

He took a seat in Mary Anne's office and waited while she sat at her desk. He hadn't told her much on the phone, except he had urgent questions about an abused spouse.

"Okay Jack. What's the situation?"

Jack took a deep breath and carefully measured his words, finding it hard to believe what he was going to say. "My sister-in-law is missing. I don't know if she's here, but I guess what I really want is for you to tell me she's not."

He couldn't read her expression, but knew he caught her off-guard with his question. She recovered quickly.

"Why would you think your sister-in-law was here?" Her expression was neutral, maybe too much so. "Has she been battered? Did she tell someone she was coming here?"

"If she did, nobody's told me. No one seems to know where she is. I've been searching through all the regular missing person routes for her, but it occurred to me, well, to Sheriff McAllen, she might be here."

Mary Anne nodded. "In other words, your sister-in-law is missing."

"Yes. I found out from my brother yesterday. I can't find any trace of her, even though I've explored many options."

Mary Anne said nothing for a few moments.

"Why would you and Sheriff McAllen assume she's here? Couldn't she be visiting friends or family somewhere and forgot to tell your brother? Or maybe she was in an accident? Why would you come here?"

Jack sighed. "From the sounds of it, she doesn't

have many friends. I checked on her aunt, but she passed away recently and there's nobody out at her old house. Kate doesn't have anyone else to visit, as far as I can tell."

He tried to swallow the lump forming in his throat, coughed, then met Mary Anne's gaze. "Deke also says he's noticed some changes in Kate over the years. Something made him consider abuse after going over your literature. He thinks Kate might have been the woman I talked to, the one I referred to you. I don't know if it was her. I hate thinking of Tony beating her or hurting her, but I've gotta' know. If Honey is really Kate, I need to know. I have to keep her safe, protect her from Tony. I can't let him hurt her anymore."

Jack found himself nearly in tears at the thought of Kate, the special, sweet girl he knew years ago, living in such hell. He knew the shelter demanded confidentiality and the chances of Mary Anne even telling him whether Kate was there or not were very slim. But he had to try. If she was there, he needed Kate to know he would do everything possible to keep her safe.

Mary Anne stood. "Now Jack, you know I can't tell you the names of the women in this shelter. I would be risking their safety, their very lives, if that information got out."

Jack's shoulders slumped, he'd known she wouldn't tell him. "I'm not going to put them at risk, Mary Anne. I'm trying to protect these women. I'm trying to help."

"I appreciate your concern and know when you've thought about this, you will understand it's the only thing we can do to keep these women safe. I think you'd better go."

The door clicked open behind him. He turned, expecting a security goon to escort him to the door.

Instead, framed in the sunlight spilling through the open door, stood Kate.

Mary Anne rushed to her side. "Are you sure…"

Kate stopped her with a hand, her gaze never leaving Jack's.

"It's okay, Mary Anne. Jack deserves the truth from me. I'm okay, really."

Jack wasn't sure if they said anything else. He sat in stunned silence, staring at Kate. She was thinner, paler, and more fragile than ever, but still beautiful.

If she was really standing here, it could only mean Tony—his own brother—had hurt her. Jack took a few deep breaths, trying to fight the bile rising in his throat.

"Oh my God, Kate."

His words, his pain seemed to go straight through her. She straightened her spine and broke eye contact at last.

"Mary Anne, is there somewhere Jack and I can talk privately?"

"Sure, if that's what you want. You can use the counseling room next door. Slide the sign to 'Occupied.' You won't be disturbed."

When she turned back to face him, the smile on her face filled with melancholy. The sadness in her eyes made him ache.

"Jack?"

He followed her to the hall and into the next

room. She sat in one armchair and while he slid the sign on the door and closed it behind him. When he took a seat opposite her, all he wanted to do was reach out his hand to her, hold her in his arms, and promise to make it all better.

He started to take her hand, but the protective shield around her was nearly palpable. She hadn't said hands off in words, but her body shouted it, and he stopped. He ached for her, and wanted her to say it was all a mistake.

But he knew she couldn't do that.

\*\*\*\*

He'd come back to the little white house to be sure she wasn't there anymore.

Was she still inside? He couldn't remember.

Luckily, he'd stuck to the old hunting trails running through the woods. Nobody knew those woods like he did, and nobody would see him hanging around outside the house

Last thing he needed, although why should *he* be worried if they started asking questions? A man had a right to know where his wife was.

He needed to get her alone and he could talk to her about it. She had to come home.

He had to talk to her alone. He could be patient and wait for his chance.

\*\*\*\*

"When Mary Anne told me you were coming over again, I thought maybe you had figured out who I was." Kate intertwined her fingers, trying not to squeeze too hard. "She left the door open in case you were here about me. If it had been about someone else, I would have walked away. But of course, it

113

wasn't."

Jack was staring at her as if she was a total stranger to him. Of course, he probably thought he didn't know her at all. He was must be wondering why she would make up such lies about his brother and what she was trying to prove.

"I…I didn't want to believe you were the woman calling me. I wanted my instincts to be wrong. I wanted Deke to be wrong."

Her heart did a flip-flop. "You and Deke figured out where I went? Did either of you tell Tony?"

Jack started to reach toward her hand again. He kept stopping short of actually touching her. His instinct to comfort someone in pain was probably overruled by his anger and repulsion with her.

"Don't worry." Jack shook his head. "Deke didn't talk to anyone about this but me. We didn't even know for sure if you were Honey. And I sure as hell didn't talk to Tony about it."

Kate stared at Jack, trying to remember the young man who befriended her when she was scared and lost and lonely. Trying to balance the warmth of talking to Jack with the fact she was about to serve divorce papers and an application for a protective order on his brother. No matter how nice he used to be to her, he'd hate her now. They all would.

When her gaze caught his, she realized she'd started to bite her fingernails. She snatched her hand away from her mouth. If Tony had ever seen her do that, he would have gone ballistic.

His gaze met hers. "Are you okay?"

Jack didn't even seem to notice her fingernails, but looked deep into her eyes. Maybe he thought she was going crazy. She imagined the Finelli family could accept crazy a lot easier than battered.

"A stupid question, I guess." He flushed, almost as if he were embarrassed. "I mean, you wouldn't be here if you were okay, would you?"

She shrugged. "I'm doing okay, now. The people here are very nice. They are being good to me."

He nodded. She almost thought he was going to get up and walk out, but instead he moved his chair closer to her.

"Kate, what can I do to help you? What do you need from me?"

She tried not to inch away from him. "I'm fine, really. Don't worry about me."

He slammed his fist on the table, making her jump up from her chair and dart behind it. Her hand was on the door knob when his fingertips lightly landed on her arm. She turned back to him. Could she make it out of the room fast enough?

"Oh God, Kate, I'm sorry. I didn't mean to frighten you. Really, I'm sorry. Please don't go."

She stood at the door, shaking to her boots. Her palms were sweating and her knees locked. She couldn't move if she tried.

Jack took a step back, raising his hands slowly in front of him, palms facing out. He was a little shaken himself.

"I'm sorry, Kate. So sorry. I got angry when you said I shouldn't worry about you, but only because…well, if someone had been worrying about you all along, this never would have happened. It never should have happened, but it did and now I am damn well going to worry about you, Kate. It's about time someone in this family took care of you."

Kate eased her death grip on the door knob, but made no other move to sit again. Her gaze darted around the room. Was this a trap? When she finally met his gaze, she wanted to believe him. Wanted to, but couldn't.

"This is not your concern," she said. "I'm here because I am finally taking the steps to make a new life for myself. It's up to me now, Jack, not you or anyone else in your family."

He eased back into the chair and nodded to her. She wasn't ready to sit yet, but she moved closer and stood behind it.

"Do you want to tell me about it? I mean, I understand if you don't want to talk, but I'm here for you."

She shook her head. "I really don't want to go there, Jack. Tony's your brother. I wouldn't have talked to you in the first place except Deke wasn't in and I was getting pretty desperate."

"Yeah, Tony's my brother"—Jack shook his head—"but he's a bastard. I always knew he was mean and had a rotten temper. I never had any idea he'd…he would hurt you. If I had known, well…I wish I had known."

Kate pulled her chair back and let herself settle into it again. She took a deep breath and tried to keep her voice sounding reasonable and calm.

"No one knew, no one but Tony and me. He made sure of that. And well, so did I. I mean, it was humiliating and horrible. I didn't want to believe it myself, much less let anyone else know it was happening."

His gaze switched pointedly at the bruise still evident on her cheek. As she didn't bring any makeup with her when she came to the shelter, there was no way to hide the marks.

"You mean Brenda and Tom never suspected anything? My folks, either? They live a couple miles away from you, got together with you all the time. How could they have missed it?"

Kate shrugged. "He didn't usually leave outwardly visible marks, you know. Plus, people see what they want, or expect. In their eyes, I was a beautiful, but brainless, woman who has been cheated of a baby but has a handsome and attentive husband. They don't look for more."

"No, that can't be true, Kate." Jack shook his head. "You are much more than beautiful and so far from brainless. Your friends, your true friends, would know the real you."

Now she did laugh, although it was a bitter sound. "Friends? Do you think I was allowed to have friends? Brenda was acceptable, because she's Tom's wife, but I couldn't allow her to get too close."

"Didn't you make friends at work? What about Ruby? How could she fail to realize what was happening?"

"Ruby's special. I think she might have suspected, but didn't know what to do. Besides, until I was ready to leave, there wasn't anything she could do."

Jack eyes were suspiciously damp. He seemed genuinely concerned, but she'd fallen for a similar

117

act many a time and wasn't naive anymore.

"Well, you're out of there now and that's what matters. You can find a new place to live, go back to work, and start your life over without Tony. I want to do everything I can to help you, Kate. Tell me what you need."

She stood again, pushing her chair back under the table.

"Get real. You cannot get involved in this. Tony is your brother. When I drag him into court, whether for the order of protection or the divorce, your family is going to hate me. Tony is the golden boy. You know that as well as I do. Your parents aren't going to take kindly to my dragging his name through the mud. Don't let me and my problems with Tony come between you and your family."

Jack stood, facing her but not getting too close.

"There's nothing between me and my family, Kate, as you well know. I'm not Tom or Tony and I never was. I'm useless to my father, and my mother has never been willing to fight him on the issue."

"But you came back to Harper's Glen. You have a chance to make peace with your family. Taking sides with me won't help your cause with any of them."

"If they side with Tony on this, then I don't want a relationship with any of them. If they aren't able to face the truth about him, then to hell with them. Your safety is more important to me, Kate. You're more important."

She took a step back and pulled open the door. She couldn't let him make promises he would come to regret. And she couldn't listen to promises he wouldn't want to uphold. It would only make it harder in the long run.

"Thank you for helping me, Jack. You gave me the chance to get out and probably saved my life."

"I want to go on helping you, if you'll let me."

She wiped the tear slipping out of the corner of her eye. She had promised herself she wasn't going to cry. But then again, she had expected him to be angry, not sweet. She thought he'd want nothing to do with her, not offer to help.

"I can't let you destroy your chance to be a part of your family now you're living in Harper's Glen again. My problems have nothing to do with you. But if you help me escape him, Tony and the rest of your family will never forgive you."

He reached out and gently ran a finger down her cheek, following the path the tear had made. She held herself still, realizing she wasn't afraid of his touch.

"But Kate, don't you realize? If I don't help you, if I don't protect you, I will never forgive myself."

He leaned in, feathering her cheek with the faintest whisper of a kiss as he walked by her and out the door. She placed a hand over the spot and watched him walk out the front door. Then she found herself sinking to the floor as the tears began to flow in earnest.

## Chapter Seven

"When do you think we'll have something back from the coroner's office?" Jack tried to keep his concern for Deke out of his voice.

Back in the office, Deke was pale and out of breath, his eyes looked as if they were sinking into the recesses of his skull. Violent crime affected everyone in a community this small, but it could turn out to be more than Deke could handle right now.

"Well, she said she'd have something for us before dinner, at least a preliminary. Cause of death seems pretty obvious, but I guess we'll have to wait for details of any traces of blood or semen or anything else to identify our killer."

"Okay. The command post is set up in the basement of the jail. I have all ten investigators assigned to follow up on various leads. The data we have received from the forensic team and crime scene is being input into the computer. And I met with the state police investigator from Horseheads. He's overseeing the operation at the moment."

The murder investigation was proceeding slowly. Deke and Jack met with Bob Standish to break the news about his wife and his dog, and offered Bob protection from Ed Michaels. Larry and the other deputies scoured Ed's trailer, locker at the salt plant, and regular hang-outs. But still, they had no leads.

"As long as we have to wait a few hours for the report, how about we head over to the diner for some lunch?" Even if Jack wasn't very hungry, Deke could use the break.

"Okay. We'll have a chance to talk a bit about what you're going to do."

Deke pulled himself to his feet and hobbled to the door. Jack held it open for him and followed him out onto the sidewalk.

"You mean, what I'm going to do with the investigation? I thought we covered it all. I'll head back over to the command post after lunch."

"No, that's not what I meant." Deke pulled open the door to Minnie's and headed to their booth in the back. "There's no need for you to go over there until something new turns up."

Jack hung up his jacket and took a seat. "Then I don't get it."

"I'm asking what you're going to do about your brother." Deke motioned to the waitress and asked for two of today's specials.

When Jack didn't answer, Deke pushed again.

"What are you planning to do about your brother beating his wife for the past ten years? Have you confronted him yet?"

Jack looked at his friend, his mentor. Deke understood what role Tony had played in Jack's life and his decision to leave Harper's Glen. He never knew, though, that Jack had been in love Kate.

No one knew.

He doubted anyone had ever even suspected. Everyone knew the beautiful cheerleader didn't marry the skinny nerd. She married the football star, even if he ended up beating the hell out of her. While Jack always knew he wasn't good enough for Kate, he should have realized his super-jock brother wasn't either.

The waitress dropped off their food and filled their coffee cups. Jack dug into his food, but Deke mostly picked at it.

Deke pounded his index finger on the table between them. "Well, have you?"

"I don't know if I can confront him without wanting to kill him."

"Then you'd better get a handle on your temper. He might be a bastard, but he's still your brother and you're still the undersheriff in this town. You can't go beat the crap out of him."

Jack laughed, although the sound was low and rough. "You have a lot of confidence in my ability to beat a man half a foot taller than me."

Deke set his fork down and leveled his gaze at Jack. "I have complete confidence in you, boy. I know you are seething over the way he's treated that little gal all these years. I don't think a little thing like the difference in your size would stop you from knocking him flat."

"I could knock him flat, if I tried."

Deke shook his head. "Listen, this is not about you or any ghosts from the past you're still carrying around with you. You have to figure out how to help Kate the most. Then you're going to have to help the rest of your family deal with this, which won't be easy. You can't go off half-cocked and beat up your brother, even if you want to."

"I know." Jack shrugged.

"Of course you do. So, what are you going to do?"

Jack took a swig of coffee, hissing as the hot liquid burned his tongue. Swearing softly, he put the cup down.

"I'm going over to talk to him today. I can't wait any longer, even if the bastard still hasn't filed an official missing person's report. Now I know Kate isn't really missing, my only concern is making sure he can't find her, at least, not until she's ready."

"Well, there's no time like the present. Why don't we head over to his office now?"

Jack nodded and threw some bills on the table.

As they approached the bank office, Jack's cell phone vibrated in his pocket. "Finelli."

Once he finished his conversation, Jack caught up to Deke and reached for his elbow to stop him from entering the bank.

"That was Thelma. She thought we should know Kate's lawyer filed the petition for an order of protection this morning. Tony's about to be served with the papers. I think we should go in first, but I wanted you to be prepared."

"Okay. This should be interesting."

Deke was almost smiling, his weathered face twisted into a wry little grin.

"What do you mean?"

"Sorry, but you know Tony has a pretty high opinion of himself and his importance in this town. He will not be pleased to have his domestic dispute aired in public and he'll be madder than a hen if you and I are here to witness it."

Jack tried to tamp down the satisfaction at the thought.

Almost, except then he remembered Kate's shaky voice as she described the years of abuse, the shame in her eyes.

There was nothing they could do to Tony that would satisfy his debt.

\*\*\*\*

Tony had an office in the back of the bank. Given the importance of his latest position, he had real walls, not a cubicle or partition. His walls were mostly glass, visible to his subordinates and the customers of the bank, who were supposed to be impressed and intimidated by the sight of him.

Jack wasn't sure the bank knew or cared what effect Tony had on people, as long as everything was business as usual. Unfortunately for Tony, his signature charm would get him nowhere today.

As Jack and Deke approached the door to Tony's office, he rose and slipped his hands into his pockets. Although his politician's smile was in place, Tony's eyes showed wariness. This was no friendly family visit.

"Well, this is a surprise. Things a little slow in the sheriff's office today, guys? What, did the state troopers take your murder investigation away from you and now you have nothing to do?"

Tony motioned for them to come in but didn't move from the doorway. Jack wasn't playing games today, so he pushed right on by and he and Deke sat.

Tony walked back around his desk to sit, apparently amused with his own humor as he was the only one smiling.

"Actually Tony, we're here to talk about your wife. Remember, the wife you said went missing two days ago. Now, since you haven't come to the office to file a missing person's report, I have to wonder whether or not she's come home."

Tony's smile dimmed slightly, but Jack might have missed the malevolence behind it had he not been watching for the evil glint in his brother's gaze. Tony definitely did not want to discuss what he considered personal matters.

"No, she hasn't come home. But, as you said, she didn't take her car and there's no report of any accidents, so I'm sure she's fine."

"And has she called you?"

"No, but it's not unusual. Kathy's not the brightest girl; I don't have to tell you Jack. She probably hasn't even considered I might be worried about her. I'm sure she will call eventually."

"Disappearing for days is not unusual for her?"

Jack knew Deke chose that moment to cough in an effort to break the building tension in Jack's voice. He wanted to let Tony back himself into a hole, but Jack had to remain calm.

"Well, she's never been terribly reliable or responsible. I've worked with her as much as I could, you know, to help her keep her job and be able to run the home. But when it comes right down to it, she's nothing more than a dumb blonde, as the saying goes."

Tony had the audacity to snicker at his own joke. Jack seethed, so Deke took over.

"I don't think Ruby ever complained about her. Seems like she's done a good job over at the salon."

Tony turned to the old man, his gaze filled with distaste.

"Well, I guess she's a competent hairdresser. She's a pretty girl who knows about hair and makeup. Not brain surgery, but it's enough for her."

Jack stood and turned to the glass, trying to get a hold of his temper. How could his family not know what a jerk Tony was?

"You don't seem too worried about her, Tony. I got the impression you were very upset at Ruby's, but now you seem somewhat resigned to Kate's disappearance."

"Of course I'm worried about *Kathy*. But I've come to realize she's probably fine. I don't think anything has happened to her. I mean, Harper's Glen's not a hot-bed of violence like DC now, is it?"

Jack walked back to his chair, sat and leaned forward, resting his forearms on the edge of Tony's desk. He wanted to be close enough to watch him sweat.

"Actually, Harper's Glen has plenty of violence, Tony. As I'm sure you are more than aware. In fact, the level of violence in your own home would amaze the residents of DC or any other big city. At least those residents not involved in domestic abuse themselves."

This time, Tony didn't smile.

He didn't even blink.

"What in hell are you talking about? What do you know about my home?"

Jack's gaze didn't waver. "I know you beat your wife and have for as long as you've been married, probably longer. She isn't missing, Tony; stop the game. You know as well as I do, she left you. Probably the only reason she's still alive."

Tony jumped to his feet, leaning his tall frame over the desk until he towered over Jack. Jack stood and met him glower for glower.

"You don't know shit, Jack. You'd better shut your damn mouth. I don't know who has been filling your head with such garbage, probably that bitch Ruby, but she doesn't know what the hell she's talking about. Neither do you."

"Ruby didn't tell me anything. She's afraid enough of you to spread it out over the rest of the Finelli men, as well. I don't think she'd tell me the time if I asked her."

Tony seemed to stop in his tracks. He crossed his arms and glared down at Jack.

"Then who?"

Jack said nothing, but his gaze locked with his brother.

"Kathy." Tony ground out the name. He almost vaulted over the desk, but must have realized the scene he was creating for the peons beyond the windows. Panic raced through Tony's gaze, while he visibly battled to control his fierce temper.

Tony edged around the desk and came toe to toe with Jack. His voice was soft but menacing, his face distorted with rage.

"Kathy is *my* wife. You stay out of this and away from her. You have no right to interfere with what goes on between a man and his wife. Which you'd know if you hadn't gotten yours killed."

"At least I didn't kill her with my own fists, like you've been trying to do for years."

Jack put his right hand on his hip. He didn't expect to need his service weapon, but he wouldn't underestimate Tony's rage. Again, pure hatred seethed from Tony's very pores and hit Jack in waves. He waited for Tony's fist to do the same. Apparently his brother was better at acting than Jack would have given him credit for. The expected punch didn't come.

"This is none of your damn business, Jack. Tell me where my wife is, I will go take her home, and we can discuss whatever problems we have privately."

"I think she's tired of your private discussions. Battered, sick and tired, to be exact. In fact, I believe there's a deputy standing outside your office door right now to prove my point."

Tony seemed surprised at the sight of the deputy. He pasted his charming smile back on and opened the door. He flinched when the deputy served him with a complaint and summons. His gaze flew to Jack, filled with anger and hatred.

"What the hell kind of trick are you playing here, Jack?"

Deke finally stood and took as step toward Tony as he closed the door behind him.

"This is no trick, and Jack had nothing to do with it, Tony. Your wife has filed an application for an order of protection from you. You are required to appear in court to answer her complaint."

"Why that little bitch…"

Jack stepped forward, his right hand clenching into a fist. "Don't go there, Tony. You brought this on yourself. If you weren't such a monster, your wife wouldn't need the courts to protect her from you. But she does. Stay the hell away from her."

Jack motioned Deke toward the door. Tony was a volcano ready to blow, and Jack had no intention of letting Deke get in the way.

Tony opened the door with more force than necessary, sending the woman in the adjoining office racing across her desk to catch the painting that came crashing to the floor. Tony never flinched.

After Deke walked out, Tony grabbed Jack's arm. Jack whipped his arm away and stood toe-to-toe with his brother.

"Don't threaten me, little brother. You know nothing about life in this town or my marriage or anything else you're trying to stick your nose into. Take your Ivy League education and your FBI resume and get the hell out of here."

"Remember Tony, this is a legal matter now. Kate is under our protection and you cannot go near her. Don't, or you'll make me explain to Mom why I had to throw you in jail."

Tony's smile grew so wide and tight his face nearly shattered. He leaned in closer to Jack's face and whispered.

"Don't mess in this, Jack. Stay the hell out of my marriage. But if you talk to my lying bitch of a wife, tell her I expect her to drop this nonsense and be home by dinner. Otherwise, I won't be too forgiving."

The chilling glint in Tony's eye had nothing to do with forgiveness and everything to do with evil. The heat of Jack's anger settled into his bones. However it happened, his brother had become a monster and it was long past time someone put an end to it.

"You stay the hell away from Kate."

He turned and followed Deke from the office, past the stunned stares of the other employees. Small town gossip being what it is, he knew his parents would learn about this incident soon.

****

Kate tried to be patient knowing Jack had to clear security before he could enter the shelter. But as soon as Mary Anne told her Jack had been to Tony's office, Kate began to chew on the corner of her thumbnail. It was all but bloody now.

She took a tentative breath when he finally walked through the front door and met her in the living room.

"What's wrong, Jack? What happened with Tony?"

Jack smiled, his face full of concern that could not hide the anger and tension obvious in the cool depths of his eyes.

"Let's sit down, Kate, and we can talk."

He motioned to the sofa, but Kate lit on the overstuffed arm. Jack took a seat on the edge of the cushion furthest from her.

"Jack?"

"Okay, here's the thing. Deke and I were in Tony's office when the deputy came to serve him with the request for an order of protection."

"Oh God." Kate sank to her knees on the cushion.

"Yeah, well, as you can imagine, he was livid. I thought…"

Her pulse raced as the possible outcomes flew through her mind. "He didn't hurt you, did he? Or Deke?"

"Relax. We're fine. It's you I'm worried about." Jack settled into his seat and leaned his left arm across the back of the sofa. He turned to face her more directly.

"I'm fine. I'm safe here." She crossed her arms over her chest.

"I know you're safe here, but you can't stay forever. I'm worried about when you leave the shelter. Tony's eyes were full of pure evil today. I don't think he's going to let you go easily."

"I've known that all along."

"I guess I'm starting to realize exactly how twisted he is. He told me to tell you he *might* forgive you if you forget the whole thing and are home by dinner time tonight."

She started to chuckle, but the mirth died in her throat. No matter how ironic she might find Tony's offer of forgiveness, the true danger behind his words was unmistakable.

"I'm going to be *here* for dinner tonight, tomorrow, and the next night. Mary Anne said I can stay here as long as necessary, but I want to get out on my own once the order of protection is in place."

"That's not good enough. You are scheduled to go to court in three days. You could be out of here on Monday. Where are you going to go?"

Kate stood and walked to the fireplace. She knew Tony. If no one knew where she was, there was no way Tony could find out. She wanted to trust Jack, but she couldn't afford to risk her safety or her life.

She turned back to face Jack. "I have something arranged for after I leave the shelter. I'm taking an extended leave from Ruby's to give Tony time to cool off before I start showing up in town again."

He sat forward. "What do you mean, you won't be around? Where are you going? I know you don't have any family left. Who will be taking care of you?"

"It's time I took care of myself."

He jumped to his feet, all of the forced calm drained from his face. He strode toward her at the mantel.

"No, I definitely do not think this is a good time for you to be alone. Tony is furious and it's only going to get worse once it becomes a matter of public record. You need to be guarded, by me and the rest of the department. That's why you get the order of protection in the first place."

"The order of protection is to put Tony on notice that I am not going to take this anymore. I need the law to make it clear he has to leave me alone. I'm not foolish enough to think he would stay away if I said I'm leaving and walked out. But, I also don't want to publicly rub his face in it. I'll stay out of town for a while. To give him time to cool off."

"You won't be in Harper's Glen at all?"

"I won't be coming into town for a while, no."

She didn't want him to think she'd left the area, in case she needed his help, but couldn't let anyone know where she was unless absolutely necessary.

Kate had to stand firm despite the sad or even confused expression on Jack's face. She'd survived this long by learning how to protect herself, whatever it took. Sometimes it didn't work, but she would never let her conscience bother her anymore. This wasn't about family or relationships or even hurt feelings. It was about staying alive.

"I want to accompany you to the courthouse for the hearing."

"Thank you, but don't you think your family would be upset?"

He surprised her by grabbing her left hand. She had to stop herself from pulling away. He pulled her hand up until her gaze met his.

"My family is not what matters here, Kate. You are. I don't think you need to worry about them. Let me deal with them and you just worry about staying safe."

"Besides, it's your job, right?"

His right hand reached softly to the hair slipping from her ponytail, gently brushing it back behind her ear.

"This isn't about my job."

She tried to fight the tears that threatened to come crashing through her defenses. She was used to abuse and ready to fight. But she was not prepared for kindness or caring or gentleness.

And damn Jack; that was just what he was giving her now.

She couldn't get a word around the lump in her throat, but needed to break the connection and end the moment. She pulled her hand away.

Jack turned and cleared his throat, reaching for his jacket.

"Well, I had better get back to work. I wanted

you to know Tony's been served and is mad as hell. Don't think about leaving this building for any reason until I come to pick you up for the hearing, okay?"

"I won't. I'm not that stupid, Jack."

She must have sounded more sarcastic than she intended, because he turned back before he reached the door. He walked back and placed his hands on her shoulders.

"You're not stupid, Kate. You couldn't have survived this long and gotten this far if you were. But I do want you to be careful. I'll do everything I can, everything you let me do to keep you safe. Let me help you."

Again the lump. She nodded.

"Okay."

He leaned in and feathered the soft hint of a kiss on her cheek. She might think she imagined it, but her skin was on fire.

"Bye, Kate."

"Bye."

She pressed the door closed and waited for the locks to click into place. Then she rushed to her room and collapsed on the bed. She would need strength to survive Tony and her plans for divorce. But she could tell already she would need nearly as much strength to resist Jack and the comfort and security he offered.

**\*\*\*\***

He hunkered down in the woods, pulling the edges of his sleeping bag around him. She didn't leave the little, white house with the sheriff, but she might still be in there. He had to be vigilant.

Since she wasn't at home, he had to figure out what she was doing, and he could only do that by keeping a close eye on her.

\*\*\*\*

When Jack pulled into the driveway, his mother stood in front of the kitchen window. Her tense gaze greeted him as he walked to the door.

They knew, all right. At this point, it was more of a question of what they believed.

His mother opened the door, wiping her hands on a dish towel before pulling him into a hug.

"I'm glad you came, Jack. We have to figure out what to do about this mess. Take off your coat and I'll get you a beer."

"No thanks Ma, I'm still working. How about coffee instead?"

"Sure. Why don't you go into the living room and I'll bring it to you? Let's get comfortable while we talk."

Jack hesitated. "Has Tony been here?"

"Yes, he left about half an hour ago."

"Anyone else?"

She turned, her confusion clear on her face. "What do you mean? Who else should we be expecting?"

Jack took the coffee mug she held and took a sip. "I haven't been back to the office. I didn't know if any more subpoenas were going to be served."

Rose put her now-empty hand on the counter, almost as if for support. "What subpoenas?"

Jack guided his mother to a chair at the table and sat beside her. "Ma, it's possible Kate's lawyer will call you or other members of the family as witnesses.

It might not come until later, but I was wondering if you'd been called."

Rose's hand flew through the sign of the cross, as it always did in time of stress.

"No, thank God in heaven. Tony's news was bad enough. I can't imagine how Dom would react if one of us had to get involved."

"Aren't you involved anyway? I mean, Tony is your son, and Kate has been his wife for ten years. How could you two live this close, visit with them as often as you do, and never know what was going on between them? How could you be blind to the pain Kate's been in all these years?"

Rose sprung to her feet, horror-stricken, and backed away from Jack.

"What are you talking about? You can't mean you believe her lies? Kate's confused or ill or just plain evil," Rose said. "But for whatever reason, she's lying about Tony. She's trying to hurt him and I'm not helping her by doubting my son."

Jack spun away from her, biting back the profanity on the tip of his tongue. "What are you talking about? What reason would Kate have for lying? Do you think she wants to show the town how she's been a victim for ten years and let Tony walk all over her? Is that the story Tony's tried to feed you?"

"Your brother is not feeding us a story. Obviously Kate wants a divorce and is using this story to take Tony for everything he has. I don't know, maybe she has found someone else. Who knows?" Rose shrugged her shoulders. "All I know is Tony said she's making up this whole thing, and I want it to stop."

Rose turned and fled through the swinging door. And even though Jack would rather be anywhere else right now, he pushed it open and followed.

As he passed the dining room table, home to many shouting matches and scenes of humiliation, his father's voice was already rising with anger. Jack squared his shoulders and turned into the living room.

Dominick Finelli was rising out of his recliner when Jack entered the room. As Jack knew from years of experience, there would be hell to pay if Dom had to get out of his chair.

"What did you say to upset your mother?"

The days were over when that tone of voice from his father made Jack cringe. He'd long since given up hope of winning his father's approval.

"I asked how it was possible for you two to live so close to Tony and Kate all these years and never know what was happening between them?"

Dom turned on Jack.

"They had problems. Every married couple has problems. You should know as well as anyone. Your problems managed to get your wife killed."

Rose gasped, but Jack didn't even flinch. He hadn't expected any better from the old man.

"At least I wasn't the one who killed her. If Tony isn't stopped, he'll kill Kate. What I don't understand is how you two could stand back and let it happen." Dom's eyes fired with rage, but Jack refused to back down. "Don't you care that Tony beats his wife? Don't you care Kate has to run to a battered women's shelter to escape him before he could kill her? And what are you planning to do to stop him from killing her now you know?"

Dom's right hand snaked out so fast toward Jack's face that he almost didn't have time to stop it. Almost.

Unlike all those years when he was a young boy, this time Jack stopped his father's slap in mid-air. Dom's eyes nearly popped out of his face, but his expression showed no remorse, only anger. Again, no worse than Jack should have expected.

While his father prided himself on never using his fists on the boys, he didn't think twice about slapping them until they were black and blue. Must be where Tony learned it.

This time, Jack wasn't backing down.

"Okay, that's how you want to play it, is it? Either you know and want to pretend you don't, or Tony has you so snowed and you actually believe his bullshit." Jack shook his head.

"Don't you talk to me that way." Dom started to raise a hand again, but instead crossed his arms over his barrel chest.

"Sure, Dad. Kate is taking Tony to court to make him stop beating her but you're more concerned about my choice of words."

"You'll show respect to your parents or you'll leave this house."

Jack swore. Tears were slipping from his mother's eyes, but Jack wasn't going to be swayed by them.

"Fine. Any family willing to hide the horrors that have been going on here is not worth my time anyway."

Jack walked back to the dining room doorway and stopped. He turned back, hoping his words were getting through.

"I believe Kate. I've seen her bruises, listened to her story, and I know she's telling the truth. If you choose to believe Tony, then you are nearly as bad as he is. You might as well have been beating her yourselves, for all the help you two have been to her."

Dom started stomping toward Jack. "That's it. Get out of this house. If you cannot support your brother in his time of crisis, but can only insult your mother and me, you are no longer welcome here. You are no son of mine."

"Fine by me."

Jack walked to the kitchen door and turned back as his mother started to stand, only to have Dom push her back into her seat. Then Dom turned and glared at Jack, waiting for him to leave.

So he did.

He left his parents' home. He should have known it would come to this, he should have seen it coming. The fact he hadn't didn't change his resolve to protect Kate with everything he had.

He knew in his gut Kate was telling the truth. He'd seen the evil in Tony's eyes, and had experienced his nasty temper more times than he could count. His parents had seen it too, even if they chose not to notice.

Backing out the driveway, he headed down Main Street to the office. Kate was safe and there was nothing Jack could do for her right now.

Instead, he had to try and help another battered

woman by putting her murderer away. Debbie Standish's murder would not go unsolved, not if Jack had anything to say about it.

## Chapter Eight

"All rise. Family Court for the County of Stevens is now in session. Judge Donovan presiding."

Kate stood and smoothed her dress while the judge took his seat. She glanced back at Jack as she sat down. He tried to convey his support through his smile and position directly behind her in the courtroom. Hopefully, it would help her get through this.

Tony sat at the defense table with his lawyer, Greg Matthews. Greg oozed good-old-boy from the tip of his shiny, new boots to the fuzzy top of his balding head. Jack hated him on sight. Probably had the kind of mentality to believe Tony's lies or at least figure Kate deserved what she got.

The bailiff called the case and Kate's lawyer read her petition to the court. Kate sat ramrod straight, ankles crossed, and hands folded in her lap. Her hair was pulled back into a ponytail, and without any makeup on, per her lawyer's orders, she looked about eighteen.

Jack did some research on Kate's lawyer over the weekend. He was impressed with the woman's credentials and the results she generally got for her clients. She was professional, intelligent, and experienced. And she was making old Greg come across like a buffoon.

Although Tony was still smug and superior when he took his seat at the beginning of the hearing, his smile slipped a bit when the judge took his lawyer to task for making derogatory remarks about Kate and her lawyer. The muscles in Tony's jaw clenched repeatedly at the sound of a few snickers from the back of the courtroom. Jack began to think Tony would grind his teeth to dust before the hearing was over.

From his vantage point in the front of the courtroom, only the profiles of Jack's parents showed, as they sat with Tom and Brenda across the aisle. While Brenda stopped to speak to Jack on their way in and mentioned she and Tom wanted to talk to him afterward, his mother had turned her head only once, making eye contact with him briefly.

His father ignored him completely, but the strain showed in the old man. His shoulders weren't as straight as usual, his skin more flushed, and his hands were moving erratically throughout the hearing. He seemed more than agitated, and Jack wondered if his father could survive the fall of his golden son.

Kate rose and walked to the witness chair. When the bailiff offered the bible, Kate placed her hand on it and solemnly swore to tell the truth. Her earnest gaze seemed to pierce Jack's heart. How could his idiot brother ever hurt such a tender soul?

It was hard for him to listen to Kate's testimony.

"Was Tony Finelli abusive to you when you were dating, before you were married?"

Kate shook her head. "I never thought he was. I

mean, he had very definite opinions about what I should wear and who I could talk to, but he never hit me or anything."

Her voice was fragile. Jack feared it would shatter. She sounded like a young girl again.

"Do you remember anyone in particular he told you not to talk to?" Her lawyer motioned toward Tony.

"Well, he wasn't happy I was working with Jack, you know, that Jack was helping me with my homework. Tony started doing my homework with me, well, really, he did most of it for me."

"And who is Jack?"

"Jack Finelli, Tony's younger brother. He's very smart and had always been really nice to me. Tony said he didn't want his little brother helping me when he could do it himself."

"Did Jack Finelli get upset when you stopped working with him?" her lawyer asked.

"I think so. I mean, he'd helped me since I moved to Harper's Glen. He was my friend." She spoke through pain in her voice. "I don't think he understood why I didn't want his help anymore."

She looked at the judge, her lawyer, and even the bailiff, but not at Jack. He was dying to let her know, even silently, that he'd always understood. He'd never been mad at her.

"But Jack wasn't violent with you, was he?"

Kate shook her head. "No. Jack would never do that. That's not the kind of man he is."

"Not like his brother you mean?"

Nearly everyone in the room craned their necks toward Greg, expecting him to jump to his feet and object. Obviously, old Greg must have been sleeping during law school because he just kept on smiling.

Kate was staring at her folded hands in her lap, despite Jack's wish to catch her eye. "Tony and Jack are nothing alike."

Listening to Kate describe the early years of her marriage to Tony was difficult, but nothing compared to her testimony regarding her desire to have a baby.

"And did you ever get pregnant, Mrs. Finelli?"

Kate's voice became softer. "Yes, I got pregnant the second year we were married."

"Did your husband ever hit you while you were pregnant with his child?"

Kate paused, wiping her eyes. When she finally raised her face, the pain in her gaze speared right through Jack and he had to force himself not to run to her.

"He did."

Kate's lawyer placed a hand on Kate's chair, leaning toward her. "I'm sorry, Mrs. Finelli. I know this is hard for you, but can you explain what happened during your pregnancy?"

Kate visibly swallowed, but her voice remained soft. "I had terrible morning sickness from the very start, so it was hard for me to get things done in the morning. I missed a lot of work, and wasn't able to keep the house as clean as Tony liked it."

"Did he hit you because the house was dirty?"

Kate shook her head, and took a moment before answering.

"Not really, but it made him angry."

Her lawyer turned, facing at Tony. "Why did he

hit you then?"

"When I was four months along, I was still terribly sick every morning. On the last morning, I had to drag myself out of bed to make Tony's breakfast. Even on the mornings I could, the smell of it was enough to send me back into the bathroom in a hurry. Tony was getting pretty tired of me being sick all the time."

"What did he do, Mrs. Finelli?"

Kate stared straight ahead. "Well, Tony was getting dressed for work and couldn't find any clean socks. I was supposed to do laundry the day before, but I had come home from work so sick I couldn't do it. He didn't have any clean socks to wear to work and he was really mad. I was trying to make his breakfast when he came thundering into the kitchen. When I tried to explain how sick I'd been, he pushed me back against the wall of the kitchen. I started to tell him how sorry I was, that I would go buy him some more socks, but he was beyond any of that by then. He punched me hard, in the stomach, and stormed out the door."

Kate was calm, her voice even, but the silent tears running down her cheeks nearly broke Jack's heart. His stomach ached for the pain she endured.

"Did you lose the baby, Mrs. Finelli?"

With tears running down her face, Kate nodded slowly. "Yes. I was bleeding. I called Brenda and she took me to the hospital, but it was too late."

"Do you mean Brenda Finelli? Wife of your brother-in-law, Tom Finelli?" Her lawyer gestured toward Brenda.

"Yes."

Jack glanced at Brenda whose cheeks were smeared with tears. Tom pulled her into his arms, both of them otherwise motionless in their seats.

"Did you tell Brenda what happened?"

Kate shook her head. "No, I told her I fell down the stairs. I had been dizzy on and off, so I said I went to put some laundry in and fell on the stairs."

"Why didn't you tell Brenda the truth?"

"I was too worried about my baby; I didn't want to lose it. And I knew Tony wouldn't want anyone to know what had happened."

Kate paused again, blowing her nose and taking a drink from the cup of water next to her.

The lawyer turned back to Kate again, standing between her and Tony. "Did your husband come to the hospital while you were there?"

"Yes. I had to have a D and C after the miscarriage. Brenda called Tony, and he came right away. He was there when I came out of surgery."

"Was he repentant?"

Kate's smile was so sad, it made Jack's eyes tear up. "Of course. He was always sorry afterward, at least in the beginning. This time more than ever, when the doctor told us I couldn't have any more children because I'd been damaged too badly."

The ache started as pain in the vicinity of Jack's heart but turned to anger by the time it reached his brain. Brenda gasped and buried her head in Tom's shoulder. His mother's shoulders shook, but his father sat still as a rock.

"Was Brenda still in the room?"

"No, she left to call Tony's parents. When she came back, Tony said he was upset because we lost the baby, but didn't tell her I couldn't have any children."

"Did he ever tell his family what happened?"

"No, of course not." Kate shook her head. "In fact, when his parents arrived, he told them it was my fault because I was trying to do the laundry even when I was sick. He said he wasn't angry at me, though, since I was sad about losing the baby and...well...also since I wasn't smart and probably didn't realize I was risking the baby by going down those stairs."

"He blamed you?" The lawyer motioned toward Tony.

"Yes. Even when we were alone, he said he wouldn't have been forced to hit me if I wasn't so lazy about doing my chores around the house."

"Why didn't you leave him then, Mrs. Finelli?"

Kate bowed her head again. "I loved my husband. I was sad about losing the baby, all the babies I dreamed of having, I couldn't bear the thought of losing my husband, too. Even when he got mad at me, I loved him."

Jack had to physically restrain himself from jumping over the rail and wiping a smirk off Tony's face. He glanced around the room, wondering if anyone else recognized the evil in Tony's eyes.

Tom and Brenda whispered between themselves, but his parents never moved. Jack couldn't imagine what his father must be thinking during this testimony. What Kate had lived through ripped Jack's heart right out of his chest. He could only hope his father was listening.

As Kate described the progressively increasing

amount of violence in her marriage, Jack once again wished he had come home more often over the years. He might not have seen what was happening, but there was a chance he would have recognized the signs. Maybe he could have helped her, maybe he could have stopped it somehow.

But he stayed away because he never measured up in his father's eyes, he could never compete with Tony and Tom. It all seemed trivial and selfish now. All the while he thought there was nothing in Harper's Glen for him anymore; he failed to consider what he could have done here. He failed Kate due to his own selfishness, just as he failed Melanie.

When he married Melanie, he knew she loved him more than he loved her. He was able to rationalize it because she wanted a home, a family life, something he thought he could give her. Her family had all the money in the world, but never spent any time together. All Melanie wanted was kids, a husband, and a normal suburban life.

The first disappointment came when the doctor said there would be no babies. Melanie was devastated. She offered to divorce him because she was defective, but Jack assured her he didn't mind. He was happy in the Bureau and enjoyed their active social life, and figured someday, when they were ready, they could always adopt.

But when Jack's career took off at record speed, sending him whizzing up the ladder at the Bureau, Melanie started to resent the long hours and frequent travel. He missed a lot of holidays and social engagements, and she grew sick of being alone.

Things deteriorated rapidly from there. He began

to suspect Melanie was having an affair. He even confronted her about it, on the last morning. She was in a snit because he neglected to get her tire fixed. She was yelling and carrying on, and he lost his temper. She wouldn't admit to having a lover, but said, even if she did, she was entitled since he was never home. She stormed out of the house and got into his car instead of her own, telling him he could deal with her damned flat tire if he wanted to get to work.

When she turned the key in the ignition, his car burst into flames and Melanie was killed instantly. Because she was in his car.

The bomb was meant for him. One of the serial killers Jack had arrested hired a hit man to keep Jack from testifying. The fact they tracked the killer down and sent him away, as well as getting the serial killer quickly to death row, did little to ease Jack's guilty conscience.

It was his fault Melanie was dead. He couldn't escape the fact, even if he escaped Washington, the Bureau, and the apartment they shared by racing back to Deke as soon as he asked.

He let Melanie down. And he let Kate down by ignoring her and his obligation in Harper's Glen for too many years. But that was over. He would have things straightened out here before he left again. And this time, Kate would be safe.

****

When the gavel hit the bench, the mere sound shattered all the bones in Kate's body. The bailiff called, "All rise" when the judge left the courtroom, but Kate was unable to move. Her lawyer elbowed her, but Kate couldn't have stood even if the building was on fire. She was stunned.

She felt one hand on her shoulder, another on her arm. Her lawyer was talking, others were talking too, but Kate couldn't make out the words. She was cold. Deep to the bone, shaking in her shoes, cold.

As she sat, huddled against the cold, her teeth clattering so loud it was the only sound, Jack was there. He spoke in soft tones, held her with gentle hands, and wrapped her in his coat. Whatever else was going on in the courtroom was beyond her comprehension. But Jack she could see, she knew Jack was there. At the moment, nothing else mattered.

"Kate? Kate, honey, are you all right?"

Jack's voice cut through the fog, a warm breeze to ease her shivering bones. Kate tried to speak but merely nodded.

"Kate, you won. The judge agreed with you. You won your order of protection. It's over now and we can go."

Sounds and lights slowly started to come into focus. Her lawyer was packing up the pictures and papers had pled her case. Mary Anne was talking to the lawyer, smiling at Kate and nodding. Kate smiled back.

Jack was crouched by her chair, concern and worry etched into his handsome face. A lock of his shiny, black hair had slipped into his eyes, shadowing the brilliant blue staring out at her. Kate reached forward and swept the hair back, pleased his gaze softened and some of the worry eased.

"Earth to Kate. Are you with us now?"

She let her hand drop, for just a moment, onto his hand where he leaned on the arm of her chair. The merest touch helped warm her to her toes.

"Sorry. I didn't mean to space out, but I couldn't handle the fact that the judge believed me. I really never thought anyone would."

"I don't think anyone could have listened to you today and not believed you. The whole courtroom was on your side."

Kate turned her head slightly, toward the table where Tony sat minutes ago. Thank God he'd left already.

She shook her head. "Not the whole courtroom."

Jack stood and offered her a hand. Deciding her legs had regained the strength to hold her, she placed her hand in his and stood.

"Don't even think about him. He's legally required to stay at least one hundred feet away from you now. Don't hesitate to call 9-1-1 if he even comes within a breath of that limit."

Kate thanked her lawyer, accepted a hug from Mary Anne, and pulled her coat on. "Let's get out of here."

Jack put his arm behind her and ushered her out of the courtroom to where Tom and Brenda were waiting in the hall.

"Kathy—"

Jack put his hand up, stopping Brenda in mid-sentence. "This is not the time or place."

"Now, listen, Jack," Tom said. "Brenda and Kathy have been friends for a long time. I think it's up to Kathy whether she wants to talk to Brenda or not."

Jack dropped his arm from around Kate's waist and shouldered his way between Kate and his brother. Tom had never been anything but nice to Kate, but Jack was ready to slay a few dragons for her.

"She has had a hell of a day, don't you think?" Jack turned first to Tom and then to Brenda. "If you two want to talk to her, and she wants to talk to you, why don't you do it some other time? She needs to rest now."

Kate knew he was only trying to help, but she didn't need another Finelli man telling her when to sleep or when to talk. She put her hand on his arm and not-too-subtly pushed him aside.

"Jack, I'm okay. You don't have to run interference for me." She turned to Tom and Brenda, not certain what to expect.

Brenda's eyes were red and puffy. She stood back, hovering behind Tom in a submissive stance totally unlike Brenda's usual nature. She almost seemed to want extra space between Kate and herself, as if abuse was something she could catch.

"I don't understand." Brenda was almost whispering, her eyes watery again. Tom reached his arm around her shoulders and pulled her close to his side. Brenda cleared her throat and started again.

"Kathy, I don't understand how this could have been going on, all these years, and Tom and I never knew. I mean…you and I are best friends, aren't we? How is it possible you lived through this kind of abuse and we never knew?"

Kate tried to keep her expression calm, her stance relaxed. Brenda hadn't come right out and said she thought Kate was lying. Her expression seemed more hurt than angry, but not nearly as hostile as Kate had feared.

"I couldn't tell you, Brenda. I thought about it many times, but I couldn't do it. I couldn't tell anyone."

"But you lied to us." Brenda raised her voice. "You lied to me." Brenda looked torn and lowered her volume again. "I mean, when you lost the baby, and you told me you'd fallen down the stairs. And ever since, when we talked about why you couldn't get pregnant. You never told me the truth. Why did you have to lie to me?"

"This isn't about you, Brenda." Jack's voice was gentle, but the censure was obvious nonetheless. "Kate doesn't need recriminations from you. If you really are her best friend, she needs your support and love, now more than ever."

Big, watery tears slid silently down Brenda's cheeks. She turned her face into Tom's chest and he wrapped his arms around her. Tom bent his head and murmured in Brenda's ear. They turned slightly away.

Kate tried not to let her disappointment show. She hadn't expected Brenda to understand. She knew the chances were great Tom and Brenda would never speak to her again, the same as Dominick and Rose. If that was the price she had to pay to be free of Tony, as high as it was, she was willing to pay it.

After a few moments, Kate turned to Jack and motioned to him she wanted to leave. It had been a stressful day and she wasn't up to any more confrontations. If Brenda was winding up for more accusations or blame, she'd have to save it until later.

Jack wrapped his right arm around her waist and started to walk her past the tearful couple. Before they passed, a hand reached out and grabbed Kate's arm. Fear raced up Kate's spine and she instinctively crouched, hoping to duck whatever blow was coming her way.

"Oh my God," Brenda cried. "I'm sorry, Kathy. I'm sorry I didn't see… I'm sorry I never knew."

Kate relaxed a bit, meeting her friend's tearful gaze. "It's Kate. I'm not Kathy anymore."

"I can't believe I let you down like this, but I promise to be a better friend to you from now on. Can you ever forgive me?"

Kate looked up at Tom, worry etched into his face, and then turned to Jack. His face showed the slightest bit of smile, which was the only thing that made Kate think it possible she'd heard Brenda right. She turned back to her friend and suddenly her own eyes filled with tears. Brenda pulled her into a hug that spoke volumes.

Kate had never been a hugger. She couldn't let anyone get close, even when it wasn't the pain the embrace might cause. She always watched in envy those who hugged easily, wishing she connected with people so well. Maybe now she could.

When she and Brenda finally broke apart, most of their tears had dried. The four Finellis walked out of the courthouse as a unit, Kate wrapped in the safety and security of their warmth.

Even though Brenda and Tom wanted to help, Kate needed some time alone. After promising to call Brenda the next day, Kate got one last hug before they parted. She accepted Jack's offer to drive her back to the shelter, where she would spend one more night. Climbing into his car was like scaling a mountain. Just one more of the mountains she'd scaled today.

"Are you okay?" Jack glanced at her before pulling out of the parking lot.

She nodded, weakly. "I'm exhausted. You were right. I need to rest."

"But, other than that, are you okay?"

The muscles in his jaw were as tight as a drum, and his gaze was glued to the road. She had taken all the comfort she needed from him today, without even seeing the stress he was fighting.

"Yes, I'm okay."

"Now, you heard what your lawyer said, about filing copies of the order with my office as well as the village police? You should keep one in a safe place and always carry one with you."

Kate nodded. "I know. She talked to me about it all last week, knowing I'd be a little dazed today."

He turned long enough for her to catch the tight ghost of a smile on his face. His dark brows drawn together, making his expression more concerned than reassured.

"When are you leaving the shelter?"

"Tomorrow, around noon." Kate turned to the side window and then back at Jack. "I want to get myself settled in my new location, and make room at the shelter in case someone else needs the space."

His jaw was wired so tightly his teeth must be ready to burst from the pressure. She reached across the bench seat and gently touched his arm.

"I'll be okay. I know what I'm doing, maybe for the first time ever. But I promise, if I get scared or worried, I'll call."

He brought his left hand down and covered hers. "I hope you'll call no matter what. I'll be worried about you and…uh…thinking of you. Can you give me a cell number?"

The warmth of his touch spread quickly up her arm and down through the core of her. He was solid and steady and safe. She pulled her hand away before it became too much for her.

"I'll call you, I promise. I don't want to give out my number, yet. I think it'll be safer that way. Besides, there's no way your family can put you on the spot if you don't know."

As Jack pulled the car to a stop in front of the shelter, he turned to face her.

"Don't keep things from me in an effort to ease things between me and my family. Tom and Brenda are on your side now, and Tony and my parents are not my concern. I can't control what my parents think, and I don't care what Tony thinks. You're what's important. You and your safety."

Kate leaned in and brushed a soft kiss on Jack's cheek. Then she opened the car door and slid her legs out, turning back to Jack.

"Thank you. I appreciate your support and protection more than I can say. And I promise, I will call you. But I need to be alone right now. I need to do this on my own. Please, don't try to find me until I'm ready. Okay?"

She got to her feet and closed the door before he could say a word. Her speech sounded stronger than she was, and she didn't want to give him the chance to change her mind. She walked to the front door, pushed it open, then turned and waved to Jack. He waved from inside his car, and watched as he pulled out and left. Now she really was alone.

\*\*\*\*

Kate pulled the door to her aunt's lake house closed and breathed in the still, musty air. The only sound was the slight rustle of the wind through the falling leaves. At this time of year, there was rarely a boat on the lake, especially in the middle of a weekday. Kate walked from room to room, soaking in the stillness and solitude. There was definitely something to be said for peace and quiet.

She carried her groceries to the kitchen and started to unpack. The food stamps the shelter had given her covered enough soup and staples to last her for a while, especially considering what she'd left the last time she was here. When she resurfaced in town, she could get her hands on some of the money her aunt had left her. Then she'd be able to donate some to the shelter, so they could help other women in need. But for now, it was more important she stay hidden away, and safe.

She unpacked her clothing, such as it was, and stored it away in the cherry armoire. On the nightstand, she placed her CD player and three new audio books she borrowed from Mary Anne. She couldn't wait to get a library card of her own and borrow every audio-book the library owned.

Kate checked the locks on the front door and let herself out the back, making sure to lock up behind her. She jogged down the steps from her deck to the bank, and didn't stop until she reached the shore.

Her aunt's house. Her house now, was located in a tiny cove created by two walls of shale and slate on either side of the stretch of beach. The rocky cliffs made great climbing and protected her strip of shore from the harshest winds off the lake. That is what made it such a great spot for a year-round house.

The cliffs also protected Kate. It was as if she were hidden from the harsh realities and peering eyes of the world. She had to remind herself she really wasn't invisible and still needed to be careful, even here.

Kate spent her first day of freedom skipping rocks and collecting tiny shells washed up on the shore. She curled up on her porch swing in a thick, cable-knit sweater to watch the sun slip slowly behind the western hills. She was nearly hypnotized to sleep watching the bright orange swirls on the lake. But as the sun went away, so did the warmth it generated and the sudden chill was enough to drive Kate back inside.

After eating some soup and bread for dinner, Kate took her tea into the living room. She changed into the boxy flannel pajama bottoms she got from Mary Anne and pulled on a sweatshirt to match. The outfit made her smile, Tony would have gone through the roof if he found her dressed like this, which made it all the sweeter. She wasn't on display for anyone here. She didn't have to be anyone but herself.

By the time Kate finished her tea, she decided to call Jack. He would be worried and she wanted to reassure him she was okay. At least, that's what she told herself was her reason for calling. It couldn't be she needed to talk to him again.

"Hello."

"Jack? It's Kate."

He sighed. What a wonderful sound it was. "Kate, I'm glad you called. I've been thinking about you all day. Is everything okay?"

"Everything is fine." Especially since Jack had been thinking of her all day.

"Good. You checked the locks on your doors and windows?"

"Yes."

"Do you keep your phone near you at all times?"

Smiling, she said, "Yes."

She pushed her hair behind her ear and lay back on the couch, curling her legs up beneath her.

"Does someone know where you are?"

"Yes, Jack. Mary Anne knows where I am. But I don't want you, Ruby, or anyone else to know, yet. I don't want Tony hurting anyone trying to find out where I am."

"I can understand protecting Ruby or Brenda, but don't you have enough confidence to believe I can handle myself against Tony?"

He sounded hurt more than mad, which was definitely not her plan. Did he really doubt her confidence in him?

"Of course I know you can handle yourself. I'm not worried about Tony hurting you, but I don't want him causing a bigger rift between you and your parents because of me."

"I told you not to worry about it. My father has disowned me. I'm 'no son of his' anymore. There's nothing Tony can do to make that worse."

She frowned. "I'm sorry, Jack. Your father has never seen you clearly. I don't know why, but he's not objective about you...really, about any of you."

"Well, I've never been the kind of son he wanted or expected, that's all. We have nothing in common and he's finally given up trying."

Kate ached to take his hand, wrap her arms around him, whatever it took to ease his pain.

"It's his loss. He's been too blind or stubborn or stupid to realize what an incredible person you are. That's his problem, not yours."

Jack didn't answer for a moment and she began to wonder if she'd gone too far.

"Thanks. You're sweet to say so. The thing is, it is my problem. If I want to live in Harper's Glen, it's going to be damn uncomfortable if I'm not speaking to my father or allowed in my parents' home anymore."

Kate picked up the throw pillow and worried the fringe while she spoke. "He's what drove you out of town in the first place, isn't he? Well, not just your father, but the way he worshipped Tony and Tom. I guess I saw it happening back then, but there didn't seem to be anything I could do about it."

"There's nothing anyone can do about it. He values size, sports, hunting, and the manly things he shares with Tony and Tom. He doesn't value brains, education, law enforcement, or any of the things I have always stood for. It's the way it is, and I can deal with it."

What an idiot Dominick Finelli was. Couldn't he understand Jack was twice the man Tony ever was?

His height had nothing to do with the size of the man inside.

"Are you going to stay on after Deke passes away?"

Again, he was quiet for a moment. She must have surprised him.

"Why do you ask?"

"I figured you came home as a favor to Deke, but when he's gone, there probably won't be much to keep you in Harper's Glen."

His voice sounded unsure. "Well, I expect I'll be appointed to finish off whatever's left of Deke's term as sheriff. And then, Deke is hoping I'll be elected sheriff myself."

"That's what Deke is hoping. What about you? Do you want to live in Harper's Glen?"

He was almost whispering now. "I don't know."

She expected the answer, but not the twinge of pain it caused her.

"Would you ever think of leaving Harper's Glen, Kate?"

Now he surprised her.

"Well, I don't know. I can't imagine why. This is my home, even without Tony."

"This home town of yours hasn't done right by you all these years. Someone should have seen what was going on long ago." His tone had more heat to it. "Someone at the hospital or the beauty shop. They should have known you were in trouble and helped you long before this. Are you sure you want to call these people your own?"

Kate took a breath, trying to envision what she would have done if someone asked about her bruises, tried to help her out.

"It's not their fault. It's Tony's. And it's a little bit my fault, for taking it and not telling anyone. But it wasn't up to the people of this town to save me. What matters is people are helping me now."

His breath rasped in her ear, where her pulse pounded out the length of his silence. She wished she could see his face, know what he was thinking behind those bright blue eyes.

"Yeah, I guess you're right."

She sat in silence with the phone to her ear, listening to Jack breathe and wishing he were there, next to her on the couch. Not the kind of thought she should be having on her first night of freedom, but it was there nonetheless.

"I'm going to let you go now, Jack. I'm pretty tired. It's been a long couple of days and I need to get to bed."

He mumbled something she couldn't make it out.

"What?"

"I said, I wish I was there to tuck you in. You know, to make sure you're safe and everything."

She smiled. She wished he was too.

"Goodnight, Jack."

"Goodnight, Kate. Be careful."

After she clicked off her phone, she held it to her chest for a while longer. It wasn't as warm and strong as Jack would be, but it eased her empty.

****

He'd followed her from the small, white house to the courthouse, and from the courthouse to this tiny house on the lake.

162

He ducked out just in time to avoid being seen and concealed himself in the tree line. People didn't expect someone walking by the water at night, especially at this time of year, so she'd never even known he was there.

He'd have to watch for a couple of days to make sure no one else was around, but he should be able to get her attention here. That small, white house was very busy, with people going in and out at all hours.

There better not be any other men showing up around here.

When the time was right, he would let himself in and make her understand she needed to come home. She was supposed to be with him. It was God's law. She was his wife. She'd have to listen to him; he was the husband.

Even if she didn't listen to him, she'd learn real quick he was in charge.

## Chapter Nine

"I got here as quickly as I could. What's the status?"

Jack walked through the waiting room to the hall outside the ER. Thelma had called him fifteen minutes ago, saying Deke was on his way into the hospital after collapsing at his desk. What he'd been doing at his desk so late in the evening, Jack didn't know.

The normally unruffled Thelma was as agitated as Jack had ever seen her. This had to be serious. "They won't tell me anything, yet. The nurses keep saying the doctor will come talk to me as soon as they know something."

Jack lightly placed a hand on her shoulder. "Let me try to get some answers."

Jack strode to the doorway of the emergency room cubicle Deke was in. He was shocked at how much Deke had deteriorated over the course of a few hours.

The old man's face was ashen and his breathing was so loud Jack could hear it from the doorway. The doctor and nurse hovered around the edges of the skinny hospital cot, checking tubes and valves, adjusting and conferring. Jack was about to holler at one or the other of them when they noticed him.

"Are you here with the sheriff?"

"Yes." He walked closer to Deke's bed, and Thelma followed him into the room.

The doctor walked toward Jack with his hand outstretched, gently pulling him back into the hall as they shook hands.

"And you are?"

"I'm Jack Finelli, his undersheriff…his friend. Thelma and I are as close to family as Deke has."

The doctor nodded. "Okay, then you know where we stand with Deke's illness?"

Jack, silent as he tried to swallow the lump in his throat, was grateful when Thelma spoke up.

"We know Deke's cancer is terminal and there isn't a lot of time left, if that's what you mean."

The young doctor nodded. He checked the chart he held and motioned Thelma and Jack to a nearby couch.

"Deke's condition is deteriorating rapidly. I'm going to recommend we keep him here for at least a week, if not two. Then, depending on how he's doing he might be able to go home with a full time nurse, but he's not going back to work anymore. If he takes it easy and gets excellent care, he might have a month left, maybe six weeks at the outside."

Jack turned and stalked down the hall. He couldn't process this now. He couldn't think about Deke dying. How would he tell the old man his days as sheriff of Harper's Glen were really over.

When he turned back, Thelma was leaning slightly on the arm of the doctor with tears running down her face. She'd aged ten years in the space of a moment. This was going to be very hard on her. Jack walked back to the couch and sat next to Thelma, trying to be of comfort.

"I'm sorry; I needed a second there."

Thelma wiped her nose and nodded. The doctor nodded, too.

"This is not going to be easy on any of you, and, if necessary, we can keep Deke here until the end. We may be able to extend the time he has left if he stays in the hospital."

Jack shook his head. "No. I know he'd rather be home. In fact, he'd rather be at the office, but since that's out, I want him to be home."

"He's going to need good care, round the clock. It's a very expensive proposition, Mr. Finelli. I don't know how good the county's insurance is…"

"Not to worry." Jack shook his head. "Get Deke the best care available and send the bills to me." At least some of the money he inherited after Melanie's death would come to good use after all.

"That's very generous, Mr. Finelli. The nurse will let you know what needs to be done."

Thelma turned and placed a hand on Jack's arm. "Why don't I handle the details of getting the nurses, a hospital bed, and whatever equipment is necessary sent to Deke's house, and smooth out the insurance issues? You don't need to worry about those things, Sheriff."

Sheriff. Oh God. It was true. Jack was now the Sheriff of Stevens County.

He couldn't think about that right now, though. He needed to talk to Deke. He needed to be the one to tell him what the score was. It was the very least he could do for his friend.

****

"How's it going down here?" Jack walked into the basement, hoping some breakthrough on the murder case could take his mind off of his dying friend. The command post was humming and Scott Randall was right in the thick of things.

"We're making progress, slowly. We got confirmation from the forensic unit that Ed Michaels is our man. There are officers watching the house, the salt plant, the local bars, even the Standish house, hoping Michaels will show his face somewhere in town. He's got to be feeling the squeeze about now."

"Good. Make the bastard sweat. I don't want him to find a single spot in this county where he can stop to take a leak without worrying about who's looking over his shoulder."

Scott tilted his head, his gaze questioning. "Is everything okay?"

Jack coughed. "You mean, other than a murderer on the loose, a wife-beating brother, and a man who was more of a father to me than my own father who happens to be dying of cancer?"

Scott stood and grabbed the leather coat from the back of his desk chair. "Let's you and me go get something to eat. I haven't been out of this basement in hours and I don't even remember the last time I had food. Can you find me something good to eat in Harper's Glen at this time of night?"

Jack welcomed the distraction he knew Scott was trying to offer him. He needed a chance to blow off a little steam and, frankly, couldn't remember when he'd last eaten either.

He and Scott entered Minnie's when only a few truckers were chowing down. Unwilling to sit in

Deke's regular spot, Jack was glad the place was empty enough for him to have his pick of tables.

"Now, what brings a ten-year veteran of the FBI back to Harper's Glen?"

Jack smiled, surprised Scott had heard about his time with the Bureau already.

"Word gets around fast, doesn't it?"

Scott chuckled. "Well hell, have you been away from small towns so long you've forgotten what it's like?"

"I guess." Jack nodded. "I left town when I went off to college and never came back. I went straight from there to the Bureau and stayed until Deke asked me to come back."

"What made him think you'd agree?"

Jack paused, having never really considered that before.

"I don't know. I mean, I think Deke knows I would do anything for him. But I guess he also knew before I did that I wanted out of the Bureau."

"Did you have problems there?"

"Only if you consider having my job follow me home and my wife ending up dead because of it a problem."

"Wow, sorry." Scott picked up the menu and held out his coffee cup for the passing waitress.

"No, I'm sorry." Jack closed his eyes briefly and then met Scott's gaze. "It's been a hell of a day and I guess I'm not fit for man nor beast tonight." Jack started to rise, thinking to take his sarcastic self-pity and go be miserable alone.

"Wait. Unless you have something urgent to get to, why don't you stay? I'm tough enough to handle it, and it sounds like you could use a sounding board."

Jack sat back and stared at this man across from him. He wasn't a big man, although bigger than Jack, probably close to six feet. He had to be mid-thirties, and had spent his life, as far as Jack knew, working his way up in the Horseheads Office of the State Police. He seemed like a straight-forward guy with more than a few brains in his head.

"Thanks. If you're willing to take your chances, I think I could use the company."

As they ordered their food, Jack brought Scott up to speed on Deke's condition and what it meant for Jack in the office. When dinner arrived, Jack realized how hungry he really was.

"I'm sorry to hear Deke is sliding downhill so quickly," Scott said. "He's been a fixture in this town for a long time and I know he will be sorely missed."

"I know." Jack grimaced.

"He wouldn't have asked you to take the job if he didn't think you were the right man for it. And from what I've seen on this investigation, Harper's Glen is lucky to have you."

"Thanks. I hope the town fathers agree when the news of Deke's retirement hits the grapevine in the morning."

"Is there some reason they wouldn't?" Scott took a sip of his coffee and finished off his dinner.

Jack laughed out loud. "Are you kidding? Didn't you hear about the fiasco in court yesterday? My brother, the wife-beater? Does that make a good reference for sheriff?"

"You are not your brother's keeper, as the saying

goes."

"No, that's for sure. I'm not my brother's anything, when it comes down to it. We couldn't have been more different, from the very get go."

Scott finished his coffee and waited for the waitress to leave the check before continuing.

"Well, it seems to me the fact you are so different is more reason for your brother's problems to have no reflection on you as sheriff."

Jack set down coffee and the waitress picked up their dishes. "I guess. I want to be able to find Ed Michaels, get him off the street, and put things to rights in this town, preferably before Deke passes away."

"Does that mean you're not planning to stay on once Deke is gone?"

Jack hadn't meant to tip his hand, especially since he didn't know what he thought about staying in town anymore. His ambivalence must be obvious.

"I'll finish out Deke's term if I get the governor's appointment. But I'm still not sure this is the place for me. I don't want Deke to worry, so I haven't said anything to him. I need to wait and see how things go with my family before I decide whether to stay."

"That seems fair." Scott nodded in agreement. "But, from what I've learned, you'd be an asset here and go a long way to replacing Deke's role in this town."

Jack nodded, unable to imagine why someone he'd known a short time would have such faith in him. He'd gotten used to people judging him on the merits of his work when he was at the FBI, but it was different here in Harper's Glen. He was different here. Or, was he?

"Well, we'd better get back to work if we want to get Michaels behind bars. Then we can all rest a little easier."

"Okay, Sheriff. Back to the basement, you slave-driver."

Jack slapped Scott on the back, laughing for the first time all day. Letting off a little steam had been a good idea. He'd have to remember to do this more often.

**\*\*\*\***

"He thinks he's so smart. He thinks I'm beaten, but he's fooling himself."

Picking up the gun he polished hard and long enough to bring a shine to the barrel. Neat rows of ammunition were counted off and packaged.

*I have to wait until the right moment, so they don't know what's coming, don't know it's me. Then I'll show them all what he's really made of. I'll make him regret he ever brought his sorry butt back to this town. Should have stayed away, that's all. He shoulda' stayed away.*

**\*\*\*\***

"Yes, Thelma?"

Jack glanced up from the files before him, still a little uncomfortable to be sitting at Deke's desk. Thelma, bless her professionalism, continued on with business as usual.

"I think you're going to want to see this, Sheriff."

Thelma, wearing rubber gloves, was holding an open letter, made with cutouts from a magazine, just like in the movies.

"What is this? Is it some kind of joke?" Jack looked at it and then back at Thelma.

"It doesn't seem to be." She placed the letter in front of him on the desk. Jack was careful not to touch it.

"*'Keep your nose out of another man's marriage, Sheriff. What God has joined together no man should put asunder. Or else.'* Where did this come from?" His gaze met Thelma's.

"It was waiting for me on my desk this morning. I thought it unusual, especially since the mail hasn't arrived yet, so I put on the gloves before opening it."

Jack stood. "This was on your desk? It didn't come through the regular office mail delivery?"

"No, it was just sitting there."

Jack walked out into the outer office. He had spoken to Deke once about the lack of security in the sheriff's offices, but they hadn't had a chance to make any changes yet.

He turned back to Thelma. "Who has access to this office overnight? Who has the keys?"

Thelma ticked off names on her fingers. "The only ones with keys are you, me, Deke, the deputies, and our investigators."

"Not the extra officers working at the command post?"

"No. Only our regular, full-time staff. Well, and the maintenance crew that comes in to clean up."

"Get me a list of the people on the maintenance crew. I want to find out if anyone noticed anything unusual. Also, I want to start implementing the increased office security plan Deke and I discussed.

Can you pull that out for me and we'll figure out where to start?"

Jack walked back into his office. He really wanted to talk about this note with Deke, but he didn't need it enough to jeopardize the man's health. He picked up the phone and called Scott Randall instead. Within minutes, Scott was at his door.

"Hey, Jack." Scott came in and took a seat. "Helluva' way to start the morning, huh?"

"Thanks for stopping in. I don't know if this letter will really amount to anything, but it is enough to get me thinking we need additional security around here."

Scott read the letter. "I'd say this definitely qualifies as a threat."

"Yeah, but I'm not sure if it's directed at me or Deke, or maybe at the office in general. And it's not very specific."

"True, but I think you're right about needing to increase security. Pretty much anyone off the street can walk into your office with very little to stop them." Scott motioned toward the outer office. "And that goes for any of the county employees, as well. Not a good idea for social services or other sensitive departments. For any of the departments that piss people off."

"Deke and I talked about ways to improve security. I think we need to start working on it now."

Jack and Scott discussed the plans and called Thelma in to get started on the improvements. Before the end of the day, a contractor was in the office installing a bullet-proof glass partition and intercom system.

Deputies had been stationed at the doorway into the building and at the top of each landing. Metal detectors were ordered and would be installed within weeks. It was impossible to make a perfect system, but at least it would be better.

By the time he finally took lunch, Jack was glad to escape the dust and chaos of the office. He traded it for the grease and chaos at Minnie's.

He ordered the blue plate special with coffee, and opened the files he'd brought with him while he waited for his food. He became absorbed in the report of the state forensic unit; he didn't notice it wasn't the waitress standing at his table until he finally looked up.

Then he had to look way up, into the angry eyes of his brother.

"What's new, Jack? Trying to ruin someone else's life today?"

Tony slid into the booth opposite him, although obviously not interested in sharing some light lunchtime conversation.

Jack closed his files. "I did not ruin your life, Tony. If it's ruined, it's your own fault."

Tony's eyes gleamed and his face was more animated than Jack remembered ever seeing it.

"If it's ruined? Are you kidding? I have a responsible position in the bank in this community. I'm not the kind of man who deserves to have my name dragged through the mud in open court. To have my crazy wife making up all kinds of lies about me in public and then seeing my own brother waiting on her hand and foot. Come on, Jack. Get real."

Jack almost laughed out loud, but he didn't want

to sound as crazy as Tony did.

"Real? This is real, Tony. You don't deserve a wife, especially not one like Kate. She wouldn't have been forced to air your dirty laundry in public if you didn't beat the crap out of her every chance you got. She had to go to court to make sure you don't get any more chances."

"You don't know what you are talking about, Jack. This is my marriage. It is between me and Kathy, and maybe God." Tony's hands fisted on the table top. "You are not a part of it, and need to keep your damn nose out of my business. Kathy would never have gone to court with this if you didn't push her in that direction."

Now Jack did laugh. "I didn't push her one way or the other. I'm not you. I recommended she get out of your house, and that was before I even knew who she was. Fortunately, she took my advice and went to the shelter."

Tony raised his fist, pounding on the table and spilling Jack's coffee.

"You have no right to interfere in my marriage. Not you or those pansies at the shelter. I have to be able to talk to my wife if we're going to work out our problems. Now, thanks to you, I can't even find her."

Jack moved his coffee out of range of Tony's fists. "No, you can't go near her, even if you do find her. I will be happy to throw your butt in jail if anyone even whispers you are anywhere near Kate. Don't forget, Tony." Jack pointed a finger in his brother's face. "Violation of an order of protection is a felony. If you think the bank is unhappy with you now, wait and see what happens then."

Tony leaned forward and grabbed Jack's shirt. Jack instantly knocked Tony's hand away and got to his feet.

"You really want to get arrested today, Tony?"

Tony stood and glared down at his brother. "Oh yeah, you're such a hot shot, you really worry me."

"Get the hell out of here. I have nothing to say to you and you're disturbing everyone's lunch."

Tony turned and glanced around the diner. Apparently the fact everyone had stopped talking to watch the two brothers didn't please him. He turned back to glare at Jack, his gaze filled with hate and menace, then he stormed out.

Jack slid back into his booth and straightened out his files. When the waitress approached with his meal, she gave him a shy little smile.

"I'm sorry to say it, Jack, but I'm awfully happy for Tony to get what he had coming to him."

Jack looked up and smiled. Behind the waitress, other customers were smiling at him. Maybe the people of this town hadn't been as blind to Tony's true nature as he thought. Maybe only his father was.

"Thanks. I'm happy he left, myself."

The waitress giggled as she walked away.

****

"Okay, where is she?" Even if his goddamn brother sent his wife to a women's shelter, Ruby would know where she is. Kathy probably came crying to Ruby all the time.

"Tony, she's not here, I don't know where she is, and I don't want you in here."

Ruby tried to block his way, but Tony shoved her aside.

He stormed into the back room and rummaged around in the bathroom, but found no sign of her. The place wasn't big, so it would be hard for Kathy to hide. But even if she wasn't in the shop, Ruby knew where she was. He had to get the old broad to tell him.

Tony walked back to Ruby, determined to get some answers. "Listen, she is my wife and I have a right to talk to her. Tell me where she is and I will leave you alone. I don't want to talk to you anyway."

Ruby stood at the main desk, as if protecting something. Tony stormed back over there and grabbed her arm, pulling her out of his way.

Ruby gasped.

"What do you have here, her phone number? She's got to have a new number." He ripped apart the files and papers on the desk, but couldn't seem to find anything that might lead him to his wife.

He turned on Ruby, towering over her as she crouched against the wall.

"Where is she, damn it!" He grabbed her arms and shook. "I have my rights and not you, my damn brother, or some stupid judge can't tell me otherwise. Tell me where she is and I'll leave."

"I don't know where she is, and I wouldn't tell you if I did."

His hand instinctively flew up and smacked her across the face. He didn't have to take sass from anyone, especially not some middle-aged bat who made her living cutting other people's hair.

He raced back into the back room and searched for Ruby's purse. She'd have to have Kathy's phone number somewhere.

After dumping it out on the floor, he found nothing. He rifled through some boxes on the shelves, but still nothing.

When he came back into the front of the store, Ruby was dialing the land line. Tony stormed to the desk and yanked the damn thing from her hands.

"You know where she is and I will find out, one way or another. When you talk to her, tell her I've had enough of this shit and it's past time for her to get her ass home."

As he opened the door to leave, he turned around. Ruby was cowering by the desk, dabbing some blood from the corner of her lip.

"I'll be back. Next time, you better tell me what I want to know."

With that, he stormed out of the store.

Chapter Ten

"Are you getting settled in? Do you need anything?" Ruby called to check on Kate every day, saying she couldn't sleep until she knew Kate was all right.

"I'm fine, really." Kate took a seat at her little kitchen table, admiring the view of the lake. "I have been getting a lot of sleep, listening to my audio-books, and sketching out some plans for the day spa. I am anxious to get moving on the expansion. I called a contractor for ideas and he'll meet us at the shop next week."

"Are you sure you should come into the shop already?"

Kate paused concerned by the nervous twinge in Ruby's voice.

"Do you think it's too soon?"

Ruby was breathing but made no sound. Finally she answered, "Maybe. You might want to give Tony a little more time to calm down and get used to this situation."

"Ruby, did something happen?"

Ruby's voice went up almost an octave, to a phony-sounding surprise pitch. "Now, why would you say that? It's just, you know, he has to be embarrassed and angry about how things went in court. I don't want you to rush things; it'll make him madder."

Kate shook her head. "I don't want to rush things either, and I know it would be better to stay out of Tony's way for the near future. But this is a small town, and unless I plan to move, he's going to have to deal with me now and then. As long as he stays one hundred feet away, we should be fine."

"I'm not sure he puts much credence in the order of protection, honey. A man like Tony isn't going to like having the law tell him how to treat his wife, you know?"

Kate's voice became almost a whisper. "Yeah, I know."

"If you want, we can meet somewhere out of the way, some place he'd never go. That way there's less chance of him seeing you."

"But I want the contractor to examine the shop as it is now, with the empty space next door. It would be nice to get his feedback on how to expand, how much it'll cost, and how soon it can be done."

"Well, maybe we can bring the floor plan along for our meeting and he can draw it out for us."

Kate tilted her head, trying to think of their options. "No, I want him to be able to envision it through my eyes, to hear what we have to say, to check out what you've already done there. He can't get that from a piece of paper. Besides, it's not like Tony's office is next door or anything. There's no reason to think he'll know if I come in through the back door."

"Well…"

Kate had a niggling feeling Ruby was still holding back. "What is it, Ruby? What happened?"

"It's… Tony was here, wanting to know where to find you."

"That's why I didn't want you to know. It's better you didn't have to lie to him, right?"

Ruby hesitated.

Kate's breathing picked up sharply. "What did he do?"

"He got angry when I couldn't tell him where you're staying. He didn't believe me and I antagonized him a bit. He wasn't pleased."

"What aren't you telling me? Did he threaten you?"

Ruby's voice became a little shaky. "Well, he threatened you, and me too, I guess. He's acting crazy, Kate. You need to stay out of his sight. He could go off at any minute."

Kate tried to remain calm, reminding herself Tony did not know where she was, and he couldn't find her. She took a deep breath and asked the question she was afraid to ask.

"Did he hurt you?"

Ruby almost disguised the catch in her voice, but again sounded a little too cheerful. "He tried to push me around some, but he can't hurt me. I'm too tough and too old to put up with his kind of crazy."

"Oh, Ruby. I'm sorry. I never dreamed he would touch you. I thought you'd be safe, you know. I should never have dragged you into this."

"Now you listen to me, missy. Your crazy husband did not hurt me and he won't. I am not afraid of him, at least for myself. And even if I was, it would be worth it to help you get freed of him."

Kate's shoulders sagged. "I know, but there

should have been some other way, instead of putting you in harm's way."

"I told you, I'll be fine. I am afraid for you, though. Tony is not right. Maybe he never has been, but he hid it better than he has now. I think you need to stay clear of him for as long as possible."

Kate sighed. She wanted to get on with her life, make something of herself; start again. She could see now it was her fear of Tony and total belief in him that allowed him to treat her the way he did. She didn't make it happen, but she let it happen.

"I will give it a couple of weeks, but I can't hide out here forever. I have to get back to work, go to the grocery store, the bank, the library. I didn't leave my prison in Tony's house to have him make me a prisoner here, too. I can't hide forever, or he wins."

"I understand, honey. I really do. I want you to be careful. Freedom is only a great thing if you're alive. Right now, I think Tony is close enough to the edge he could kill you if he gets his hands on you."

Shaking her head, Kate frowned. "No, he'd never go that far. If he killed me, he couldn't control me anymore, and I've figured out it's what's most important to Tony. Control. He might beat the crap out of me, but he wouldn't try to kill me."

"Well, you know the man better than I do, but I want you to be careful. How about I call the contractor and tell him to meet us at the coffee shop on Buffalo Street in Ithaca? It's a bit out of the way, but you won't take the risk of running into Tony there."

Kate didn't have a car. Her aunt's car was in the garage, but if anyone saw her driving it, her hideout wouldn't be a secret anymore. "I don't know, Ruby…"

"Do you need a ride? I can pick you up somewhere in town or wherever, if you tell me where."

"Okay. That sounds like a good idea." Nodding at the possibility, Kate continued. "If the contractor can meet us, why don't you pick me up at the park at the end of the lake? I'll be in the baseball dugout. No one will know I'm there."

"Sure, that'll work. I'll talk to the contractor, get some floor plans for this shop and the space next door, and we'll be good to go."

"Great. I really appreciate your help, Ruby. You're a life-saver."

"I'm not doing much, really."

She smiled. "Not true. If not for you and Jack, and of course Mary Anne and everyone at the shelter, I could never make it on my own."

"Have you talked to Jack since you left the shelter?"

Kate chuckled. It seemed like all she did these days was talk to Jack, think of Jack, dream of Jack. Even in her sleep, she couldn't seem to let him go. At least the nightmares hadn't returned.

"Yeah. I talk to him every day. He's a big help in keeping me calm and centered. And he's being sweet about all this."

"Sweet, huh? How sweet is he?"

Ruby's sarcasm made Kate realize how wonderful it was to tease and joke again, to have something to giggle about, even if only in her own mind.

"He's concerned and caring and very cautious. He is desperate to know where I am staying, so he can make sure I'm safe. He really seems to care."

"Of course he cares, honey." Ruby's voice softened. "You are a sweet, loving, and beautiful person. Any man with half a brain would care about you and we both know Jack has more than his share in that department."

"And I am learning how much more important and sexy a brain is on a man than anything else."

"Sexy, now that's not a term used often in connection with Jack Finelli. Not that he doesn't deserve it. He's fair, not like the rest of the dark Finelli men. He's good looking enough, you know, but compared to Tom and Tony, well, at least compared to their looks, I don't think anybody ever stopped to think about Jack."

Kate ached for Jack, for the truth in that assessment. "I know, and what a waste. Tom's a nice guy, but it has nothing to do with his looks. Jack is wonderful and Tony's a monster. While I was drawn to Tony's dark hair and eyes when I was young, Jack has filled out and his lighter hair and eyes are much more appealing now. Go figure. If I'd only realized this ten years ago, I could have saved myself a lot of pain."

"Well, I guess the question is, now you figured this out, what are you going to do about it?"

Kate paused, shaking her head. "What are you talking about? What am I going to do about what?"

Ruby's voice seemed to have a hint of mischief in it. "I mean, now you know how special Jack is, and you're soon to be a divorced woman, what are you going to do about him?"

Kate walked to the window scanning the lake. The moon reflected on the still, cold water. The sky was so dark it looked like black velvet sprinkled with a few shining lights.

"Nothing. There's nothing for me to do. Jack will never be able to see anything but the victim his brother made me. He'll never consider me a whole person; a strong or independent woman. I don't even know if I can be those things. But I know he deserves someone who can make him understand his incredible gifts and potential, someone who can help him believe in himself again. Not someone he has to rescue."

"You won't need rescuing forever."

Kate smiled a sad but resigned little grin. "I'm glad you think so."

She checked the locks on the back door and turned off the kitchen lights, walking back into the living room.

"I know so, honey. You and me are going to have a booming little business here, just you wait and see. And we'll get started on it real soon, don't worry."

"Thanks, Ruby. You're the best."

"I'll meet you at the park, at the dugout right?"

"Yep. See you then. Goodnight."

Kate checked the locks on the front door, and shut off the rest of the lights. She still wanted to call Jack, but she'd call after she got into bed. She liked the idea of talking to him in bed.

**** 

That dumb cow didn't even realize he was

listening at her window. He knew Ruby would rush to tell his wife he pushed her around, just another nagging woman.

He was smart, though. He knew if he waited around, he might pick up some hints as to where his wife was. He didn't hear anything to make him think Ruby knew, but they were going to meet up. All he had to do was watch them return and follow her back to her hide-out.

Then he could find his wife, bring her home, and show her where she belonged. For good.

\*\*\*\*

Jack grabbed the phone before he headed out the door. This couldn't be good news, coming so soon after the last call.

"Hello?"

"Hi, Jack. It's Kate."

Jack stopped in his tracks. Thank God. "Kate, hi. Listen, I can't talk right now. Can I call you tomorrow?"

"No problem. But…is something wrong?"

He balanced the phone between his shoulder and his ear, and pulled his coat on. "I'm on my way out the door." He tried to keep his voice from cracking. "The hospital called. Deke slipped into a coma."

"Oh, Jack. I'm sorry. What did the doctor say?"

"They don't know much, but he might not wake up. I gotta' go. I'll talk to you tomorrow. Bye."

"Okay. Bye."

Jack pocketed his phone and raced out the door.

He sat in the waiting room outside the I.C.U. while Thelma sat on the couch opposite him. She brought knitting, prepared for a long night. Jack wished he had something to occupy his hands and his mind. Anything but the thoughts of losing Deke.

"Jack?"

He immediately stood and turned toward the vision in blue standing in the doorway. He had to touch her, just to be sure he wasn't dreaming. He reached out and took her hand in his.

"Kate? What are you doing here?"

She shyly smiled and walked to him. "I didn't want you to be alone. I thought you might need someone with you."

A jolt went straight to his heart. He almost smiled, until he remembered why they were here.

As he pulled her into the waiting room, Thelma looked up and said hello. Kate stumbled, glancing back at Jack.

"I didn't think. Of course Thelma would be here. How silly of me. I thought of you alone and didn't think it was right."

Jack stroked her arm, easing her onto the couch as he did. "I'm glad you're here, Kate. Thelma and I only have a few minutes with Deke each, and it's nice to have someone else to talk to. I think I've bored Thelma long enough."

Kate smiled in obvious discomfort.

"Why don't you two go get some coffee or something," Thelma said, looking at Kate. "I am going in to visit Deke in five minutes, and I promise to come find you if anything changes. I think Jack could use the distraction for a little while. Plus, I doubt he's had anything to eat tonight."

Kate turned to Jack and tilted her head toward the door. "What do you think?"

Jack nodded. "I think it's a good idea. Thelma's right. I haven't eaten a thing all day. I've always loved hospital food, so let's go find out what they've got."

Kate actually laughed. "You have got to be kidding. I never knew anyone who loved hospital food."

Jack drew her hand through his arm and escorted her down to the cafeteria. Their little jokes and teasing eased his ache a bit.

After they got some food and took a seat, Kate reached across the table and laid her hand on his. The feather-light weight of her was warm and soft. A little of her warmth seeped through his skin.

"You know you've made Deke a happy man. You're the son he never had. He spoke of you often over the years, always beaming with pride. And I know how much it means to him you came back when he needed you. Don't have any regrets. You helped make his life a happy one."

Jack shook his head. "From three hundred miles away? I don't think so."

She squeezed his hand, but didn't let go. "You don't have to live near someone to be a part of their lives, a part of their heart. You called him, sent him gifts, and spent time with him when you could. He knows you love him, and that's what matters."

Jack took a sip of coffee to help dislodge the catch in his throat. "I'm the lucky one. He's been good to me, better than anyone in my family ever was. He's my best friend and I don't know what I'll do without him."

He couldn't break down and cry in the hospital

cafeteria, but the tears in Kate's crystal blue eyes almost did him in. He made quick work of his turkey and mashed potatoes, gulped down his coffee, and stood. "Let's get back upstairs."

As they walked back down the hall, Kate slipped her hand into his. Just a little thing, barely a touch, but it reminded Jack he wasn't alone.

Thelma looked up when they walked into the waiting room. If she thought it unusual he was holding hands with his brother's wife, it didn't show. She said there was no change when she was in with Deke, but that wasn't necessarily a bad thing.

Jack and Kate sat on the orange vinyl sofa, trying to get comfortable. He knew he should tell Kate to go home, but he didn't want to. She was a better distraction than any book or TV.

"I'm going to take a break, as long as you're back." Thelma stood and gathered her knitting into a bag. "I think I'll go get some coffee and make a few phone calls. I need to walk around a bit and get the kinks out of my legs. Please call me if anything changes."

After Thelma left, Jack became more restless. He stood and paced the small waiting room, flipped through the magazines on the coffee table, and sat again, crossing his legs in one way then the other before Kate reached over and took his hand.

"Why don't you tell me how things are going on the murder investigation?"

Jack marveled at the strength in her delicate hand, the fine bones clearly defined through the ivory skin. She squeezed gently and he looked up into her eyes.

"Come on, Jack. Tell me what's going on. Unless you can't, I mean…unless it's classified, of course."

Jack shook his head, smiling sadly. "There not much to tell at this point. We have proof Ed Michaels killed Debbie, and probably killed her dog, too. We have an A.P.B. out on him, and are watching all of his regular hang-outs. It's only a matter of time until we find him."

"Poor Debbie. And how horrible for her husband and son. It's hard to understand why Ed would kill her now, when they'd been divorced and she'd been remarried for many years."

Jack sat forward, arms resting on his knees, but didn't release Kate's hand.

"The hardest part of all of this is trying to think like Ed is now. We have some profilers and psychologists working up a profile for us."

"Have they come up with anything?"

"As far as we can tell, Ed has a drinking problem, although it's not a daily thing. He seems to go on benders a few times a year, particularly around the times of his wedding anniversary to Debbie, her birthday, and the time she left and divorced him. We have witnesses who told us he gets abusive when he drinks, especially toward Debbie, and he's been arrested for disorderly conduct and assault several times over the years."

Kate shivered and Jack realized this was a little too close to home for her. It was hard enough to get away from an abusive husband. Kate certainly didn't want to think about what happened when the husband wouldn't let go.

"Listen, why don't you tell me about your idea for a day spa with Ruby?" He laced his fingers with hers. "Have you drawn up plans or gotten financing figured out? What kind of services are you going to offer?"

"Oh, it's going to be great. You can get your haircut, of course. But we'll also offer manicures, pedicures, facials, body wraps, Vichy baths, aromatherapy, massage, and even mud baths. We'll have to add a few more employees, and get some more training ourselves, but it should be a big hit, especially with all the tourists in this area during summer."

Jack nearly gasped at the light radiating from Kate's face as she talked about the spa. Her eyes sparkled in a way he hadn't ever seen before and her skin actually glowed. Anything that could make her happy right now had to be a good thing.

"And we are going to set up some weekend packages in the winter, to pull in more tourists from Rochester and Syracuse, maybe even New York City. We'll work with some of the local hotels and the wineries, give people lots of things to do over a weekend, including some pampering. I think those will go over really well."

"It sounds like a great idea. If you don't mind me asking, though, how are you and Ruby going to secure financing for all of this?"

"Well, Ruby has the building as collateral, and she already has the business. I have some family money to invest, and she applied for a business loan for the rest. I think it'll work out. We may have to start smaller, offer fewer services, but the best, and then build gradually."

He nodded. "It's going to be a big hit, Kate. Ruby's location on Main Street is a huge plus. Sounds like a good investment and should get you on your own feet financially, after you divorce Tony, at least when combined with alimony."

She slipped her hand away from his, pulling both of hers into her lap and staring at her fingers as she twisted them together.

"I don't want Tony's money."

He touched her shoulder, leaving his hand here. "But it's your money, too. You've always worked, right?"

"Yeah, but he makes a lot more than I ever did and he's way more obsessed with money than I am. I don't need much." When she glanced back up at him, the truth was in her eyes.

"The money's not as important as getting away, right?"

She nodded. "I don't want to have any contact with him after this is all over."

"This is a small town. I don't know if you're being realistic."

"You're probably right, but at least if he can't play control games with me over sending money, I'll have a better chance of avoiding him."

He leaned in. "Will you be able to get by on your own without his money?"

"Yes, because it *is* a small town." She nodded. "Things aren't as expensive as they are, say, in DC, I bet you had to take a big pay cut, coming back to Harper's Glen after being in the FBI."

Jack cleared his throat. "True. If not for the fact

that Melanie left me a sizeable estate, I might never have considered it."

She looked up. "Melanie left you a lot of money?"

"Yeah." He shook his head. "Her family was very well off and she had a trust fund. When she died, it all came to me. It's been hard to deal with, since it's my fault she was killed."

"Jack, it is not your fault. You didn't kill her."

He pulled his hands back, crossing his arms over his chest. "Yeah well, I didn't protect her from the scum I came in contact with, did I?"

"You can't keep blaming yourself for Melanie's death." She leaned in to put her hand on his arm again. "You are a smart man; you always have been. Do you truly believe, in your immense brain, you could have stopped a maniac from rigging your car to explode?"

Jack chuckled. "Immense brain, huh? Are you saying I have a big head?"

Kate smiled. "Answer the question, Jack."

He took a deep breath and made himself think before speaking. "No. I don't think anything could have stopped him from trying to kill me. But, it was my fault Melanie took my car, because I hadn't fixed her tire."

Kate nodded. "Why didn't you? For that matter, why didn't she? Did she know where to take the tire to get it fixed? Could she have done it herself?"

Jack stopped, cocked his head to one side. He'd never really thought about it. "Yeah, I suppose so."

Kate took his two hands in hers. "Okay. Isn't it possible she took your car that day because she was angry, or selfish, or trying to punish you in some way?"

A ripple raced up Jack's spine. Melanie's face on the last morning, the anger in her eyes, the viciousness of her voice, came crashing into Jack's mind. She had wanted to punish him, whether for failing her or accusing her of having an affair, or something else, she definitely chose to take his car purposely to make him suffer.

"Oh God." He began shaking, despite Kate's small hands trying to hold him together. "She didn't even know her anger at me was going to get her killed. She just wanted to spite me. Oh, Melanie."

Kate pulled him into her arms and rocked him as she might a young child. She ran her hand over his hair as he buried his face in the crook of her neck. She murmured something, but he couldn't make out the words over the anguish rushing through his brain.

When the memories began to fade and the tears he let fall had dried, Jack began to realize how soft Kate was. Her warm skin smelled of soap and goodness. Her arms held him tightly but gently and her hair tickled his nose.

Next thing he knew, he pulled Kate closer into his embrace. He knew he shouldn't, but he couldn't make his arms cooperate. She didn't fight him, whether because she was still trying to comfort him or she wanted to be there, he didn't know. And he was ashamed to think he didn't care.

Jack buried his nose in her long, blonde hair, breathing in sunshine and beauty. His hands held her back carefully, not wanting to scare her or bruise her, but wanting to be closer still.

Kate must have sensed the change in their embrace, as her soothing murmurs ended and her breathing picked up. Her hands twined behind Jack's neck and she leaned ever-so-slightly against his chest. Her breasts were pressing against his flannel shirt, nearly sending Jack rocketing off the couch.

He was playing with fire and had to stop.

If he was smart, he would let her go, stop touching her, stop sniffing her hair. If he was smart, he'd pull back and put some space between them. Maybe he wasn't smart after all.

Suddenly Jack realized someone else was in the room. He released Kate and looked up at the I.C.U. nurse.

"You can go in now, Mr. Finelli."

Guilt washed through Jack again.

Not for Melanie, no, not anymore. Kate had helped him understand that situation for what it really was, and he would be eternally grateful to her.

But here he was to see Deke, to will his friend back from the edge of death, and instead he's trying to think of ways to get into Kate's pants.

He jumped up from the couch, quickly walking into Deke's room. The beeping machines and gurgling tubes hadn't changed from the last time he was allowed in. The gray cast to Deke's face was the same as was the rasping of his breath.

When Jack took the old man's hand in his, the dry, cold skin was the texture of worn leather. Nothing had changed in here, even though all hell had been breaking loose on the couch in the waiting room.

"Come on, Deke, wake up. I need you. I'm

afraid I'm falling in love with Kate, or maybe I've always loved her, and I need you to kick some sense into me again. She's my brother's wife."

He gently squeezed Deke's still hand between his two.

"My head tells me to stay away, but the rest of me isn't listening too well. I need you, Deke, to keep me strong. To remind me I'm the acting sheriff, and I should only be concerned with protecting Kate; keeping her safe, and helping her start over. I shouldn't be concerned with kissing her, touching her, or smelling her hair. And I definitely shouldn't be thinking of taking her to bed. Wake up and knock some sense into me, okay?"

Jack leaned over the edge of the hospital bed and laid his head on their clasped hands.

"Wake up, Deke. Please wake up."

## Chapter Eleven

He walked through the woods, following the dry creek bed to the road before crouching down in the ditch until he was sure there were no cars around. In the still of the crisp, fall air, his breath was the only thing in sight. He darted across the road and once again was lost in the stand of trees.

Nobody knew the woods like he did. He could get to her wherever she was.

They thought they were so smart, using those damn computers to stick their noses in a man's job, his marriage, his life. Some things are supposed to be sacred. What happens between a man and his wife is nobody else's business.

They would be sorry for interfering in his marriage. If they'd minded their own business, his wife would still be where she belonged, in his house, cooking his meals, and washing his laundry. The way it was supposed to be.

But they took her from his house. She never would have left on her own. She knew her place.

Now they had to pay. And soon, very soon, he'd make sure they did.

**\*\*\*\***

"Hey, Jack. You got a minute?"

Jack looked up from the files he hadn't really been reading. He could use a break from telephone watching. Like a pot of water, a watched phone never rings.

"Sure, Scott. Come on in. Anything new on Ed Michaels?"

Scott took a seat in the guest chair facing Jack. "Not much, sorry to say. We have been through his bank records, phone calls, employment records, everything, but we still haven't found the s.o.b."

Jack nodded. "He'll turn up. I doubt he's left the area. He knows the back woods trails and hiding places. We just have to be watching and ready."

"We've got teams watching damn near every place in town. We'll nab him if he shows even one scraggly hair on his head."

Jack chuckled. From the photo they had on their wanted posted, Ed Michaels didn't have too many hairs to spare.

Scott hesitated. "Anyway, I'm here about something else."

"Okay."

Scott shifted in his seat, glancing down at the paperwork in his hands and up at Jack again.

"Oh man. Is it Deke?"

"No, no. Sorry. I didn't mean to make you think that. Deke is the same, as far as I know."

"Okay, what is it?"

Scott cleared his throat, thrusting the pile of papers onto Jack's desk.

"I did some more research on your brother, like you asked. I've uncovered some discrepancies in his financial statements."

Jack pulled the papers in front of him. "What kind of discrepancies?"

Scott stood and walked around the desk, pointing to columns on his spreadsheet. "Well, something is draining away all of Tony and Kate's money. Their income level doesn't match what they have in the bank, which is next to nothing. With both of them working, and Tony a manager at the bank, they should have more to show for it."

Jack glanced back up at him. "What about the house? Do they have a mortgage?"

"Yeah. In fact, Tony took out a second mortgage last year and is way behind on payments. But that doesn't explain what happens to their monthly income, which should be more than enough to meet their expenses."

Jack sat back in his chair, almost afraid to ask the next question. "Have you gotten a line on what the problem is yet? I mean, Kate said nothing about alcohol, but is there any indication he's into drugs?"

Scott shook his head, moving back to the chair. "From what I've been able to come up with, there is nothing to indicate drugs or alcohol."

"What, does he have an expensive girlfriend or something?"

"Actually, I think he might be a compulsive gambler."

Jack sat up quickly, both feet hitting the floor hard.

"Gambling? How could he get into trouble gambling in Harper's Glen?"

This time, Scott was the one who chuckled. "You have been away a long time, haven't you? Over the past ten years, the fastest growing businesses in this area have been farm wineries and the reservation casinos."

"How close is the nearest one?"

"There's one in Oneida. It's not far, and I know a lot of people from the area go up there regularly. There are even bus deals from Elmira and Corning."

"Why do you think Tony's gambling?"

Scott leaned over the desk and pulled a sheet from the stack. "Here's the amount of money draining out of their joint bank accounts."

He pulled out another sheet and laid it next to the first one. "And here's Tony's latest credit card statements, showing cash advances taken at the casino."

As Jack leafed through the paperwork, he tried to remember what he knew about compulsive gamblers. He had to agree with Scott. The numbers certainly supported this theory.

"I want to call Kate and go over some of this with her, ask if she has any ideas about where their money goes."

Scott stood and grabbed his jacket. "Okay. Call me when you're finished and let me know what you want to do from here."

"Why don't you stay? I might need you to go over some of this with her, if she has questions, which she probably will. I'm willing to bet she has no idea what the status of their finances is."

Scott nodded. "I think it's a safe bet. Especially since everything is in Tony's name."

As Jack started dialing the number, Scott smiled. "Hey, I thought she wouldn't give you her phone number."

"She finally did last night at the hospital. I had to

promise not to trace it to her location. She wanted me to be able to call her, especially if something happens to Deke."

"Hello Kate, it's Jack."

"Hi Jack. Is Deke okay?"

Jack smiled, turning slightly away from Scott. "He's the same, but at least he's not worse."

"I'm praying for him."

"Good. Listen, I'm at work and Scott Randall from the State Police is here, too. I want to put you on the speaker phone because he found some discrepancies in your financial records, yours and Tony's, and it would help if we could figure out what's going on."

When she answered, her voice was much softer. "Why is Scott checking our finances?"

"I asked him to, as a personal favor, to check for anything to help you in the divorce. I also wanted to be prepared, in case he tries to violate the protection order."

"Okay, I guess. Sure, put me on the speaker and ask away."

"Okay."

"Hi Kate." Scott sat up in his chair, leaning toward the phone.

"Hi, Scott. Thanks for helping in all this. I will be indebted to you if anything you find helps me get my divorce finalized quickly and easily."

Scott looked uncomfortable, but murmured, "You're welcome."

When Jack explained the status of the mortgage payments, Kate seemed shocked to learn there was a second mortgage and payments on both mortgages were months behind. Jack shook his head. "You didn't know anything about this?"

"No… I can't believe it. Tony always had our mail sent to a post office box. He said it was easier for him, since he can pick it up and deal with it at work. Our bank account is at his bank, of course, and he pays the bills from there."

"He handles all the finances?" Jack knew what the answer was going to be before she even spoke.

"Oh yes." Her breath was coming faster now. "As long as we've been married. He said…well, he said since he's in banking, it was his job to do our bills, and besides, he always said I wasn't smart enough to do it."

Son-of-a-bitch. Jack took a few deep breaths before continuing.

"You don't know where your money goes?"

"What do you mean, Jack?"

He glanced at Scott. "I mean, your check goes into the bank every week, as does Tony's direct deposit from the bank. As far as you know, what happens then?"

"He deposits my tip money, too. Then he pays the bills twice a month, I think. Whatever's left stays in our checking account. I mean, other than what goes into his 401(k) at work. I don't really know anymore, but there should be a good amount in the checking account. I can't understand why he hasn't paid the mortgage."

Scott was shaking his head, but didn't speak.

"Kate, honey, there is next to nothing in the checking account."

She gasped. "I don't understand. Where is all our

money?"

"We think Tony may have a gambling problem. Do you think that's a possibility?"

"Gambling?" Her voice soft again.

Scott spoke up. "Does he travel often? Is he an avid sports fan, getting unusually upset over the outcome of football or baseball games or other sporting events?"

Kate was murmuring recognition.

Scott continued. "Have you ever noticed him making bets with friends or family?"

"He doesn't really travel for work, you know, but goes on hunting and fishing trips with the guys, usually at least once a month."

"Do you know where they go?" Scott asked.

"Somewhere north of here. I'm not really sure. He never told me because he didn't want me to bother him."

Scott tried again. "What about sports? Does Tony watch a lot of sports?"

Kate laughed soft and low. "Yeah, I'd say so. Nothing else is ever on the radio or the TV, every season of the year. We attend most of the local high school games, and Tony never misses the car races in Watkins Glen. He uses most of his vacation days going to sporting events of one kind or another."

Scott reviewed with Kate the common signals of compulsive gambling, and she agreed it was possible. She didn't see any alcohol or drug abuse, but acknowledged she might not know about it. Jack didn't even want to think what else Tony might be spending their money on.

He looked up at Scott, who had stood again.

"If it's okay with you, Kate, I'm going to keep digging. With the information you've given me, I can probably find something to show us what is happening to all your money."

Kate's voice was still quiet. "I can't thank you enough, Scott. I appreciate all your help."

Scott walked to the door. "Don't worry about it. I'll catch you both later."

Jack picked up the receiver again as Scott closed the door behind him.

"Still there?"

Kate sighed. "Yeah, I'm here."

"Are you okay?"

"I think I am. I'm mad, but I also don't care too much. I didn't expect to walk out of my marriage with anything. As long as I walk out alive, it's all that matters."

Jack sat up in his chair, thrumming his fingers on the desk. "What about your day spa? Were you planning on using the house, or your half of it, as collateral for the business loan?"

"No. I have some money of my own."

Jack had to wonder where Kate came up with her own money, but it wasn't his place to pry.

"Okay. Well, I wanted to ask what you knew about all this before we go forward with it."

"Thanks, Jack. It's a huge relief to me knowing I will have something to barter with when it comes time to get this divorce finalized. I don't want to be the weak one anymore."

He leaned back and took a deep breath. "You're not, Kate. You're one of the strongest women I know. You have survived, and not only have you come out alive, but you have friends, a new business to build, and the strength to make a new life for yourself. You should be proud of yourself."

Her cough couldn't mask the tightness of her voice. "Thanks, Jack."

"Well, I'd better get back to work."

"Oh, before I forget, I'm going to Ithaca with Ruby tomorrow to meet with our contractor. And yes, Ruby and I will be careful. I'm sure it'll be fine, but I wanted you to know."

He smiled, although a bit leery about her going anywhere right now. "Thanks for telling me. Call me when you get back from Ithaca. I'd like to know you're home safe and sound, okay?"

She chuckled. "Okay. Bye Jack."

After he hung up the phone, he leaned back in his desk chair again and closed his eyes, letting his head fall back on the chair.

He was furious at Tony for taking all of Kate's money, including her tips, and throwing it away on card games and sports. Compulsive gambling helped explain the missing money, and it also jibed with Tony's violent temper and insane need to control everything.

Kate had taken it all pretty well. He had to admire her desire to simply be rid of Tony, whether or not she had any money left after the divorce. He couldn't imagine what kind of money she had of her own, or where she'd gotten it, but he was glad to know she did.

Did Tony know she had money of her own? Jack made some notes in the file. He would have to do everything he could to make sure Tony stayed the hell away from Kate and her money.

He knew this protectiveness was more than duty. He was drawn to Kate in a way he'd never been drawn to another woman, including Melanie. Whenever he saw her, talked to her, hell, even thought of her, a surge of adrenaline, a weird, edgy tightness filled in his chest. Once he'd helped her escape his brother and start a new life, he would have to figure out if it was possible for him to be a part of it.

**\*\*\*\***

He crouched down behind the abandoned concession stand. Waiting. Listening.

It was insulting to think he had to hide out here like a common criminal. She'd pay for this.

He pulled the collar up on his jacket, wishing again he'd thought to put on a hat, when the car pulled in. He crawled to the edge of the building, moving as slowly as possible into a position where he had a good view of the end of the parking lot near the dugouts.

Why the hell didn't she get out already? No, they had to sit there and talk some foolish nonsense. Probably what they did all day at work, too.

The passenger door finally opened and the dome light shone briefly on her face. The door closed and someone raced into the dugout. He wasn't fooled. She was never smart enough to even fool a child. Why did she think she could hide from him?

After a few minutes, she peeked her head out from the dugout and looked around. Pulling her hood up, she took off on foot down toward the water's edge. He followed, making sure to stay back in the trees, away from any light, but close enough to keep her in his sight.

When they got to the edge of the park, she turned and scanned the area around her again. He flattened himself to the ground, waiting. Cold stones and small sticks cut into his cheek and palms, but he didn't care. He'd do what he had to do to get his wife back, to take her home, to show her where she belonged.

He watched her climb up the bank and follow the line of trees along the edge of the lake road. Whenever a car came, she stopped and pulled deeper into the trees. She wasn't smart enough to hide from him, making it was easy to follow her trail.

When she approached the turn-off, he had to bite his tongue to stop from swearing out loud. Of course she would hide at the lake house, to keep away from her lawful husband. He should have figured out where she would run. He would have, given time.

He trailed behind, sticking to the tree line and dirt shoulder of the road. She didn't turn unless a car approached, and he ducked deeper in to the trees whenever headlights approached. She was too stupid to realize the moon was lighting her path all the way to the front door.

Once she started moving around inside the house, turning on lights and such, he skulked up to the kitchen window, hoping to overhear her conversation with the batty old aunt. He made himself as comfortable as possible and settled in for the duration. There was no talking in the house. Maybe the aunt was already asleep.

By the time she finally spoke, it was clear she

was on the phone with someone. He moved in closer, careful not to miss a word.

****

"I think it went really well. He made some preliminary drawings for us, and it's clear he understands what we want. Whether or not he can do it, and keep it under budget, is another thing."

Kate stirred her cocoa, tested the temperature, and took a sip.

"What do you know about this guy" Jack asked. "Have you talked to other people he's worked for? Has he done anything like this before? If you want, I can check him out for you, talk to some people around town, and ask what they have to say about him."

She tried to keep the irritation out of her voice; sure he meant to be helpful.

"Ruby and I would never have wasted our time meeting with the guy if we hadn't checked him out ahead of time. She talked to several of his former customers who were very happy with his work. In fact, they all rave about him."

"Does he do a lot of commercial work?"

Kate hesitated, knowing he wouldn't like the answer.

"No. He usually does residential remodeling. But the people Ruby talked to couldn't say enough nice things about him. He only takes on one job at a time and works on it until it's finished."

Jack scoffed. "Yeah, but he probably overcharges you because he can't get the job finished."

Kate took a deep breath. She didn't know why

Jack's questions were making her anxious, but she didn't like it.

"If that were true, his customers wouldn't be satisfied, right?"

"Unless he only gave you the names of his family members to use as references."

She couldn't understand why he was being belligerent. "I don't think it's possible in this town. Ruby knows everyone in the county and she would know if he was trying to pull one over on us. I trust her judgment, Jack. I wish you would trust mine."

When he didn't immediately reply, Kate started to think she ticked him off. When he finally spoke, it was in a much softer tone of voice.

"I'm sorry, Kate. You're right. You are an intelligent, capable, grown woman. I didn't mean to make it sound like I don't trust your judgment. I do. I want to protect you, however I can. If it came across as insulting, I'm sorry."

She was conflicted by his words. "I'm glad you think I'm intelligent and capable, but I don't want you to give up protecting me entirely, okay? Sometimes, I'm going to need a shoulder to lean on and I was hoping it could be yours."

Silence again. Had she gone too far?

"I'd like that. But I don't want to disappoint you."

"You won't."

"Uh, Kate, I'm not sure where this is going, or if I'm reading some signals wrong, but I know you're vulnerable right now and I don't want to take advantage of you."

Kate smiled. At least he said vulnerable, not

pitiful.

"And I appreciate your honesty. I have a long way to go to getting back on my feet again. But just because I am finally standing up for myself doesn't mean I want to be alone."

"Yeah, but your marriage to Tony, and, well, the way he's treated you; it has to leave you a little hesitant to ever trust a man again, right?"

Kate took a sip of the cocoa, trying to find the words to answer a question she had been asking herself for days.

"I don't think it has. I mean, yeah, I would never go near a man I thought was abusive. I know now what kinds of signs to look for and I'm learning how to stand up for myself. But I also know not all men are like Tony, and I still want the same things I've always wanted: marriage and a family, even if it means adopting."

He paused a moment. "Have you considered taking a self-defense class?"

Her jolt made her spill her cocoa. "What? Where did such an idea come from?"

"I think it would be a good idea for you, to make you feel more secure and stronger. You know, to give you more self-confidence in knowing how to protect yourself. I think it would be good for you."

She licked the cocoa from her thumb, sucking gently on the nail. "I don't know. It never occurred to me. Do you really think it's a good idea?"

"Yeah, I do. There's got to be a class in town or at least in Elmira or Ithaca you can take. I can check into it, if you want me to."

She smiled, the mental picture of him finding a

class for her, or even thinking of it in the first place, making her warm inside.

"Thanks, Jack. I really appreciate you thinking of it, thinking of me."

His chuckle was low and deep in his throat. "I've been thinking about you a lot." He hesitated before clearing his throat. "More than I should, considering Deke is in a coma and there's a murder investigation going on. Never mind the fact you're my brother's wife. I can't seem to get you off my mind."

A tingle of current shot from her head and down her spine, to a part of her she had shut down long ago.

"I'm glad. I've been having the same problem and I wouldn't want to be alone in this." She sighed. "Seriously, I know I am in no position right now to be thinking of anyone but myself and my own survival. I have to get free of Tony and start a new life without him. But I'd be lying if I said I haven't thought of you and anticipated talking to you or seeing you every day."

"What do we do about it?"

She closed her eyes and shook her head. "I don't know. Nothing right now, I guess. I'm not sure I'm ready for more than what we have. Although I want to be."

Before he could speak, she continued, "I am attracted to you. I didn't think I would be, but the fact is I am. I'm not ready to do anything about it right now. I hope you can understand and I hope you're still here and still interested enough to talk about it, later on, after I find out who I am."

"Take your time. I'll be here."

Kate released a breath she didn't know she was holding and smiled into the phone. "Thanks, Jack."

"My pleasure, Kate. Although I would be happier knowing where you are, while I wait."

"I don't want Tony to pressure you to find out where I am."

"He's not going to find out from me." His voice had a bit of an edge to it. She knew she'd offended him.

"I'm not implying you'd let it slip or anything."

"Then why won't you tell me? I wouldn't come there if you don't want me to, but I'd feel a lot better knowing where you are."

She set down her mug. "I know, and I'm sorry. I was sure the key to keeping myself safe was to stay hidden. But I'm not sure anymore. I don't think it's going to make much difference to Tony when he finds out where I am. He's going to be mad no matter what. Maybe I'm isolating myself for no reason."

"How did Ruby pick you up to meet with the contractor if you haven't told her where you are?" His voice sounded defensive again.

"I met her at the end of the lake. I waited in the park and she picked me up then dropped me back off there. She doesn't know where I am, either."

Jack sighed.

"I don't know if isolation is the answer. Maybe you should call the shelter and talk to Mary Anne or your lawyer or someone and ask for advice. I know they have the expertise to help keep you safe, which is the most important thing, no matter where you are."

"Please know it's not that I don't trust you, Jack. I know you could find me by tracing my cell phone, or even without it, if you tried. And I appreciate the fact you haven't done it."

After a moment, Jack spoke. "Listen, I'm going to let you get some sleep. Call me if you want to talk or anything. And call Mary Anne, talk to her about your concerns. She'll be able to guide you. In the meantime, I'll research a good self-defense class for you. I could even go with you if you want."

Kate yawned. "I think I will go to bed and pop my latest book in the CD player, so I can relax. I feel like I've been hit by a bus."

"It's the stress, Kate. Sleep it off and you'll be chipper again tomorrow."

She smiled. "Thanks, Jack. For everything. I'll be up for a while. You can call me back if you want. I'm not going anywhere, and I'm always glad to hear a friendly voice."

"Okay, goodnight."

"Goodnight."

She walked to the sink and rinsed out her mug. After washing off the kitchen table and turning off the light, she went into the living room to check the locks and turn out the lights.

She never made it that far.

"You two-timing bitch." She registered Tony's voice, coming from her living room at the same time as his slap came in contact with her face.

She recoiled, but he stepped in close again, grabbing her arms and shaking her.

"You are my wife, but here you are flirting and teasing with my own brother on the phone. You've probably been sleeping with him too, haven't you?"

The same old fear raced up her spine, wiping out the strength and peace that were building there.

"No Tony, no. I haven't been with anyone but you. Ever."

He glowered at her. "I don't believe you, you lying slut. You ran out of our house and betrayed me in front of the whole town. You've probably been screwing every guy in Harper's Glen behind my back for years."

"That's not true. I have never been unfaithful to you."

Another slap. Why did she think she could argue with him now?

"You were unfaithful to me the first time you talked to someone else about what goes on in our marriage. It's sacred and nobody's business but ours. You had to come crying to your old, pitiful aunt. Did she convince you to run to Jack?"

He pulled Kate along the hallway, back to the bedrooms. "Where's she hiding?" He started kicking the doors open and slammed Kate into the wall while he searched the closet.

When he grabbed her arms again and started to pull her up the stairs, Kate gave in. "Aunt Linda's not here. She died. I haven't talked to her in years."

This made him stop. He didn't release the pressure on her arms, but he seemed to size up the room.

"The old broad is dead?"

"Yes. She died a few weeks ago."

"Then whose house is this now?"

Kate tried to avoid meeting his eyes, but he

wrenched her chin back up until their gazes met.

"She left you this house, didn't she?"

"Yes."

A strange light shown in his eyes. Kate could almost see the wheels turning inside.

"What else did she leave you?"

Kate shrugged, staring back at the floor. "Not much. Her furniture and stuff."

He gripped a little harder. "And money?"

Kate winced at the pain. "Ah, a little money. I'm not really sure how much."

He was silent for a minute and Kate started to sweat. When he dragged her toward the door Kate went limp, hoping the dead weight of her body would make it impossible for him to pull her. He turned back, pure evil glowing in his eyes, and lifted her off the floor.

After he tossed her over his shoulder, he grabbed her keys off the hook on the wall and carried her outside, plopping her in front of the garage.

"You shouldn't have done it, Kathy. You shouldn't have embarrassed me the way you did." His voice was calmer, but higher than usual. The menace in his tone sent chills through her.

"But, Tony—"

"Shut up! You have to pay for your sins and now I know the best way to deal with you. I'll be a poor, grieving widower and a richer man, and you'll have eternity to contemplate your deeds."

"No, please Tony, no!"

## Chapter Twelve

"It's really quite perfect, you know." He turned briefly to her and the crazy was obvious in his eyes. "By the time they find your body, there will be no way to tie it to me."

Tony pulled Aunt Linda's car to the edge of Rock Cabin Road. The narrow, twisted pathway ran along the base of the cliff at the edge of Black Water Swamp. Little used in the best weather, the road became practically deserted as winter approached.

Their headlights reflected in the runoff from fields at the top of the cliff. Streams of water wound their way down the cracks and crevices of the bank and formed small ponds of mud in the huge potholes that riddled the old dirt road. In another month or two, everything would be frozen. For now, it was dark, dank, and cold. The cold seeped all the way to her bones.

"It's too late in the year for any more canoe tours of the swamp. No one should be nosing around here until spring." He shut off the car and headlights.

Tony's voice was calm, an eerie calm. Kate knew he was at his most dangerous when the yelling stopped and the calm set in. But even she'd never experienced such a chilling edge to his voice.

Kate tried desperately to find any lights or other signs of life outside of the car, but the dark was complete and consuming. She tried to swallow the panic lodged in her throat, but couldn't shake the knowledge she was about to die.

They sat in the quiet darkness of the car for several minutes. The waiting was wrenching and Kate nearly begged him to get on with it. But ten years of survival training kicked in and she wisely kept her mouth shut.

"Okay. I think it's safe to say we haven't been followed." Tony opened his car door, and in the quick flash of light, glared at Kate before climbing out and shutting the door.

She struggled to swallow the cry springing from her lips. She had seen Tony angry, furious, menacing, and mean. She never understood his anger, but knew it was real. This was different.

His face didn't show the quick tempered, calculating anger she was used to. In its place, was something more.

Something beyond anger and more unstable.

Something bordering on the insane.

He wrenched open the door on her side and reached in to yank her out onto the road. Her arms were again caught in his crushing grip as he pulled her down the bank.

"You should have known better, Kathy."

He stood farther down the bank, his face mere inches from hers. His stale, hot breath stung her eyes.

"After all the years I've spent trying to teach you how to be a wife, how to take care of me and my home, for you to go and make our marriage a joke in front of the whole town proves to me how stupid you really are. I thought it was getting through, but you're as dumb as a post. Next time, I'm going to pick a wife who's pretty *and* smart."

Next time? Kate began to shake and tried desperately to calm her frenzied muscles. Tony began to laugh.

"Just figured it out, huh? I guess I should have been clearer in my meaning so you could understand. I wouldn't want you to go blindly into the swamp, too stupid to know you're about to die." He pulled her to a stop at the edge of the water.

She stood still, numb from the panic clenching her muscles and chattering her teeth. In many scenes of her memory, over all the years of their marriage, she often feared for her life, but she never expected the end to come like this. She knew Tony might end up killing her with his fists, but she never thought he'd plan her death.

"Don't you have anything to say for yourself? Don't you want to beg me to spare your useless life? Or are you too stupid to even spit the words out?"

As Tony shook her, her head fell forward and crashed into his. He swore, she gasped, but he didn't loosen his grip.

"You bitch. You did that on purpose."

His right hand released her left arm and came crashing into Kate's jaw. The impact snapped her head back and wrenched her neck. The sudden explosion of pain brought tears to her eyes and a throbbing in her head, but still she said nothing.

If she could do nothing to control Tony or to save her own life, she could at least withhold any pleasure he got from her pleading and whimpering. It wasn't much of a consolation, but at least she'd die with more dignity than she'd lived the past ten years.

****

"What are you doing here this late, Jack?"

Jack stopped, the phone in his hand. Scott leaned against his door frame with a can of cola in his hand.

"Working late. What's your excuse?"

"The same, of course." Scott walked in and sat in one of the side chairs. "Who are you trying to call at this time of night?"

Jack still held the phone. "Kate, but she isn't answering. I'm starting to get worried."

"Any reason to think she's not fast asleep?" Scott placed the can on Jack's desk.

"She told me she wasn't going anywhere and she'd be awake listening to a book. That wasn't too long ago, but now she's not answering."

Scott leaned forward, resting his forearms on his thighs. "Maybe she decided to take a bath or something. Give her a few minutes and try again."

Jack nodded and hung up the phone. Scott was probably right, although Jack still couldn't shake the sense of shivers down his spine when Kate's phone went unanswered.

"Anything new on the Standish case?"

Scott described the latest efforts being made to track Ed Michaels and the reports filed by the coroner's office and the forensic specialists. They had received many tips about Ed Michaels from the public after opening a hotline. It was taking the investigators days to track down all of the leads, but none had panned out as of yet.

Jack and Scott discussed the increased security measures being taken in the sheriff's office, at the command center, and throughout the county offices. Although not everything was in place yet, Jack was confident the county employees were better protected than before.

"Why don't you call it a night?" Scott stood and headed for the door, pitching his can into the recycling bin next to Jack's desk.

What was the sense, when he wasn't going to get any sleep? "Is that what you're going to do?"

Scott laughed. "No. I'm going to head back downstairs and try to get a few more of the leads processed so the teams can follow up on them tomorrow."

"Well, I think I'll wait until I get a hold of Kate before I head home. You know, to make sure she's all right."

"Okay, then, I'll let you make your call. See you tomorrow."

As Jack reached for the phone, it rang.

"Hello, Jack Finelli here." After Jack heard the report, he slammed down the phone and ran to the hallway door.

"Scott, you still there?"

Scott's muffled answer came from down the hall. Jack ran back into his office and started the dialing the phone while waiting for Scott to return.

Jack put the phone on speaker as Scott entered the room.

"What's up?" Scott walked into the office and stood by the desk.

"I got a call in from one of the patrols. Tony's car is parked down at Lakeside Park. They said it's been there long enough they got curious. They stopped to check it out, but he's nowhere to be seen."

"Do you think something's wrong?" Scott looked on in concern.

"I know something is." He clicked off the phone in disgust. "I tried Kate again, and she's not there."

"What does Kate not answering her phone have to do with Tony's car being at the park?"

Jack checked his weapon and cell phone, grabbed his jacket, and motioned Scott toward the door. "Ruby dropped Kate off at the park a few hours ago. She walked home from there."

Scott nodded and followed Jack out the door.

"Do you know where Kate is staying?"

They both climbed in Jack's car, he started the engine and tossed his cell phone to Scott.

"No. But now I have reason to check. Call in and check if you can get a ping from her cell phone. The number is on my phone." He started driving toward the end of the lake.

Scott clicked off his phone. "Kate's phone is pinging on the southeast side of the lake. Any ideas where she might be?"

Jack nodded. "Her aunt lives along the east shore, not too far from town. Call 911 to get the address."

In a few more minutes, Scott held his hand over the phone. "It's 4249 Route 53. Do you know where that is?"

"Yeah. Tell them we may need backup if we find anything."

Jack gripped the steering wheel tightly as they flew past the end of the lake. Tony's car sat off in the far corner of the lot, the sheriff's patrol car still parked beside it.

"I told the guys on patrol to do a check of the area while we go to Kate's house. I have a bad feeling about this."

Jack spun into the windy dirt road, his ears ringing with the pounding of his heartbeat. There was no telling what Tony might do if he got his hands on Kate now. He tried to focus on the road, tried to erase the image of Kate's face, bleeding and bruised, that came to mind.

It was all Jack could do not to drive the car right up the front steps in his rush to get inside. He pulled to a stop and jumped from the car. He motioned to Scott to circle around to the back of the house. Jack stood at the door, listening, and tried the knob.

When the door slid open easily, a violent chill raced up Jack's spine. He knew Kate well enough to know she wouldn't leave her doors unlocked, even if she thought no one could find her. She promised him every night to double check her locks before going to sleep.

She wasn't there.

Where was she?

Jack ran through the house, pausing outside each doorway to listen for voices, but found none. When he made it back to the kitchen, Scott was coming in the back door.

"I checked the porch, the dock, and the shoreline; no signs of Kate."

"She's not in here either."

Jack turned back toward the living room and stopped in the doorway. He spotted a cup of cocoa sitting on the edge of the piano and stuck his finger in it.

"It's still warm."

"Look at this." Scott crouched down, examining a spill on the floor near the piano. "The hot chocolate spilled."

Jack examined the furniture in the living room, walking from the piano to the door. The rug at the base of the stairs was bunched up and there was a dirty hand print on the wall by the door. Even more telling was a splash of blood on the doorknob.

"He's got her. He grabbed her here." Jack raced back outside, scouring the doorway and yard. "Footprints leading to the garage."

He pulled open the garage door and his stomach dropped. Empty.

"Any idea if her aunt had a car?" Scott walked the edges of the garage while Jack crouched down over the oil stain on the floor.

"This oil is fresh. And I can smell the exhaust in there. They haven't been gone long."

They raced back to Jack's car and jumped in. As Jack whipped the car around and started back down the drive, Scott pulled out his own cell phone and called into dispatch for more back up.

They got to the end of the road and stopped. Jack leaned his head back and squeezed his eyes shut. If he didn't stop and think, he wouldn't be any help to Kate.

****

"Where the hell would he take her?" His voice was the roar of a wounded animal.

The possibilities raced through Jack's mind. Where to start? How could they find them in time?

What was Kate going through right now?

Scott looked at him. "Is there any place you can think of, where Tony might think it's remote or private or special?"

"How should I know?" He took a breath before continuing. "Sorry. It's not your fault. I don't know much about Tony anymore, if I ever did."

"Who does?"

Jack turned to Scott. "What?"

"Who knows Tony? Who might know where he'd take Kate?"

Jack grabbed the cell phone and punched in Tom's number. He held his breath until his brother picked up.

"Jack?"

"Tom, listen. This is serious. Kate's missing and I have reason to believe Tony might have her."

"Oh God. What can I do?"

Jack took another deep breath. "I need to know where he might take her. We can't search the whole damn county fast enough. I need somewhere to start. Can you think of a place Tony might think was remote enough no one would find him?"

"Geez, Jack. We've been hunting all over the county. I can think of lots of places. Can you narrow it down at all?"

The panic rose in Tom's voice. Jack tried to keep his own wits about him.

"He grabbed her at her aunt's house, down at the end of the lake, on the east side. Remember where she lived?"

Tom didn't answer immediately and Jack clenched his fist. He imagined himself reaching through the airwaves to choke some kind of response from his brother. "Tom, I need something fast, man."

"Jack, I can think of a lot of places. Can you give me something more to go on?"

Jack squeezed his eyes shut, reaching for more ideas. "It looks like he took her in the aunt's car. If she's fighting him, like I hope she is, he's going to have to go somewhere accessible by car. He can't carry her too far into the woods."

"Try Skyline Drive or Rock Cabin Road. Somewhere down by the swamp. We have been turkey hunting down there. It's one of our favorite spots because it's like we're the only ones left on the planet. It's pretty remote, but easy to drive to."

Jack turned the car and headed back toward the swamp.

"Okay. We'll start down there. You keep thinking and call me back with anything else you come up with. Maybe you can ask Mom and Dad. They don't have to believe he'd hurt her to know where he'd go if he had something to hide."

"Okay Jack. I'll talk to them and Brenda and I will think of some other places, too. I'll call in whatever we come up with. But shouldn't I search for them, too? I mean, if you're looking down by the swamp, maybe I can head up the hill."

"I'll call you if we don't find them. For now, just come up with some more spots he might go. Bye."

Jack snapped the phone shut and shoved it back in his belt clip. He made a left turn and drove over a rickety old bridge onto a dirt road that went back to the edge of the cliff.

Skyline Drive went up, Rock Cabin road went

down. Which one should he take?

"Why don't you hop out and walk up Skyline a ways. I'll follow this one along the bank. Call or text me if you see anything and I'll do the same."

Scott grabbed a flashlight and jumped out. Jack eased down the twisting dirt road, searching for signs of life. Praying Kate was still alive.

After about three minutes, he found a tire track in the deep, muddy runoff along the edge of the road. He stopped and jumped out.

It was wet and new.

Jack stopped and listened, straining to pick up Kate's voice somewhere over the sound of blood racing through his brain. Nothing.

He got back in the car and edged forward, squinting into the darkness of the swamp. He unrolled the windows, trying to quiet his own breathing, but there wasn't a sound.

Suddenly, his headlights picked up the license plate on a car in front of him. He immediately shut off his own headlights and turned off the car. He grabbed another flashlight and slid out the door, running low up to the rear bumper of the car.

Amazing. Kate's aunt had been driving this car when he and Kate were in high school. He hunched down behind the car, flipped open his cell phone, and punched in Scott's number.

"Get down here now and let the back-up know where we are."

He shut the phone and inched his way along the back of the car. He paused at the corner, scanning the road in front of the car. Nothing. Suddenly, a rustling started in the bushes along the edge of the road about twenty-five feet ahead.

Staying close to the side of the car and then the wall of the cliff, Jack edged his way toward the sound. With the help of the crescent moon up above, two black forms were visible in the bushes.

"...think they have a right to interfere with a man's marriage, break up his home. They're a bunch of stupid cows anyway. The only reason they work at that damn shelter is because they don't have a life of their own."

The dangerous tone of Tony's voice, both calm and crazy, sent shivers down Jack's spine. His brother had lost it. Jack crouched down and began edging toward the bank.

"I can't believe you were stupid enough to fall for their line of crap. You should never have told them what goes on between you and me. It's private. No one else has a right to know anything about our marriage. You should never have told people those bad things about me, Kathy."

Jack stopped and listened carefully, praying she would say something, anything, to let him know he wasn't too late.

"Why did you do that? Why did you leave me? You're my wife. You promised to love me forever. How could you break your promise?"

An edge of desperation started to creep into Tony's voice. Jack wasn't certain, but thought Tony was crying as well.

"Answer me, bitch!"

The sound of skin on skin contact meant Kate was taking a beating, but at least she moaned. She was still alive!

When he got to the edge of the bank, he held as still as possible while he judged the distance to Kate huddled on the edge of the swamp. Tony stood over her, shaking her. When she didn't answer him, he began ranting and raving like a madman.

Tony raised his arm, poised to take another swing at her, as Jack jumped over the bank and switched on the flashlight.

"It's over, Tony. Let her go."

Jack stood with the flashlight in his left hand and his service revolver in his right. Tony stared at him, uncomprehending, like a deer caught in the headlights.

Jack took a step toward Kate, swiveling the beam of light to her huddled form on the ground. She turned to him with her blackened eyes, relief and trust shining through, despite her bloodied face. He took another step in her direction.

Tony grabbed her around the throat and hauled her up in front of him, like a shield. "Get back. It's not over 'til I say it's over. This is *my* wife and you have no business calling her, panting after her, keeping her from me. It's time you stopped interfering with our marriage."

Jack stood still, not moving any closer but not backing up either. He tried to keep his voice firm but calm. "Let her go, Tony."

Tony's face was a mask of menace and misery. "No. She's mine and you can't have her."

A wave of memory rushed through Jack. Tony, always bigger and meaner, even as kid, holding a favored toy high above Jack's head, taunting and teasing him.

"I want to help her, Tony. She's hurt. She needs a doctor. Let her go and I'll drive her to the hospital."

He pulled his right hand a hair closer to the flashlight, making sure his brother could see the gun in the beam of light, and took a step toward them.

"Let her go. Now. You know the judge ordered you to stay away from her. Don't get yourself in even deeper, Tony. Let her go and it'll go easier on you."

Tony laughed, the deranged cackling sound chilling the night air.

"I don't think so, little brother."

Jack sighed, reaching deep inside to maintain his calm.

"You're under arrest, Tony." Jack recited the Miranda warning to his brother, something he'd never imagined possible. "Now, if you let Kate go and come along peacefully, I won't have to charge you with resisting arrest."

Tony took a step backward, swinging Kate into the reeds at the murky edge of the swamp. She gasped, but said nothing.

"I'm not going anywhere with you, Jack. Leave us the hell alone. Go back to your little sheriff car and get out of here. Go bother somebody else."

Jack edged closer. "Don't you get it, Tony? You are breaking the law. I have to bring you in. If you don't cooperate, I'll have to use this." He motioned with the gun.

"Don't make me laugh." Tony cackled. "Remember, I've been hunting with you. You could never hit the side of a barn."

"That was a long time ago. Don't make me prove you wrong."

Tony pulled a gun from the pocket of his jacket. "You can't wave a gun in my face and not expect me to protect what's mine." He shoved the gun into Kate's neck and laughed at her smothered scream.

"What are you doing? You were required to turn in all your guns after the protective order was issued. Your gun permits have all been revoked. You just bought yourself more trouble."

"You don't scare me."

Jack swung his foot out, connecting with Tony's hand and knocking the gun away from Kate. Tony didn't drop the gun, but Kate was able to escape Tony's grip by sinking down into the water.

Tony turned, as if going after Kate. Jack dropped the flashlight and swung at Tony with his left fist. The shock through his knuckles upon contact with Tony's jaw was enough to send shivers of pain up Jack's arm. The contact only seemed to make Tony stronger.

Tony swiveled back, pointing the gun at Jack's head.

"Don't you get it, Jack? She's mine and no one else will ever have her. Especially you."

Jack looked down the barrel, into his brother's eyes. Whatever resided inside Tony was foreign to Jack. He leveled his own gun at Tony, praying to God he wouldn't have to pull the trigger.

"Tony, don't…" Kate broke her silence.

Tony turned slightly to Kate behind him on the ground. "Shut up, you stupid bitch. You wouldn't beg for your own life, you aren't gonna' beg for his, either."

Tony shot his foot out, kicking Kate in the head as she sat on the ground. Jack flew, lunging toward Tony with no concern for the gun in his brother's hand. As Tony turned back to pull the trigger, a gunshot exploded.

Jack watched in slow motion as the bullet his brother intended for him went high and zipped off into the bushes illuminated by the eerie glow of Jack's dropped flashlight.

Tony gasped, grabbing at his side, stunned by the red blood stain spreading across his chest. His gun slipped from his fingers and he sank onto the muddy water's edge.

Scott Randall stood on the top of the bank, shining his flashlight on Tony as he fell.

Jack grabbed Tony's gun and tossed it to Scott. Then he rushed to Kate, pulling her from the frigid water and carefully wrapping his coat and his arms around her.

He began rocking her, unable to stop the tremors in his arms or the clenching of his gut. He'd come too close to losing her. And if Scott hadn't made it in time, they could both be dead.

Scott pulled Tony from the water and dragged him up the bank. He worked over Tony's inert body while Jack tried to soothe Kate.

Within moments, the headlights of another cruiser shone over the scene. The lights and sirens of the ambulance pulled Jack from his trance.

"Come on, Kate. We need to get you some help." He lifted Kate off the ground as gently as he could but winced when she moaned anyway.

After carrying her to the ambulance, he gave the EMTs as much information as he could. They wrapped Kate in blankets and began taking her vitals while loading her into the ambulance. Jack didn't think she was conscious, although she was crying softly.

Before climbing into the ambulance with Kate, he looked back over his shoulder at Scott, still hovering over Tony. It struck Jack as somewhat surreal that he didn't even know if his brother was alive or dead. And at the moment, he wasn't even sure what answer he was hoping for.

## Chapter Thirteen

"Kate? Wake up."

The soft words emerged through a haze of pain and weightlessness. She was floating up over the bed, but for some reason everything hurt. Waking up was too much work, so she drifted off again.

"Kate, it's time to wake up. Open your eyes and let us know how you're feeling."

She didn't want to wake up. It would only make her hurt more. Whatever had happened to her was fuzzy, but Kate could remember something dark and frightening. Shaking her head caused a stabbing pain to radiate downward from her neck.

"That's a girl. Come on, Kate. Come back to me. I need you to open your eyes. Let me see your beautiful eyes."

She tried, she really did. Her eyes did not want to open, that's all there was to it. Kate pulled with all her strength, the pain almost overwhelming. When the smallest sliver of light started to edge through, a shadow appeared above her. She blinked a few times, the tightness bringing tears to her eyes. Her eyes wouldn't open any farther, but at least she could see.

Slowly Jack's face came into focus. He leaned over her, his smile hopeful and worried and exhausted all at once. He was dirty, covered with scratches and blood, and he smelled.

How had she ended up in a hospital? She tried to sit up, but couldn't find the strength to move.

"What..." Her throat was so dry she nearly croaked. Jack grabbed a cup of water from the bedside table and eased a straw between her swollen lips. Kate took a small sip and tried to swallow, but it was like jagged glass in her throat.

"What...happened?"

Jack's eyes filled with concern. He looked suddenly so sad. Kate tried to take his hand in hers, but her arm was too heavy to move. Must be all those tubes and monitors attached to her.

As if he sensed what she was trying to do, Jack reached down and gathered her hand in his.

"Don't worry about it right now. You need to conserve your energy for getting better. Just sleep, rest, and know I'll be right here. You're okay, now. Everything's okay."

If everything was okay, why did Jack look like he'd lost his best friend? And why did she hurt everywhere?

"Why..." She swallowed and tried again. "What am I doing here?"

Jack brushed his hand across her forehead, the depth of pain in his gaze enough to bring tears to Kate's own eyes. "You're okay now, but you've been hurt."

"How?" Something was niggling at the back of her brain, her poor tired brain. Something dark and evil, sending chills down her spine. "How did I get hurt?"

Jack eased himself onto the edge of her hospital

bed. He cradled her right hand in both of his and cleared his throat. When he looked her in the eye, she knew something was terribly wrong.

"Tony," was all he said.

She gasped, a new pain searing to her heart.

*Oh God. Tony.*

She remembered it all. The dark swamp, the brutal fists, the stark terror. She closed her eyes against the images, but it didn't wipe them out.

"It's okay, Kate." Jack caressed her shoulder, neck, and cheek. She opened her eyes. Jack was no longer able to hold back his tears.

But Jack came, he found her, he rescued her. She was alive and so was he. And Tony...the gun...

"Oh my God...is Tony dead?"

Jack shook his head. "No, he's alive. He just got out of surgery, and he's going to recover. Don't worry, though. I have two guards on him, even though he's still unconscious. He can't come anywhere near you. As soon as he's able, he'll be in jail."

Tony had tried to kill her. Jack fought Tony. He was shot...but— "Who shot him?"

"Scott Randall. He's the state police investigator I'm working with on the Standish murder. Remember, you talked to him about your bank accounts?"

"Thank him..."

Jack bowed his head and sighed. "I'll bring him in as soon as you're up to it. We can both thank him. He saved my life, too."

Kate was fading fast. That had to be why she was confused. She was alive, Jack was alive, and

Tony was going to be arrested. These were all good things. Why was Jack sad?

She'd have to think about it later. Now she needed sleep.

****

The young nurse working with Kate convinced Jack she'd be sleeping for a while after receiving a sedative, but also promised to call him if anything changed. He took the opportunity to shower and change, hoping to rid himself of the odor of the swamp.

When he walked back into the hospital, he stopped at the nurse's station outside Kate's door. "Has anything changed?"

The nurse looked up. "She's still sleeping, Jack. But the nurse up on ICU was asking for you."

Jack's pulse raced. "Why? Did something happen to my brother?"

"No, she said the Sheriff was waking up. Maybe you should go visit him and I'll call you if anything changes down here."

Jack raced up to Deke's room and entered as the nurse was leaving.

"He's been asking for you."

Jack pulled up a chair and laid his hand on Deke's arm. The old man's eyes slid open and he smiled. His skin was still a pasty gray and his breathing was harsh and raspy. But he was awake.

"Jack…"

Jack swallowed the lump in his throat. "'Bout time you woke up."

Deke chuckled, setting off a series of coughs. "I'm so tired."

"Rest, Deke. Everything's under control."

"The nurse…she said Tony was shot."

Jack needed to have a chat with the nurse. Deke didn't need to know all the details right now.

"Yeah, but he's going to be fine. Don't worry about it."

Deke looked up at him, reaching for Jack's hand. "What happened?"

Jack took a deep breath, trying to find the words to frame his failure without upsetting Deke more than necessary.

"Tony found where Kate was staying. He kidnapped her and was trying to kill her. Scott Randall shot him before he could. And before Tony could shoot me."

Deke was silent for a moment and Jack wondered if he was falling asleep.

"You're leaving out some parts of this story. Tell me the rest." Deke looked deep into his eyes.

Jack sighed. "Unfortunately, that's really about it. Tony would have killed Kate, and probably me as well, if Scott hadn't arrived when he did. The good news is Kate's safe, although she's been beaten up pretty badly. Tony will go straight from the hospital to jail."

"Are you okay?"

Jack wasn't sure if Deke was talking about his body or his mind. "I got dirty and banged up a little bit, but not hurt."

"What else?"

"What do you mean? Isn't that enough?"

Deke chuckled again, a low rattling sound deep in his chest. "I mean, you're being kinda' hard on yourself, aren't ya?"

Jack lowered his eyes and took a deep breath. He didn't want to think he'd failed Kate when she'd needed him most, but for all practical purposes, he did.

Deke tugged on Jack's hand until Jack looked back at him. "You found her, didn't you?"

"Tom told us where to go. I just happened to pick the low road where Tony took her."

"You're both alive, and Tony's alive but under arrest. Can't you be satisfied? Or is there something more?"

Jack jumped off the seat and stalked to the window. He took a few deep breaths and turned back to face Deke, leaning on the window ledge.

"The thing is… I'm falling in love with Kate."

Deke smiled. "That's a good thing, right?"

"No." He stood up and paced along the end of the bed. "I couldn't protect her any better than I did Melanie. If it had been up to me, she'd probably be dead."

"Come here." Deke pointed to the chair.

"Deke—" Jack turned.

"Come here." The voice was soft and frail, but the will was iron.

Jack sat, resting his elbows on his knees.

"You don't know what would have happened if Scott didn't show up. Thank God you didn't have to find out." Deke placed his hand on Jack's shoulder. "This wasn't a contest between you and another man. Who cares who saved her? She's alive. You both are. That's what matters."

"But Kate is fragile and frightened and needs to

be protected. How can I make her a promise when I keep letting people down? I have no right to even think of a romantic future with her if I can't keep her from harm."

"Rubbish."

Jack looked up at his friend's outburst. "What?"

"I said that's rubbish. She couldn't ask for a better man by her side, if you'd just get your head out of the past."

"The past? What are you talking about? This happened last night."

Deke got into a coughing fit. Jack helped him get a sip of water. When he calmed down, Jack stood to leave.

"You need to rest, Deke. I'll be back later."

"Sit down, boy. I'm not done with you yet."

Jack shook his head, but sat. He reached over to take his friend's bony old hand in his.

"You think because some crazy bastard killed your wife instead of you, you have to pay for it the rest of your life? If that's the case, what's the use of being the one who survived?"

"It's not about Melanie—"

Deke started coughing again and Jack stood, reaching for the call button. Deke put his hand on Jack's arm.

"Wait."

"This is too much for you. We can talk later."

Deke took another drink of water. "I may not be up to talking later. Let me say my peace."

Jack sank back into the chair.

"I know this isn't all about Melanie. You've had a whopping chip on your shoulder from the minute you walked back into this town. Your father did such a number on you that you started to believe some of the crap he used to tell you about how you could never measure up."

"Now, Deke…"

"Hush. Let me finish. Your father's an idiot. He looked at Tony and Tom and saw athletes, hunters, fishermen, and good old boys. Then he looked at you and couldn't see the things that made you worth ten of them. Because he didn't value your intelligence, your capacity for understanding, or your sense of right and wrong, you started to believe those things are worthless. All it means is he missed the boat where you're concerned."

Deke took a sip of water, holding his hand up, motioning Jack to wait.

"I would've been proud to call you my son, Jack. Most men would've. Toss whatever baggage you're still carrying with you about your father and your brothers. It's ancient history and has no bearing on the reality of the man you've become."

Deke took a shaky breath before continuing. "Concentrate on making the most of the rest of your life. I hope you'll stay in Harper's Glen, even after I'm gone. It'll be good for you and for the town. I hope you marry Kate and make a new life for both of you, a better life and a happy one."

Jack smiled. "She might not think it's such a good idea."

The wise old eyes winked at Jack. "Well, you'll never know if you don't try now, will ya'? I'm near the end, Jack."

"Don't say that, Deke." Jack squeezed Deke's

hand even tighter.

"No, it's true. I don't have the strength to go on much longer. Promise me you'll take care of Thelma. She's a good woman and a great secretary."

Jack blinked several times, trying to tame the tingle in his eyes. "Of course. Whatever you want."

"Promise me you'll give yourself a chance at happiness. Have a life beyond your work. Think of me and know you've always made me proud. And remember, you are much more than your father ever knew. Don't let the memories of his ignorance control you anymore."

Jack bowed his head, trying to shield his friend from his agony. Deke's voice was getting thinner and weaker. His hand was cold to the touch. His every breath was a struggle.

Deke was right. He couldn't last much longer. Jack didn't want to think of Harper's Glen without Deke. He didn't want to disappoint the old man, but he wasn't sure he could stay after Deke was gone.

"Promise me, Jack. Promise you'll make the most of your life. You have so much talent. Don't waste it." Deke tugged at Jack's hand.

Jack squeezed the old man's hand slightly and coughed to cover the catch in his voice. "I promise," he whispered.

"I love you, boy, as if you were my own."

Jack looked into Deke's eyes. "I love you, too, Deke. I always will."

Deke let out a slow, deep breath and fell silent.

Jack stood still a moment, watching his friend. He reached over the bed and pushed the call button. Just when he'd accepted Deke was gone, the old man's breathing started again, slow and shallow.

The nurse rushed into the room and checked Deke's pulse and the readings on all the machines. "He's fallen asleep."

Jack bowed his head in thanks.

The nurse pulled Jack to the doorway, nodding back toward Deke.

"He won't last much longer, but he isn't gone yet. Why don't you call anyone who should be called?"

Jack pulled out his cell phone to call Thelma. He walked into the hall, but stopped in the doorway to turnback.

If the choice had been up to him, the man lying on that bed would be his father. And even though he wasn't, the ache spreading across Jack's chest couldn't have been stronger.

****

Jack spent the day and following night alternating between Kate's room and Deke's. Deke was still holding on, but barely, and Kate was sleeping and gaining strength. Periodically he got updates on Tony's condition indicating his brother was stable and expected to make a full recovery. Jack was exhausted.

Early the next morning, Jack was dozing in the armchair beside Kate's bed when a shuffle at the door woke him. Scott Randall peeked his head around the door and motioned for Jack to join him in the hall. Kate was still sleeping as Jack slipped outside.

"How's she doing?" Scott asked.

Jack leaned against the wall outside Kate's door,

242

still trying to shake off the last licks of sleep. "Good, thanks to you. She was pretty badly beaten and covered with mud and muck from the swamp. But she had a peaceful night, and the fluids and antibiotics they've been pumping into her have already started to make a difference."

Scott smiled. "Good. I'm glad. I checked on Tony and they said he should be released in a few days. Do you want me to arrange for his transport to the jail?"

Jack shook his head. "No, that's my job. I can do it."

Scott looked at Jack with one eyebrow raised. "It may be your job, but he's also your brother. I'm here to help, if you need it."

"Thanks. I'm okay with this, really. It would be different if Kate hadn't made it through."

Scott nodded and then scanned up and down the hall. "How's Deke?"

Jack swallowed hard. "He's holding on, God only knows how, but it won't be long."

"I'm sorry, Jack. The timing of this really sucks."

"I don't think it would ever be easy, but thanks." Jack pushed off the wall and walked to the water fountain for a drink.

Scott followed him. "Why don't we go get some breakfast? I really need to talk to you about the Standish case."

"I don't want to go far."

Scott raised his right hand, palm out. "No problem. Let's go down to the cafeteria. I heard a sick rumor you actually like hospital food."

Jack laughed as the two men made their way down the hall. "You must not have eaten at the right hospitals, man. I'll show you the ropes."

When Jack had filled his tray with eggs, sausage, a bagel, juice, and hash browns, he carried it all to a table and joined Scott, who picked a bowl of cereal and a banana.

Jack pointed at Scott's tray. "No wonder you can't appreciate hospital food. You didn't even give them a chance."

Scott laughed. "You got that right. No one can mess up a box of cereal and a banana."

"Tell me what's new with the Standish case."

Scott set down his spoon and took a sip of coffee. "Someone called into the hotline claiming Ed Michaels was living in the woods out past the old salt plant. I sent two teams of investigators up there to check it out."

"Did they find anything?"

"They didn't find Michaels, but there was trash and other evidence someone has been staying out there. Could be Ed."

"Could be. Let's keep a watch around the clock and see if we can flush him out."

"Right." Scott brought Jack up to date on the increasing amount of evidence piling up against Ed Michaels.

"When we find the bastard, we can nail his hide to the wall." Jack cleaned his plate and sat back, cradling his coffee.

"I have a couple other things I wanted to go over with you." Scott pulled out his notebook.

"Shoot."

"Thelma said another threatening letter came in yesterday. Basically more of the same as last time; talking about the interfering police, the sanctity of marriage, and a husband's wrath."

Jack leaned back in his chair, rubbing his chin. "I started thinking these were connected with some child support proceeding or something, but I have to wonder if Tony was behind them."

Scott took a sip of coffee. "Possible, but I can't see what he'd gain by doing this."

"Nothing." Jack sighed. "But after listening to his ranting, I realized he's not right. Somehow he became so warped, he's really unstable now. It could've been him."

"I guess we'll see if the threats stop now he's in custody."

Scott cleared his throat and set his coffee cup down. "The other thing I wanted to discuss with you has to do with Tony. I have been doing some more research, like we discussed, into his financial dealings."

Jack leaned forward. "Did you find something?"

"I think he may be siphoning funds out of some of the accounts he manages at the bank."

"Embezzlement?"

Scott nodded. "It looks that way. I alerted the bank president and he initiated an internal audit. He's cooperating completely, but also keeping everything confidential until we come up with some answers."

Jack swore. "I can't believe he's that stupid. Or arrogant."

"I'll let you know what we find."

"Thanks. I appreciate your handling this for me."

He shook his head. "My parents will never believe this. They're upset already, I'm afraid this will be more than they can handle."

"Have you been up to visit them? I saw them in the waiting room upstairs, when I was looking for you."

Jack shook his head. "They don't want me there. I'm not only the sheriff now. I'm the enemy. I threaten to burst every illusion they've ever had of Tony, the favored son." Jack stood and walked to the door. "I'm not up for another scene right now. I'd rather stay away."

**\*\*\*\***

He slipped out the door, making sure no one was watching him too close. His pockets were weighed down by muffins, apples, and small cans of juice. Those dumb clucks in the cafeteria didn't even see him. He might as well be invisible.

This stash should hold him for a while, if he was careful. He had some time now, before he could get his hands on her. She was holed up in a room on the first floor. He didn't try to go in, but watched from the doorway. She was sleeping on her side, facing the window, with her blonde hair a tangled mess down her back.

Disgraceful.

She ought to know better than go out in public looking like that. What would people think?

And what was she doing lying around in the middle of the day anyway? She should be home, cleaning the house, cooking dinner, and making it ready for him to get home.

Probably that damned sheriff was keeping her

there, sticking his nose in where it doesn't belong. Trying to come between a man and his wife.

Once he had her home, and taught her a lesson about carrying on and embarrassing him, he might let her come back to town. Once she proved he could trust her some.

But he'd never let her near the sheriff again. In fact, he might have to make sure the sheriff wasn't around anymore; just to be sure she stayed on the straight and narrow. He knew how weak women could be. Better to get rid of the sheriff and not have to worry about it anymore.

Chapter Fourteen

"Are you sure you're up to this?" Ruby hovered around Kate as if she was a hummingbird looking for a spot to land.

"I'm okay, really. Jack said Deke is really fading fast. I want a chance to talk to him, before it's too late."

Kate was moving slowly, but with Ruby's help, made the trek from her room upstairs to visit Deke. Although most of her body, and especially her throat, was still sore and swollen, she's started eating regular food again and would be discharged within a day or two.

Ruby insisted on following her, desperate to help her or better yet, steer Kate back to bed.

"Don't wear yourself out. You need rest to regain your strength, especially if you won't come and stay with me."

Kate stopped and placed her right hand on Ruby's arm. "I told you, I appreciate the offer, more than you can know. But I really want to go back to my own house and take care of myself. With Tony in custody, I'm free to really start making a new life for myself and I don't want to wait a minute more than I have to."

Ruby smiled and hugged her gently. "I guess I can understand that. But I'll stop by every day to check on you, and don't you think I won't."

Kate laughed, walking the last few feet to Deke's doorway. "I'll look forward to it." She craned her neck around the curtain next to Deke's bed. He might have been asleep, but was alone.

"I'm going to go sit with him for a while, even if he doesn't wake up."

"I'll be in the waiting room by the elevator." Ruby smiled and pulled a dog-eared romance novel from her purse.

Kate walked to Deke's bed and stood by the side for a moment before pulling a chair over. After she lowered herself into the chair, she found herself locked in Deke's sympathetic gaze.

"He really did a number on you, didn't he? But you're still here, and he's going to be in jail a long time. Looks to me like you're the victor." Deke reached a hand toward Kate and she took it.

Kate smiled, glad to find someone else who saw it her way. "I agree. He can't hurt me anymore; all the rest is gravy."

Deke smiled and closed his eyes. Kate wondered if talking was too much effort for him now.

After a few moments, he squeezed her hand and opened his eyes again. "What are you going to do about our man Jack?"

She shook her head. "What exactly do you have in mind, Deke?"

"I'd really like you to give Jack a try...for you and Jack to give yourselves a chance together."

She laughed. "You're not mincing any words, are you?"

His tired old eyes glistened with moisture. "I

don't have that luxury anymore. I want Jack to have the life he deserves, with a woman who deserves him, and I think that's you."

Kate tried to swallow the lump in her throat. "Why me?"

He started coughing, a frail, thin rattle. She helped him take a sip of water. "You and Jack were good friends once. I always thought it could've been more."

"That was a long time ago, Deke. We've both changed since then, especially me."

"You always had a light in your eyes back then. I think the sparkle you used to wear like skin is still there, even though Tony tried to beat it outta' you. With Jack, I think you'll be able to be yourself again. And he deserves someone who is sweet, smart, and determined enough to help him shed the ghosts of his past. You could help him be the man, the husband, and the sheriff I know he can be."

Kate leaned forward. "Do you think he could be happy living in Harper's Glen?"

"I know he could. He convinced himself he couldn't live in his brothers' shadows or ever satisfy his father, so he left. But the people in this town are smarter than he ever gave 'em credit for. We may not have realized what a monster Tony was to you, but I don't think many people have been fooled by his great-guy routine. At least, not in a long, long time."

"But after living in Washington, working for the FBI, won't life in such a small town be too dull for Jack?"

Deke smiled. "Jack wasn't happy in DC. And even though he did good work for the Bureau, he'll be an even better sheriff. He's smart and fair and he cares about and understands people."

Kate stood gingerly and walked around the bed, stopping to smell the bouquet of flowers on the window sill. "I know he'd be a great sheriff. But what makes you think he'd want me, even if he does stay?"

She turned back to face Deke when he chuckled. "Why wouldn't he?"

She looked down at her hands on the bed rail, unable to meet his gaze. "How can he respect me after the way I've let Tony treat me all these years? How can anyone look at me and see something other than an object of pity or curiosity?"

Deke reached out his hand and Kate walked back to the chair, taking his hand in hers as she sat. He squeezed until she raised her eyes to meet his gaze.

"Don't you dare say those things about yourself. Tony's actions, Tony's crimes, are not yours. You're the victim, but you're also the survivor. I know you're going to be fine because you're a smart girl with a good heart."

Kate couldn't stop the tears spilling from her eyes.

"Let me tell you something else. Jack doesn't think he's worthy of you right now, because he wasn't the one who pulled the trigger and put Tony in the hospital. He can't get past his guilt over Melanie, especially now he thinks he failed you, too."

"He didn't fail me, he saved me." Kate wiped her eyes on a tissue she pulled from the pocket of her jacket.

"You and I know that." Deke's voice was fading. "But you've got to convince Jack. The minute he stepped back into this town, those internal tapes of his father's rants and ravings started playing in his head again. He says he's not good enough for you because of Melanie or because of Tony, but it's really all of Dom's put downs standing in his way. You need to show him he's the kind of man you want and need. If you can do that, he'll be the best husband any woman ever had."

"I don't know if I can."

Deke tugged at her hand. "Do you want to? Do you love him?"

Kate closed her eyes and let her head fall forward. Did she even know what she wanted?

She thought back to the warmth and contentment of his nightly phone calls. She loved sharing the events of the day with Jack and talking about plans for her spa. Her cheeks grew warmer as she remembered with longing his safe, but exciting, embrace. She shivered at the thought of his fierce determination and unwavering strength in facing down Tony at the swamp.

Regardless of who pulled the trigger, Jack was the one who saved her. If she hadn't seen his face or heard his voice, she would've surrendered to the peace and serenity of unconsciousness. She never would've fought her way back to the living.

"Yes, I love him. I guess a part me always did. He was my first and best friend in this town.

When Deke spoke, his voice was quiet and hoarse. "Tell him, convince him of your love, and he'll love you forever."

Kate watched Deke drift off to sleep, awed by the old man's love for someone else's son. If only Dominick Finelli could've appreciated Jack's strengths and skills the way Deke always had. Thank God Jack had always Deke in his corner.

Well, it'd be Dom's loss now. He'd pushed Jack away like yesterday's garbage. Jack told her that even Tom was disgusted with his dad's attitude about Tony. And now, Dom's favored son was going to jail.

As she walked back to the elevator, Kate found Ruby waiting for her, as promised. They walked together back to Kate's room where Jack waiting.

****

"I'll leave you two to talk now. I have to get back to the shop and get the supplies put away before Mary Morelli comes for her three o'clock. Call me when you get your walking papers." Ruby leaned over to kiss Kate's cheek and waved to Jack on her way by.

"Did they tell you when you're going to be released?" Jack helped Kate climb back into bed. She was moving a little better than yesterday, but there was still strain in her gaze.

"Thanks." She dropped her slippers and adjusted the covers over her legs. "If everything continues to improve, they will probably spring me tomorrow. It can't be soon enough, as far as I'm concerned."

She was small and fragile lying in the bed. He wanted to build a gigantic wall around her to keep her safe. She would never stand for it, but he might be able to relax.

"Call me when you know and I'll come pick you

up. Are you going to stay with Ruby?"

"No, I'm going home."

"Home?"

"I mean, back to my aunt's house, which is my home now. I want to get to work on the plans for the spa, maybe take the self-defense class you told me about. It's time to start making a new life for myself. I don't want to wait another minute."

Jack nodded. "Well, as long as Tony's in custody, there shouldn't be any other problems. He's probably going to be released from the hospital either tomorrow or the next day. Of course, he won't be going home."

Kate nodded. "How are your parents handling this?"

Jack sighed. "When I went up to check Tony's status, my father refused to speak to me and my mother cried. My guess is; they aren't taking it well."

"I'm sorry, Jack. This has to be hard on them. And hard on you, too."

Jack stood and walked around the small room, suddenly caged in. He stopped and turned back to Kate, taking a deep breath and letting it out slowly.

"Actually, I'm sorry for my mom. I know she's suffering because she loves Tony and can't believe any of this is happening. With my dad, I expect he's crushed. He believed in a Tony who never existed. He's too damn stubborn to admit it or change anything, but it makes him seem pitiful in a way. I'm sorry for him, but I'm not really even mad at him anymore."

Kate sat up a little straighter and held out a hand to Jack. He walked to the chair beside the bed, sat and gathered her hand in his.

"I'm glad you said that. I think you're starting to understand your father more, and to accept his faults and failures. I always thought Dom was a little intimidated by you, and your intelligence. Maybe that was part of what made him defensive about you. And maybe Tony was too, although he certainly would never admit it to anyone, even himself, I'm sure."

Jack watched the sadness in her eyes, the sympathy there, and the wounded animal look was gone.

"Maybe, who knows? I guess it really doesn't matter anymore. I was lucky Deke was there for me in a way my father never was. Whatever the reasons behind it, it doesn't affect who I am now. I went to Dartmouth, joined the FBI, succeeded there, and came back to be sheriff here in spite of my father's opinion of me. If I'm successful in this life, it's thanks to Deke."

Kate squeezed his hand. "And thanks to your own hard work and intelligence, right?"

"Right." Jack smiled.

When Kate smiled back at him, there was no pity, no censure, no guile in her expression. It was pure caring and respect. A tightness filled his chest that might have been mistaken for illness but for the tingle emanating from the fingers he had intertwined with Kate's.

As she pulled slightly on his hand, he stood and sat on the edge of her hospital bed. Leaning on his other arm, he leaned down and rubbed his cheek on her hair. Inhaling the sweet smell of Kate that overpowered even the hospital disinfectant was both elation and despair.

This woman, this fragile, battered soul, was important to him, he didn't want to risk hurting her or letting her down. But she was also too important to do without.

Kate gazed up at him, bringing her mouth mere inches from his own. She softly took a breath and her gaze fixed on his lips. As if by a will of their own, they found their way to Kate's lips and softly brushed against them.

One taste, one touch, was overwhelming and would never be enough. He kissed her, tender, soft, feathery kisses, careful not to hurt her swollen lips. His right hand cradled her cheek, again, careful not to press the bruises or re-open the cuts. He lost himself in the exploration of her face.

Her hand came up and stroked his arm, squeezing gently and nearly snapping his control. He pulled back, rested his forehead against hers, and let out a breath.

"Jack?" Her voice trembled.

"Hmm, I think I'd better stop right here. You are in no condition for whatever might happen next, and, if this is going anywhere, I want it to when you're not in a hospital bed."

She chuckled softly. "Probably a good idea."

Jack leaned back, forcing himself to be content with only the contact of their two hands.

After a few moments, his pulse got back to normal and the blush in her cheeks began to fade. He cleared his throat. Back to business.

"Even though Tony's in custody, I am going to

have a patrol car come by your place on a regular basis for the next couple of weeks."

"Why?"

"We've received some threatening letters at the office."

"From Tony?"

"Maybe, maybe not. They aren't directed at you, but talk about the sanctity of marriage and the sheriff's office getting involved where it has no right to be."

She titled her head. "Do you think Tony would involve someone else?"

"I doubt it, but I'd rather be extra safe where you're concerned." Jack wrapped her hand in both of his. "It will probably come to nothing, but let's keep an eye on things, at least until we're sure the threats were from Tony."

"Okay." Kate nodded. "As long as I know the patrols are coming out there, I won't worry when I see them."

"Good." Jack stood and grabbed his coat. "It looks like we're going to get the first snow of the season. I'd better head back to the office. It could be a long night."

"Be careful."

"Call me in the morning and let me know when to pick you up. If you give me a list, I'll get you some groceries before I take you home. I want to make sure your new locks are working."

"New locks?"

"I had a locksmith install new deadbolts on the front and back doors, as well as replacing the lock Tony broke."

Kate smiled and reached for his hand again. When he took her outstretched hand, she pulled him close and kissed his cheek.

"Thanks for taking such good care of me, Jack."

He started to stand, but she pulled him back and kissed him full on the lips before letting him go.

Her eyes twinkled with promise. "That's to remind you where we need to pick up again, once I get out of here."

\*\*\*\*

The man stormed across the field behind the hospital, spitting and sputtering, kicking at rocks unlucky enough to get in his way.

The damn sheriff was talking to her again, filling her head with lies about him probably.

Then the sheriff kissed her.

What gave the sheriff the right to kiss another man's wife? Nothing, that's what. He wasn't doing his job, he wasn't protecting the good people of this county. He was chasing after a woman and trying to take her away from her lawful husband.

He had to die, no doubt about it.

\*\*\*\*

Jack walked into the command center, pleased people were still hustling and working hard to find Ed Michaels. Even though the trail grew colder every day, the teams of investigators were out following leads all over the county and had come up with solid evidence Michaels was still in the area.

Scott and Jack had dinner together most every night, often way past the normal dinner hour. They had their own usual table at Minnie's now, where they discussed progress on the case and new tactics to follow. Jack knew it was only a matter of time before Ed Michaels did something stupid and they closed in on him. Debbie Standish and her family deserved nothing less.

"How are things at the hospital?" Scott was sitting at his desk in the back corner of the room. He had six cola cans lined up on the credenza behind him and another in his hand. No wonder he seemed to work all the time. The man had enough caffeine in him to launch a rocket.

Jack leaned against the door jam, crossing his arms. "Kate's going to be released tomorrow, and Tony probably the next day. You're going to have more company down in the basement than usual, as I have extra guards lined up to cover him until the arraignment."

"Sounds good. I think we can add the embezzlement charges to the kidnapping, assault, battery, and attempted murder charges."

Jack nodded. "The bank president found proof against Tony?"

"Yeah." Scott nodded. "From their preliminary review, about two million is missing from some of their long term investment funds."

"Oh my God." Jack walked into the office and dropped into the side chair.

"I'm sorry. I know this is terrible for you and your family, but at least these charges will keep Tony away from Kate for a very long time."

Jack leaned forward and rested his head in his hands. He didn't doubt the truth of the bank's findings. He knew what addictions could do to people, and compulsive gambling was as much of an addiction as drug abuse or alcoholism. But the scandal this would bring was going to kill his parents.

"Have you discussed this with the district attorney yet?"

"No. I wanted to talk to you first."

Jack stood. "Give me the file and I'll go talk to him. I want to be there when they charge Tony with this. In fact, we'll have to call Greg Matthews and have him meet us at the hospital. I can give them notification of the arraignment."

Scott stood and handed a thick file to Jack. "I'm glad Kate is better and going home."

Jack smiled, grateful for the change of subject. "Yeah. She's still pretty bruised and swollen, but she's got a look in her eyes I never thought to see in a battered woman. She's ready to start her life over, begin again."

"Good for her. She's a strong woman. She's going be okay."

"Yeah." *Better than okay.*

Scott walked toward the door, but turned before leaving. "When this is all over, I think she might make a good speaker at the schools and such. To help young girls avoid abusive relationships and stand up to boyfriends or husbands who may be abusive. Do you think she'd want to do something like that?"

Jack nodded. "I think she'd be perfect. She's already decided to take some self-defense classes. I think it would be a great thing to tie in to a talk, as well. I'll ask her about it, after she's finished her classes. I bet she would really like to do it, you know, helping girls to avoid the kind of hell she's lived through."

Scott leaned on the bookshelf against the wall. "Does that mean you'll be sticking around her for a while?"

"I think so." Jack smiled. "I have nowhere else I'd rather be. I've come to the conclusion Deke's right. Being sheriff in Harper's Glen, taking care of the people who make their homes here, will make a pretty good life, right?"

"Sounds good to me. Throw in a little sailing on the lake, skiing in the winter, and the right woman by your side, and life doesn't get much better."

Jack smiled as he turned to leave. "You're right."

**\*\*\*\***

"We got another letter today, Jack." Thelma's calm demeanor was gone. Her hand shook as she handed him the letter, showing all of her many years.

Jack took the letter in his gloved hand and read it aloud.

"*It's too late for you now, Sheriff. You have broken God's law and man's, you who's supposed to uphold the law. You must be punished. If you stay away from my wife, she will be spared. Do not coerce her into sin any longer, or she too will have to die.*"

Jack swore under his breath. He glanced up at Thelma and immediately dropped the letter on his desk, ushering her into the nearest chair. He walked to the outer office and came back with a glass of water.

"I want you to take the rest of the week off,

Thelma. With everything Deke's going through, it's too much to deal with this lunatic, too."

"No, I'm okay. I can still do my job."

He crouched down to meet her gaze, lightly patting her back.

"I know you can, Thelma. I can't risk you getting caught in any of this. If these threats are coming from Tony, then someone else has to be helping him and that person is not in custody. If they're not coming from Tony, then we don't have much of a lead on who's behind them. I won't risk your safety unnecessarily."

Her stiff demeanor melted before his very eyes. Her features soften and she became more like someone's grandma than the barracuda she was often accused of being.

"I would like to spend more time with Deke, you know, before he passes away. I hate to think of him being alone and I know you cannot be there as much as you'd like to be."

Jack nodded, reaching out to hold her hand. "I will feel much better if you're with him, Thelma. And I put a couple of guards on his door as well. We've got some kind of lunatic on the loose and angry at the sheriff's office. I don't want to take any chances."

He took the empty water cup she handed him and helped her to her feet. At her desk, he stopped to call a patrol car to give her a ride home.

"I'll be in to visit Deke tomorrow when I pick up Kate. Let me know if you think he needs anything or if…well, if anything were to happen. I'll have my cell phone with me at all times."

He helped Thelma into her coat and walked with her to the door. When the two young deputies arrived to take her home, she turned back and kissed him softly on the cheek.

"You're a good man, Jack Finelli. Deke would be proud of you, and so am I."

Jack nodded and waved, unable to speak for the lump in his throat.

Chapter Fifteen

Kate stepped out of the car and filled her lungs with the crisp, clean air off the lake. The first dusting of snow crunched beneath her feet as she followed a path alongside her house. She walked down to the water's edge, picking up a small flat stone along the way. When she reached the shore, she pulled her right hand back and let the stone fly across the surface, like sending circles through the glass.

"Glad to be home?" Jack walked up beside her and skipped a stone of his own.

"Absolutely." She spun around, flinging her arms out. "This is home to me. The lake is peaceful and soothing, even when it's wild and rough."

A shiver raced through her as a gust of wintry air found its way inside her fall jacket. Jack wrapped his arm around her shoulders and pulled her close.

"Did you miss the lake when you lived in DC?"

"Hmm…I guess I did, though I never really thought about it when I was there. It wasn't until I drove over the hill and saw it nestled down in the valley that I realized how much I'd missed it."

Kate snuggled deeper into his embrace, wrapping her arm around his waist. "What about Harper's Glen? Were the parts of living here you missed as well?"

"Of course. There's a security which comes from

living in a town this size, where people know you and your life's history that you can't get in a big city. It's confining at times, especially when you're young. But when times are hard, and you need the support of a community, an impersonal city can't even come close."

She leaned her head against his shoulder, pulling herself into his embrace. "Like when Melanie was killed?"

Jack nodded. "Yeah, definitely then. But even ordinary stress is easier to take when you see familiar faces throughout your day."

She smiled. "You sound surprised."

"I was surprised by how nice it is when I run into someone at the Quik-Mart or Minnie's or the post office, whatever, and they ask about you or express sympathy over Deke, concern about Tony. I thought it would feel like meddling, but it's really more about caring."

Kate smiled into his chest, a spark of hope building deep in her own. "Let's go inside."

Jack handed over the new keys to her house and stood back while she let them in. She pushed open the door and then placed a quick kiss on his lips before entering. "Thanks for having the locks fixed."

She led the way into the living room, grateful all signs of her struggle with Tony were wiped clean. She walked from room to room, Jack trailing behind, touching her books, her aunt's piano, and the family photos. Any trace Tony had ever been there was gone. Even the air smelled clean and pure.

She walked to the overstuffed couch and flopped down. She patted the cushion beside her. Jack sat and leaned back, resting his arm along the back of the couch, which Kate took as an invitation and curled up next to him.

Excitement hummed inside her, both from being home again and from being close to Jack. The warmth of his arm held her tight to his chest. She heard the rapid beat of his heart beneath his shirt, and hoped the tremble she detected came from him. He had to feel it, too.

"The governor's appointment came through."

She looked up at his serious expression, unsure where he was headed.

"Which means…?"

"I've been officially appointed the sheriff, to complete the two years remaining on Deke's term."

A jolt of excitement skittered through her. "So you're definitely staying in town for two more years?"

"Yep."

"Congratulations." She leaned up and kissed him, trying to coax a response from his lips. He began to respond, but then he pulled back and stood.

"Kate, this isn't a good idea. You're very emotional right now. I don't want to take advantage of the thrill you're feeling from being home, free of Tony, and alive."

She stood, facing him with her hands on her hips. "True, but why can't you celebrate those things with me?"

He took a step back. "You are making a lot of changes in your life right now, for the good. I don't want you to be sorry later that you read more into your feelings for me than was actually there."

"I care about you, Jack—"

He raised his hand. "Wait. I care about you, too. I want to be your friend, even when I'm no longer your brother-in-law. But I don't think either of us is ready to think about anything more."

*And you're wrong, Jack.* She didn't say it, he wasn't ready to hear it, but she knew in the truth. "If you think I need more time to get my bearings, then make sure you stick around for as long as it takes."

He didn't respond, other than to grab his coat and head to the door. "I put your groceries in the kitchen and your bag in the bedroom. I want you to call me at any time, no matter what."

She followed him to the door, smiling at his obvious need to escape. "I will, I promise. And you call me if anything changes with Deke or Tony, or whatever."

"Okay. Bye Kate."

He flew out the door as if afraid of her touch. She watched him from the door, chuckling.

****

"You started the class today?" Ruby had a cart full of rollers by her side as she worked quickly, completing Mrs. Wright's permanent.

"Yeah. I went down to the club to sign up and they were about to start a new session, so I joined it." Kate was dressed in jeans and a sweater, her hair back in a ponytail and her face clean of any make-up. What a relief not to worry about passing inspection anymore.

"How did it go?" Ruby's fingers flew, comb and hair in one hand, roller in the other.

"So far, so good." Kate nodded. "We didn't

learn any moves yet, but the instructor showed us things to watch for to keep from being a victim. She showed us ways to be prepared and said if someone attacks, we should shout 'fire' instead of 'help.' She also had us practice yelling 'no' so we would be used to saying it if we ever need it. It was really very interesting."

Ruby took a step closer and lowered her voice. "Are you okay with all of this? It isn't too much, given what you've been through?"

Kate touched Ruby's arm and smiled. "Thanks for asking, but no. I'm fine. In fact, I think it's really going to help me get my head in the right place, knowing I don't have to give up without a fight anymore."

Ruby gave her a quick hug. After she moved Mrs. Wright to the dryer seat, she came back to clean up the rollers. "I know you wanted to come back to work right away, but I didn't schedule you until next Tuesday. I thought you could use a couple more days to recover and get settled."

"That's probably just as well. Jack said Tony's arraignment is tomorrow and I want to be there."

When Ruby finished her clean up, she sat next to Kate at the desk. "You have everything you need out at the house now?"

"Yeah. Jack took my grocery list to the Quik-Mart before he picked me up at the hospital."

Ruby turned her head slightly, glancing at Kate from the side of her eyes. "Did Jack get you all settled in okay?"

Kate smiled. "You're not too slick, you know. If you want to ask how things are with Jack and me, then ask."

"Okay, how are things between you and Jack?"

They both laughed.

"Good, I think. He says he can only be my friend; that I'm going through too many changes right now to consider anything more; he doesn't want to take advantage of me. I think he cares about me and it's got him scared."

Ruby chuckled. "Sounds about right."

"The biggest problem is he also thinks I deserve someone better, someone who can protect me and take care of me. Someone other than him."

"Why?"

Kate explained what happened with Melanie, and then with Tony. "Deke says it really has more to do with Dom and the way he treated Jack growing up."

"I think Deke's right." Ruby walked to the cash register and opened the drawer. "I could never understand why Dom treated Tony like he was king of the world. I mean, Tom is a nice guy, but Tony never was. He's always been a mean, selfish, son-of-a-gun."

"I didn't know you thought about him like that, you know…before."

Ruby reached out and patted Kate's back. "I wasn't going to say anything bad about your husband, sweetie. Not until I found out what an animal he really was. He has fooled some of the people in this town for a long time, but I think many of us started to see through his act in the past few years."

"I don't know how Dom and Rose will handle

the arraignment tomorrow. They were devastated enough when I got the order of protection. It'll be a tough day for them."

"And for you, Kate. You need to take it easy and get your strength back. Don't push yourself too hard."

Kate kissed Ruby's cheek and turned to go. "I won't, I promise. Once Tony's formally charged and behind bars, a huge weight will be lifted off my shoulders."

"I think a lot of people will feel better. I know I will." Ruby pushed some cash into Kate's hand. "Take this, in case, until you get everything straightened out and you're back to work."

Kate started to say no, but couldn't refuse Ruby's kindness. Instead she took the cash and pulled Ruby into a hug.

"I'm going to stop at the library to get some new books and then home to curl up in front of my fire. I'll call you later, okay?"

Ruby walked with her to the door. "And tell me all the juicy details, if Jack happens to stop by again, right?"

Kate laughed. "Sure. Let's hope I don't have to wait forever to get something juicy out of that man."

"You won't, Kate. Trust me. He can't hold out forever."

\*\*\*\*

He thinks he's smart. Putting up a glass wall in his office, as if it's going to save his sorry hide.

I can still get in.

He spends so much time chasing Debbie these days, he's hardly ever in his office. What difference does it make what kind of walls there are?

He should stay away from my wife. He has to pay for putting his hands on my wife.

But the timing has to be right. Soon. Real soon.

\*\*\*\*

Jack stood at the doorway, waiting for the van to arrive. He knew his parents were waiting inside the courtroom. Kate was there, too, with Ruby. He'd make sure the transition was smooth, but then go sit with Kate for the arraignment.

The charges against Tony were staggering. His brother violated the protective order, both by attacking Kate and obtaining a gun, but that was only the start of his crimes. He would also be charged with assault, battery, and attempted murder of both Kate and Jack. It was sad, though, the charge that seemed to upset Tony most was for embezzlement.

Jack met with Greg Matthews in Tony's hospital room the day before to review the transport and arraignment, also giving them information on the latest charges. Tony was quiet until Jack discussed the money missing from the bank and the documents proving Tony used it for his personal gambling debts. It was only then Tony went ballistic.

The department van pulled up outside the courthouse, and several deputies climbed out, surrounding the entrance to the building. Jack opened the back door of the van to help Tony climb out. His hands were cuffed in front of him; Jack released the ankle cuffs in order for him to walk upstairs to the courtroom. Tony's lawyer and another deputy got out of the van after Tony. Jack signed the necessary paperwork and then glanced into his brother's eyes.

He expected anger and hatred. He expected the condescending glint he was used to seeing in Tony's expression. He even imagined, well hoped for remorse or fear.

Instead, he didn't recognize the eyes looking back at him. Whatever had been Tony, arrogant, king-of-the-world-Tony, was gone. Now he was a caged animal, desperate and crazed, ready to panic.

"Are you ready, Tony?" Jack looked from the unresponsive gaze of his brother to Greg Matthews standing at Tony's side.

"I haven't been able to get a word out of him." Greg shrugged his shoulders and shook his head. After turning back to Tony, Greg walked ahead of them into the building, accompanied by a deputy.

Jack took Tony's arm and led him down the hall under the courtroom. Two more deputies followed behind. They climbed the back stairway to the second floor, stopping at the witness room.

"Greg, you stay here with Tony while I check if the Judge is ready for you." Jack nodded to the deputies to stay; one inside the room with Tony and two outside the door. He entered the side door to the courtroom and approached the bailiff.

"Is Her Honor ready for Tony?"

The bailiff approached the bench, and whispered to the small, middle-aged woman in black robes. Jack remembered Judge Marshall as the busy and kind mother of his friend Peter. Peter was another egghead, always on the honor roll like Jack. Apparently Peter's mom moved from district attorney to judge several years ago.

"Bring him in," the bailiff said.

Jack walked to the doorway, leaned out and nodded to the deputies guarding Tony's door. One deputy opened the door; he was followed down the hall by Greg, Tony, and two more deputies. When they reached the doorway to the court, Jack moved aside, motioning them to enter.

Tony stood in the doorway, finally looking straight into Jack's eyes. He sighed and then whispered, "I can't do it, Jack."

Jack turned from Tony to Greg and back. In that instant, Tony grabbed the sidearm of the deputy next to him and shoved it in his mouth.

Jack lunged for him, trying to push through the deputies before his brother could pull the trigger.

He reached Tony just as the trigger clicked. The explosion pushed Tony's body against the floor and carried Jack with it as he grabbed his brother's hand.

"Tony!"

One of the deputies called for an ambulance, but it was too late. Jack pulled himself off of his brother's body, wiping blood and tissue from his hands.

Tony's eyes were still open, but the back of head was mostly gone. Jack spun around, glad someone had closed the side door to the courtroom. He looked around the hall, the deputies all looking back at him, as if waiting for his reaction. Greg Matthews was huddled on the floor, softly whimpering.

Jack turned to the deputy by his side. "Secure the hallway. Make sure no one gets down here who isn't authorized. When the ambulance gets here, get Greg treated for shock. Get the coroner in here, too."

Jack pulled out his cell phone and punched in Scott Randall's number. When he explained the situation, Scott raced up from the basement, joining Jack in the hallway.

"I need to go inside and talk to Kate," Jack said, dabbing at the blood on his uniform. "I have to tell Tom and Brenda, my parents, too. They need to know what happened."

Scott looked at Tony's body and back up at Jack. "Do you know what happened?"

"I was here, wasn't I? I saw him...he killed himself."

Scott put his hand on Jack's back. "But do you know why?"

Jack shook his head. "I don't know."

He walked over to Greg Matthews, who was now sitting on the edge of a stretcher, having his vitals taken.

"Did you have any idea he was going to do this, Greg?"

Greg's eyes were watery and his face ashen. "God no, Jack. I mean, I knew he was crazy over the embezzlement charges. He went on and on about his position in the community and how it would shame your parents, but I didn't know he was even thinking about killing himself."

Jack put his hand on Greg's shoulder. "He didn't say anything about not wanting to go on or something like that?"

"No. He didn't want everyone in town to know about his gambling and debts. He was more afraid of humiliation than of going to jail." Greg hung his head. "I knew he was getting a little unstable, but I never suspected this."

Jack turned back to Scott. "Can you control the scene here for me, at least until the coroner is finished? I want to go in the courtroom and talk to my family."

Scott nodded. "Go ahead. I've got it covered."

Jack murmured his thanks and turned to grab the knob. His hand paused inches from the door.

"You okay, Jack?"

He turned around. Scott was watching him with concern.

"Yeah, I'm okay." Jack stopped and shook his head. "There's no easy way to do this." He took a deep breath and pulled the door open.

Kate came rushing across the nearly empty courtroom. "Jack, are you okay? You're bleeding."

Jack glanced down at his shirt. He hadn't been able to wipe it all off.

"No, it's not my blood. I'm fine, Kate." He rested his arm lightly on her shoulders and walked with her toward the gallery.

When Tom made eye contact with Jack, it was clear he knew what had happened. He pulled Brenda closer into his arms and nodded at Jack.

Dom sat rigid in the front row, avoiding Jack's gaze, Rose was pale and shaking.

"Where's Tony? What happened out there?"

Jack walked to the front row and sat near his mother, facing sideways. Kate sat down behind him, next to Brenda. "When we were about to bring Tony into the courtroom, he grabbed the gun of the deputy guarding him. Before we could stop him, he pulled the trigger and killed himself. I'm sorry, but Tony's dead."

Jack tried to swallow the building tears, tightening control over his own emotions. He turned when Kate's hand touched his elbow, and soaked in the show of support in her gaze.

Dom popped out of his seat, his face beat red, and lunged at Jack. Jack stood, trying to catch his father as much as deflect his blows.

"You bastard. You hated Tony and wanted him dead. You killed him, you and his lying wife. You killed my boy, my Tony."

Dom fell to his knees, shaking. Jack's arm supported his father, and kept him from falling to floor. Rose sobbed, reaching out to Dom, her slender arms strong as steel as she pulled her husband back to his seat.

Dom dropped his head into his hands, painful tears wracking through his body. Rose leaned over and wrapped her arms around him.

Jack dropped back to his seat, turning to Tom and Brenda. While both had tears in their eyes, together they leaned in to hug Jack, pulling Kate into the embrace as well.

After a few minutes, Tom stood and motioned Jack to follow him to the back of the courtroom.

"Is there anything I can do? Mom and Dad can't handle this right now. You have to know this isn't your fault."

Jack nodded. "I know. But thanks for saying it. Actually, if you could make the funeral arrangements, I'd really appreciate it. Kate is still legally his wife, but I don't think she should have to do it and Mom and Dad aren't going to be up to it."

"Of course, no problem."

Kate and Brenda walked back to join them. Brenda pulled Jack into a tight hug, her body still shaking with tears.

"I don't know what to say." She loosened her grip on him, and looked into his eyes. "This wasn't your fault, you know. Don't worry about what Dom said. He's crazy with grief right now. He can't accept that Tony was sick, but he was. It was nobody's fault." She looked pointedly at Kate as she released her hold on Jack.

Jack slid his arm around Kate's shoulders and pulled her close. As soon as she was snug in his arms, a measure of peace began to flow through his body. The day couldn't have been much worse, but her warmth was welcoming and he wanted to wrap himself around her.

He didn't, he couldn't. Her husband, his brother, lay dead beyond the door. Nothing would ever be the same.

He caught Kate's gaze briefly, tried to convey his support, and turned back to Brenda.

"No, it's not anyone's fault. Tony lost it and couldn't handle the pressure, the charges against him. Something was wrong with him, I think that's clear. It's nobody's fault, but it's not going to be an easy thing for my folks to understand."

A tremble raced through Kate, who was looking down at the floor. Jack had to get her out of there, get her home again.

"Tom, would you two stay here with Kate a moment while I check on the situation in the hall. Then I'll take you home, okay Kate?" He spoke to

Tom while looking at Kate, who merely nodded.

Jack checked in with Scott, who had everything under control. The coroner had taken Tony's body, the ambulance had treated Greg Matthews for shock, and the deputies had the area secured. Scott told Jack to go home.

He was more concerned with taking care of Kate.

****

Kate unlocked the front door, pushed it open, and walked in, soaking in the quiet. Jack followed her and closed the door behind him. Then he started to remove his blood-stained shirt.

"Why don't I make us some tea, or would you rather have coffee? I need something warm."

"Tea's fine, but let me do it." Jack followed her into the kitchen wearing only his white undershirt.

"No, I need something to do, something to occupy my hands." She filled the old teapot and turned on the stove. While she busied herself with the mugs and teabags, Jack disappeared down the hall. The sound of the bath water running made Kate shudder when she realized he was washing off his brother's blood.

Kate sank down into the chair at the end of the kitchen table. She set her mug aside before the trembling in her hands sent it crashing to the floor. Wrapping her arms around her waist, her control began to slip away.

Tony was dead. She didn't kill him, he didn't kill her, but he was still dead. She couldn't be happy about it, but couldn't mourn him either.

She was rocking back and forth in her chair,

tears slipping down her cheeks, when Jack's voice finally got through the fog.

"Kate?"

She looked up. She gasped and reached out to him and he sank to his knees, pulling her into his tight embrace. In the strength of his arms, she let herself go.

Her tears came in waves, shocking herself with the depth of her anger, pain, sadness, and relief. She was safe in Jack's arms, safe from Tony's fists, safe to start her life again.

When her tears began to subside, she looked up at Jack, whose face was also wet from tears. Trembles racked through his body, while her own began to subside. Her heart ached for his pain at seeing his brother die.

She leaned up and covered his lips with hers, whispering soft kisses while she held his body tight to hers. The firm muscles beneath his thin cotton t-shirt tensed under the exploration of her hands. His breathing kept time with hers as their kisses grew deeper and longer.

She sat up on her knees and cradled his face in her hands, kissing his eyelids, nose, cheeks, and chin. When she once again reached his lips, he moaned into her open mouth. She wrapped her arms around his neck, and he pulled her body in tight.

The skitter of excitement raced over her skin. Her skin was suddenly too tight to contain her.

His touch, his taste, his very smell; she couldn't get enough of him. Her tongue traced the line of his teeth before pulling his tongue into her mouth to suck gently. His hands moved to her hips, pulling her in close to his heat, pressing her aching breasts against his hard chest.

Kate pulled back and looked at Jack, nodding her head toward the bedroom. He needed no more encouragement than that before picking her up and carrying her off to her bed. He shed his boots and joined her atop the covers, pulling her close enough the hard length of his need for her sent a thrill through her.

Rather than the fear she anticipated, only heat and lust and love surrounded her. Jack didn't scare her, and she knew loving him wouldn't hurt. She trusted him and herself enough to know.

## Chapter Sixteen

Jack released the buttons of her shirt one at a time, kissing each new inch of skin as he exposed it. The cool moist air raised goose bumps on her flesh. His mouth on her chest sent shivers of heat searing to her toes.

Kate moaned and curled toward him, reaching for the hem of his thin t-shirt and pulling it over his head. When he was bare to her touch, she entwined her fingers in the rough, dark blond curls springing from his golden skin. She leaned forward to taste his skin, just below the collarbone, and breathe in the crisp, male heat and sweat. The scent of Jack.

He pulled her open shirt off, and made quick work of her bra. When she was bare to the waist, he cradled her aching breasts in his hands and leaned in to feather kisses along the outer edges.

Making slow circles, he tormented her with his thoroughness. She cried out when he finally closed over the tip of her left breast. Kate arched her back and dug her fingers into his thick, blond hair, holding him close enough to ease her need.

Jack moved to the other breast, giving it equal attention, before moving down her body. As his tongue invaded her bellybutton, his fingers slipped open the button and eased down the zipper on her jeans. Pushing her panties down at the same time, he slid the last of her clothing off, leaving her bare to his gaze.

**** 

Kate looked into his eyes, instantly afraid of censure or disappointment or even, possibly, disapproval. But there was only heat, desire, and love. He might not have used the words, but it was there and she and soaked it up, right through her very pores. Jack loved her, wanted her, and desired her. Jack would keep her safe.

Kate pressed her breasts against his chest, the crisp hair sending shivers through her as it rubbed her sensitive skin. Her legs intertwined with his and her hands seemed to have a mind of their own.

While she inched his zipper down, she was fascinated by the way his breathing grew more shallow and rapid. He jumped each time her fingers pressed through the opening, reaching to the soft cotton and hard flesh beneath. When his penis finally pushed free of his clothes, he moaned and wrapped his body around hers, pushing his clothes to the floor and her back to the bed.

The pace of their touching exploded into a frenzy of kissing, licking, and caressing. A tension was building within her like nothing she'd ever experienced; aching for an end, but wanting it to continue. When Jack eased his fingers between her legs, she nearly jumped out of her skin. The throbbing was so great, her muscles so tight, his caresses sent ever-increasing quakes through her whole body.

She was on the brink of simply exploding when he stopped. She looked up into his eyes and he leaned over her. He moved on top of her, poised for entry, but waited, wordlessly. His gaze held her, silently, watching and waiting.

She smiled and reached up, pulling him into a passionate kiss. Her hands slid down his body, urging him to take the final step. He slid into her, filling her slowly but completely, bringing a tear to her eye.

As Jack increased the pace, Kate began to fly. She knew what they shared was magical, eternal, wondrous, and new. She let herself topple over the edge, her muscles seizing and contracting, Jack's name ripped from her throat. Jack buried his face in her neck, plunged to the very depth of her soul and emptied himself into her. She nearly melted into him as he held her tightly in his embrace, began to slow his pace, and brought her slowly back to earth. Moments later, he rolled to her side, and she snuggled into his arms.

He never uttered a word, but the kisses he rained on her hair, the tenderness he conveyed through his hold on her, the sweetness of the afterglow all spoke volumes to her. Whether he wanted to or not, whether she was ready for it or not, Jack loved her as much as she loved him. No matter what else had happened between them, of this she was certain.

**\*\*\*\***

Jack awoke with a start, instantly aware of where he was and what he'd done.

He'd thought to comfort her, share the misery of Tony's suicide, seek some balance and understanding. Instead, he'd carried her off to bed and buried himself deep inside her. And he wanted to start all over, right now, and do it again.

He eased his arm from beneath her neck and climbed from the bed. Grabbing his jeans, he walked into the hall and pulled them on. Once in the kitchen, he filled the coffee pot and switched it on.

He couldn't walk out, not on Kate. As much as he thought about running, to try to escape his own actions, Kate deserved better. And if he was honest with himself, he didn't want to run. He was such a selfish bastard; there was nowhere else he wanted to be.

He was incredibly grateful Kate seemed to enjoy their lovemaking. Whatever memories she carried of sex with Tony hadn't frightened her away, even though he did little to help her through it. If he'd been thinking with his brain and not his dick, he might've given her more time, taken it slower. Shit, if he'd been thinking at all, he wouldn't have touched her.

Jack was startled when Kate wrapped her warm, just-out-of-bed arms around his waist and leaned her face against his back.

"Good morning." Even her voice oozed sex, the early morning raspiness deeper than her usual tone.

He pulled her arms apart and stepped away, turning to face her. "Kate, we have to talk…about last night."

She didn't seem to realize what a mistake they'd made. She smiled at him and pulled out two mugs for the coffee. He stood dumbfounded watching her putter around, pulling out sugar and milk and carrying it all to the table. When she poured them each a cup and took a seat, he could do nothing more than follow.

He took a sip of coffee, cursing the heat as it burned his tongue. She simply smiled at him and passed the milk.

Jack cleared his throat. "I'm sorry, Kate, I really am. I didn't mean for things to get as far as they did, I mean…I didn't plan to seduce you."

"You didn't." She sipped her coffee, and kept on smiling.

"No, I didn't. If you don't believe anything else, please believe I didn't come here planning to seduce you."

She shook her head. "No, I mean, you didn't seduce me. It was very mutual, and might have even been my idea. There's nothing for you to feel sorry about."

Jack was confused. She sounded content, matter-of-fact about it all; he couldn't understand.

"But it wasn't right, and I am sorry." He stood and walked around the kitchen. "You'd just found out your husband, my brother, was dead. You haven't been out of the hospital long enough to completely recover from his attempt to kill you. And you deserve someone who will take care of you, protect you, and not continue to let you down. I was out of line, and I'm really sorry."

Her smile disappeared as she slammed her cup on the table, sending coffee flying over the rim. She stood and walked to the sink. When she turned back around, he couldn't read the light in her eyes.

"You horse's ass! Do you think so little of me you believe I would have made love to you last night if I wasn't in love with you? Could I be in love with you if I didn't trust you and know you are the right man for me? Or am I too stupid to have learned anything from what I have been through in my life? Is that what you think?"

Jack turned to her, but kept his distance. "No, Kate. I don't think you're stupid at all. I'm awed by the strength and intelligence it took for you to survive your marriage, get out, and start to make a new life."

She stormed across the room, pushing her finger into his chest while glaring into his eyes. "Then give me credit for knowing my own heart, and for seeing you for who you really are, even if you're too stupid to understand yourself."

He shook his head, clueless as to how to respond to a suddenly irate Kate. She must have taken it as agreement, because she simply continued.

"Once I admitted what was going on in my marriage, got help, and got out of there, I ceased being the woman Tony was married to. That person, Kathy, doesn't exist anymore."

She turned and walked back to the sink, staring out the window. "I'm Kate." She turned back to face him. "I own this house, I am opening a spa, and I'm in love with you. That's who I am now. I'm not the victim anymore. I'm not the illiterate, idiot, showpiece Tony used as a punching bag. I'm not the worthless beauty who had nothing more than her looks to show for nearly thirty years. I have a lot to offer myself and the world, and I'm offering it to you, if you'd only accept."

His feet moved of their own accord, taking him to her. He placed his hands on her shoulders, looking deep into her eyes. "I don't deserve everything you have to offer, Kate. I know how incredible you are. I don't want to be the one who lets you down again. And I'm afraid—"

She put her hands on his arms, shaking him. "Of course you're afraid. So am I. And of course, you're going to let me down sometimes. I'm going to let you down, too. We're human. That happens. But I trust you in a way I never thought I could trust anyone, especially a man. You are everything I need to be the me I want to be, to live the life I want to live. Can't you trust me enough to know I'm right?"

He leaned his forehead in, resting it on hers. "I don't want anything to happen to you."

"Me either. But do you love me?"

He swallowed the lump in his throat, amazed by the quiver of doubt in her voice. He raised his head up and looked deep into her eyes.

"I love you more than life, Kate. If I didn't, the thought of letting you down wouldn't be so frightening."

She leaned up and kissed him softly. "I love you, too. I have the same fears, the same worries. It's part of the package, Jack."

He wrapped his arms around her, pulling her body close to his. "What if I fail you, like I did Melanie?"

"What if *I* fail *you*, like Melanie did?"

He shook his head. "You couldn't. She never loved me the way you do. And I'm not sure I loved her at all, now I know what love really feels like."

Kate leaned back and wrapped her arms around his neck, locking him in her gaze. "Let yourself love me, Jack. Don't make up barriers to keep us apart when being together is all I want, all I need, all either of us needs in life. Just love me."

He kissed her lips quickly and then whisked her up into his arms. "I do, Kate. God help me, I do."

And he carried her back to bed to show her how much.

\*\*\*\*

He was getting cold, waiting in the bushes. When he followed that damn sheriff out here last night, he planned to jump the guy as he left. But the bastard stayed all night long.

During the night, he'd stayed warm by curling into a ball and imagining the things the sheriff was probably doing to Debbie in there. She swore she'd never cheated on him, but now he had the proof.

No one would blame him for this now, killing his cheating wife and her lover. Even if it meant killing the sheriff; he was only protecting what's his.

If they didn't come out of that house pretty soon, he'd have to go in after them. He didn't want to go in there; he wanted to surprise them when they stepped outside. But he'd do whatever was necessary. And he couldn't wait much longer.

\*\*\*\*

"Are you sure you don't want me to make some soup and sandwiches? We don't have to go into town today, if you'd rather stay here."

After their morning lovemaking, Jack declared he was taking her into town for lunch.

"No, I need to stop home for some clean clothes, and then I want to check in at the office."

"No one will expect you to be at work today."

He stood in the living room, wearing his uniform pants and rumpled white t-shirt, his hair still wet from his shower.

"True, but the Standish murder investigation is heating up and I want to get an update from Scott."

"Couldn't you call him now and find out what you need to know?"

She ran the brush through her wet and tangled hair, determined to pull it back into a pony tail.

"Yeah, but I think we need to go to Tom and Brenda's, too. I want to talk to Tom about the funeral arrangements."

She nodded, her hands going still in the air. "Do I have to do something about that?"

He quickly covered the distance between them and rested his arm around her waist. She finished her pony tail before lowering her arms.

"No. I asked Tom to handle it. I don't know how Mom and Dad are reacting to this whole thing. I want to talk to Tom and Brenda to check if there's anything I can do to help make the funeral easier on everyone."

"Like not going? Is that what you're thinking?"

Jack sat on the couch and pulled her down next to him. "It's possible. I wanted to ask what Tom's thoughts are before you and I made a decision about it. I don't want my parents, well, my father, to cause you more pain because of me."

Kate pulled his hand between hers and leaned her head on his shoulder. "I want to be at Tony's funeral because I think it's the right thing to do; out of respect for the man I thought I married, the son your parents lost, and the people he's left behind.

That includes you. And if you want to be at the funeral with me, your parents have nothing to say about it."

"I also wanted to tell Tom and Brenda about us. I think it's the right thing to do. I wouldn't want them to hear about it from someone else."

Kate took a deep breath, willing any remaining insecurities down deep where they wouldn't show. She let the breath out slowly, trying to keep her voice steady. "And what are you going to tell them about us?"

Jack kissed her, his face a mix of serious and sexy. "I'm going to tell them we're in love."

Tears began gathering in the corner of her eyes, she knew she was smiling and starting to cry, but couldn't do a thing to stop either one. "Really?"

Jack leaned in and kissed the tears that slipped from each eye. Then he pulled her lips into a breath-taking kiss, stopping just when she thought he might carry her back to the bedroom.

"In case I didn't say it earlier, Kate... I love you."

When she couldn't quite force her voice to cooperate, she nodded. Taking a few quick breaths, she finally was able to speak. "This is all so hard to believe, but... I love you too, Jack."

She kissed him back, filling her embrace with all her hopes, plans, and dreams for their future. When they finally parted, the smile on his face nearly brought tears to her eyes again.

"Get off my lap, woman. The sooner we get to town, the sooner we can get back." He winked as he pulled her to her feet and headed to the door. She grabbed her purse and stopped to place a light kiss on his lips before walking out the door he held open for her.

The moment Kate stepped through the door, a hand grabbed her neck from the side and someone pulled her into the bushes. Jack rushed out after her.

"Kate?"

She couldn't answer him, because of the gloved hand over her mouth, but didn't need to. When he stepped out of the house to find her, she was pulled from the bushes and a gun shoved past her face, aimed at Jack.

"Here she is, Sheriff. Fresh from a night spent in bed with you when she'd promised herself ta' me 'til death us do part. Now you both have ta' die for yer sins."

Kate instantly recognized the voice. Though, she couldn't understand why Ed Michaels would want to kill her, or Jack.

Jack only stood a few feet away, but she couldn't get to him. She tried to squelch the panic building inside her by remembering what she'd learned in her first self-defense class. He would help her and if she remembered enough to help herself, they would both get out of this alive. They had to.

"Now Ed, don't do something stupid. Kate here…uh…might look a little like Debbie, but she's not your wife. Don't hurt her, Ed. She's not Debbie, she's Kate."

"I don't care what she's calling herself today, she's *my* Debbie and you had no right ta' put yer hands on her. She's my wife."

Kate started to tremble, started to lose control.

There was no arguing with a madman, and Ed Michaels had obviously lost his mind. He thought she was his dead wife, the woman he had already murdered. How could Jack convince him not to murder her again?

Jack kept his arms up, his hands spread in front of his body, walking toward Kate, but keeping a small distance between them.

"Don't get too close there, Sheriff. I don't want ta' shoot you both at once. You deserve ta' die a slow and painful death after the way you've hounded me these past few weeks. You've chased me like a dog, just 'cause I was trying to save my marriage and protect what was mine."

"I've been doing my job, Ed."

"No! What God had joined together let no man put asunder, remember? You got no business interfering with a man and his wife." He tightened his hold on her mouth, pulling her neck back against his shoulder.

"Oh of course, Ed. Now I understand. Explain it to me a little more though. Then I won't bother you anymore." Jack winked at Kate and nodded. She knew he was planning something, and said a silent prayer it worked.

Ed relaxed his grip the slightest bit, waving the gun in his hand as he began to lecture Jack about the sanctity of marriage. He was lost in his sick little mind, he didn't notice Jack nod his head and wink again.

But Kate did.

She pushed back with her hips at the same moment she brought her foot down on Ed's instep.

He howled in pain and tightened his hold, grabbing her neck. With his eyes and anger focused on Kate, he didn't see Jack approach from the side.

Before Ed could bring his gun around to aim, Jack grabbed his arm and wrenched it up behind Ed's back. The gun went off, but Jack was far enough to the side to avoid the shot.

He forced the gun from Ed's hand and pulled his other arm from around Kate's neck. Kate dropped to her knees when the pressure was removed, but pulled herself back up. When Jack had both of Ed's arms jabbed behind him, he pulled off his belt and wrapped Ed's hands together.

Kate grabbed the cell phone from Jack's belt and dialed 911. She handed the phone to Jack when the dispatcher answered, and he called for back-up.

Within minutes, the first cars began to arrive. Before long, Kate's back yard was full of emergency vehicles and police investigators. Ed Michaels was cuffed and shoved into the back of a cruiser. Jack's belt was returned, and, after he and Kate were checked over by the EMTs and released, he wrapped his arm around Kate's shoulder. He guided her over to where Scott Randall was talking with another deputy.

Scott slapped Jack on the back and shook his hand, then leaned in lightly hug Kate. "You two okay?"

"Yeah, but I'm glad it's over." Jack smiled down at Kate, who nodded.

"We're fine, thanks to Jack." She reached up and touched her lips to Jack. The rest of the world disappeared.

She didn't notice if Scott Randall walked away, or what happened to everyone else, or how they got back in the house. Next thing she knew, Jack was carrying her again, lowering her onto the bed, pulling her close to him.

She snuggled in as close as could be, soaking in his heat and his strength. The rest of the world could wait; the police reports, funeral plans, well-wishers, and casserole-bringers. Nothing else mattered right now.

## Epilogue

The Town of Harper's Glen had really outdone itself. When Jack and Kate planned their wedding, they wanted something small and quiet. Just a simply ceremony to make legal the bond they already shared, the commitment they'd forged to each other with love.

But small and simple wouldn't do for the sheriff and his beautiful bride.

Ruby pumped Kate, just as Scott pumped Jack, for all the details of the impending nuptials. Both friends were vocal in their disappointment over the simple ceremony.

Next, Judge Marshall wouldn't perform the ceremony in her chambers, insisting they use the courtroom instead. Jack had his suspicions at the sight of Bill Grant's florist truck outside.

Before Jack and Kate knew what was happening, they were standing in the courtroom surrounded by a good portion of the town's residents, being cheered and congratulated and blessed. Jack's heart was full when Deke, accompanied by his nurse, sat in the courthouse to witness the beautiful event.

Kate, ever the beauty, looked like an angel on earth, dressed in a winter white suit with an emerald green blouse. She carried his bouquet of white roses.

Kate smiled up at Jack with the light of love's

own promise shining from her eyes, and he fell mute. There was no way he could ever tell this woman all the love he had for her in his heart.

Thank God, from the way she looked at him, she already knew.

**A word about the author...**

Barb Warner Deane was born and raised in the small town of Watkins Glen in the beautiful Finger Lakes area of New York. She graduated from Cornell University, where she met and married her husband, on graduation weekend, later getting her law degree from the University of Connecticut.

Barb, her husband, and three wonderful daughters have lived in the Chicago area for the past twenty-five years, other than two years in Frankfurt, Germany and two years in Shanghai, China. She draws a lot of writing inspiration from her experiences, and the incredible people she met, as an expat. *On The Homefront*, her historical women's fiction novel, coming soon from The Wild Rose Press, was inspired by a trip to Normandy, France.

After giving up the practice of law, Barb has worked mostly as a mom, but also as a paralegal, bookstore owner, book merchandiser, travel writer, proofreader, writing consultant, high school media guru, IT specialist, and avid volunteer: for Girl Scouts, including a leader for five troops on two continents, the American Women's Club in both Frankfurt and Shanghai, as President of the Windy City Chapter of Romance Writers of America, and high school PTA president.

In addition to writing, Barb is a genealogy and WWII buff, loves to read, of course, is a huge fan of The Big Bang Theory and Harry Potter, and is crazy for both U.S. and international travel. Now that she and her husband are empty-nesters, she's making plans to expand on her list of having visited forty-six states and thirty-seven countries on six continents.